The Day of the Moon

Also by Graciela Limón

In Search of Bernabé
The Memories of Ana Calderón
Song of the Hummingbird

The Day of the Moon

Graciela Limón

Arte Público Press
Houston, Texas
1999

This volume is made possible through grants from the City of Houston through The Cultural Arts Council of Houston, Harris County.

Recovering the past, creating the future

Arte Público Press
University of Houston
Houston, Texas 77204-2174

Cover illustration and design by James F. Brisson

Cover illustration based on photographs from
Mexico's Sierra Tarahumara: A Photohistory of People on the Edge
by Dirk W. Raat and George R. Janacek
copyright 1996 by the University of Oklahoma Press
Used by express permission of the publisher

Limón, Graciela.
    The day of the moon / Graciela Limón.
    p.   cm.

    ISBN 1-55885-274-3 (pbk. : alk. paper)
    1. Indians of North America—Mexico—Fiction. 2. Tarahumara Indians—Fiction. 3. Mexican Americans—Fiction. I. Title.
PS3562.I464D39   1999
813'.54—dc21   98-47015
                                                                                   CIP

♾ The paper used in this publication meets the requirements of the American National Standard for Information Sciences—Permanence of Paper for Printed Library Materials, ANSI Z39.48-1984.

9 0 1 2 3 4 5 6 7 8   10 9 8 7 6 5 4 3 2 1

Xipe Totec was skinned alive by a destructive spirit.
She did not die. Instead, she put her skin back on
and was restored to life.

(A Mexica Belief)

The Ancient Ones believe that while we sleep our soul
joins the spirits of the dead, and that together they work
hard, harder yet than during the day when we walk
about in sunlight. They also believe that during
the night, when we are sleeping, we do wonderful,
mysterious things with those who have gone to
the other side of the sierras. They say that it is
at this time that we make new songs and poems,
and that we discover who we love. This is what
is meant by The Day of the Moon. It happens,
they say, every night when we are dreaming.

(A Rarámuri Belief)

To
Mary Wilbur
who has been an inspiration to my writing.

Preface

This novel touches upon the Rarámuri people of Mexico, who, scholars believe, are among those who have most fiercely resisted the incursion of European ways. Early in the Spanish conquest, the Rarámuri took refuge in the high ground of the canyon caves, where they live to this day. This place, known as El Cañón del Cobre, lies between Los Mochis on the Pacific Ocean and the city of Chihuahua, Mexico. The Spaniards named the tribe *Tarahumara,* but they call themselves *Rarámuri,* which means foot runners. I have chosen to call them by the name which they prefer.

G.L.

Acknowledgments

My sincere gratitude goes to Paz Tostado Vandeventer for the conversations she and I have had on the miracle of healing. It is to Paz that I owe my reflections on Xipe Totec as a symbol of the restoration of the human spirit. Because of her, I have written of Xipe Totec, usually viewed by scholars and admirers of Mexica mysticism as a male god, as a feminine deity.

I am grateful also for Mary Wilbur's generosity in giving of her time and effort in editing the first draft of this manuscript. It is a hard and demanding task, and she has never said no to me. I also thank Crystal Williams for assisting me in recovering valuable information on the Rarámuri people. Finally, my gratitude to Dr. Shane Martin, colleague and friend, and his research assistant, Ernesto Colín, who have read *The Day of the Moon* and written many good things about it.

Don Flavio Betancourt

Chapter 1

Don Flavio Betancourt sat in the armchair, staring through the lace curtains of his bedroom. His gaze was vacant as his eyes scanned the rainy landscape; he was vaguely aware of the swishing sound each time a car drove past his house. His mind, however, was somewhere else. It had escaped, as it did nearly all the time now. The old man's thoughts ran away from him, skipping west, skittering over rooftops, dashing upward, spiraling over the Sixth Street Bridge, then turning south and rushing headlong toward Mexico.

He was eighty-five years old and he had grown frail. He was no longer tall, as he had been during most of his life; he had shrunk. His once muscular arms now sagged. His shoulders were thin and hunched. When he walked his head drooped and his small belly jutted out. Don Flavio looked down at his spotted hands, squinting, trying to focus his blurred vision. He turned them over, palms up, and saw that the skin was wrinkled and yellowish. Then he put them on his thighs, and he saw the dark blue veins; they reminded him of spider webs. He closed his eyes for a moment, aware of the vague discomfort that pressed against the pit of his stomach. When his lids snapped open, his mind returned to his memories.

"It didn't happen all at once," the old man mumbled as he reached out to take hold of the curtain. He moved it to the side so that he could look through the window. Tiny rivulets of rain streaked the glass but he could make out the reflection of his once handsome face. Now withered folds of parched skin hung off his jowls, pulling the corners of his lips downward, and giving his face an intimidating frown. What had been thick, nearly blond hair was almost gone; only a few strands of yellowish gray hair lay plastered to his skull with pomade. The color of his eyes, too, had been transformed by age. What was once blue was now a faded translucent gray.

Don Flavio's reflection began to recede from his eyes, becoming smaller until it seemed to have been sucked in by the watery glass. Suddenly another image appeared in its place, one that recurred in his brain at unexpected times, making him squirm in the armchair or wherever the memory assaulted him. The apparition mesmerized him, paralyzing his will to shut his eyes, or even to rub away the reflection.

The specter usually began with what appeared to be the hooves of a deer. These blurred and mixed until it became clear that they were not hooves but the feet of a man. They moved so rapidly that the *huaraches* that bound them seemed hardly to touch the earth on which the man ran. Above the feet came the legs and thighs, the loin cloth, the muscular belly, the heaving chest and shoulders, the taut neck with its bulging vein. Then the head began to take shape with its long, black hair flowing behind the runner.

It wasn't until then that Don Flavio was able to focus on El Rarámuri, the detested Indian. That face haunted the old man: the square jaw, the straight lips partially covered by a thin, drooping mustache, the aquiline nose framed by the eyes of the nomad. And once whole, the specter ran ceaselessly, brush and rocks flashing by with indescribable speed, the coppery earth moving with him, increasing his velocity. The image did not move from the watery glass, but Don Flavio knew that the distance being covered by the native was enormous, impossible for most men. The reflection moved with a grace that disguised the strain on the runner's body. The old man's eyes dilated as he remembered the first time he saw El Rarámuri seemingly surpass the wind that gusted through the crevices of the canyon.

Don Flavio finally covered his face with his hands; a soft moan slipped through his lips as he felt the discomfort in his stomach turn into pain. He tried to think of something else, but the vision burned somewhere behind his eyeballs. He wiped a circle into the blurry glass with his palm. He peered into the encroaching winter evening, deliberately concentrating on the steel gray color of the sky. Then he stretched his neck to look down the street; he wanted to fill his eyes with ordinary things. There, across the street, was the two-story frame house of the Miranda family. To the right, the old man saw the tree that had been threatening to die for the last twenty years. It had finally dried up in September. To the left was Third Street. On the corner was the tire garage, its grime spilling out to the sidewalk.

Don Flavio strained to see if any people were out on the street, but no one was there; it was raining too much. When he leaned back in his chair he grunted in frustration. His hands were sweaty. He realized that looking out onto the street had only interrupted the native's run and that the nagging reflection had returned to taunt him. The old man's head sagged backward onto the high back of the chair, his eyes shut tightly and his mouth clamped shut as he tasted the bitter saliva coating his tongue.

There was a muffled rap on the door.

"*Entra.*"

"*Buenas noches, Don Flavio.*"

"*Buenas noches.*"

Don Flavio's terse reply to the old woman was characteristic; he rarely spoke anymore. When she placed the tray on the table by his side he only nodded. It was time for his early evening chocolate. He grunted as a sign of gratitude, but as she was about to leave, he turned to her.

"Ursula, I won't have dinner tonight."

Ursula Santiago paused as she adjusted her deep-set, small eyes to the growing darkness in the room; the gray that streaked her coarse hair caught the last glimmering of daylight. Her head was small and well-defined, as if chiseled in stone. High, bony cheekbones accentuated her beaked nose, as did the wrinkles that circled her thin lips. In the gloom, her skin was brown and auburn. Ursula was a small woman, but she held herself erect and moved with confidence, even when facing the old man.

She nodded. She knew that he was in pain. She had noticed his skipping the evening meal more frequently during the past months. What Ursula did not know was that for the moment Don Flavio was not concerned with the biting discomfort in his belly, because he was more aware of relief. Her coming into his room had finally stopped El Rarámuri. The image had vanished from the window.

As Ursula began to leave, Don Flavio stopped her again. "Where's the girl? I haven't seen her in days."

"*Alondra* is in the kitchen." She resented his not uttering the name. "Do you want me to call her?"

"Yes. Tell her to come for a moment."

Ursula looked at the man she had served since she was seventee. Once she had been in awe of him, but the years had wasted him, snatched away his arrogance, leaving only the shell that now sat in front of her. When he and his sister, Brígida, had fled Mexico with Samuel and Alondra, Ursula followed as well because she had made a promise. She had spent the rest of her life fulfilling that vow.

"Wait! Tell my sister that I want to speak to her, too."

"Don Flavio, you've forgotten. Doña Brígida is dead."

"Ha! What does it matter? I don't speak to crazy women anyway!"

Ursula snorted through her nose, thinking that Doña Brígida had not been crazy, that she had been understandable most times, even though she had her moments at the end of her life. When that happened, everyone smiled or giggled, knowing that her mind had wandered again. Ursula shrugged her shoulders and left the room, closing the door softly. Don Flavio waited, refusing to look at the window. In a few minutes, he heard the rap on the door.

"Come in."

He did not look up. He knew who stood in front of him, and he kept quiet for a long while.

"Don Flavio. I'm here."

"Yes. I know."

"Do you want me to turn on the *lámpara?*"

"No. And don't mix languages!"

Again he fell into silence, hunched deep into the armchair thinking of how much her way of speaking annoyed him. He finally sucked in air through his mouth as he looked up at the young woman. He first saw the feet, shod in worn tennis shoes. Then he scanned the legs, thighs, hips; they were clad in faded jeans. His eyes moved up, covering the abdomen, breasts, shoulders, neck. He noted the cotton shirt tucked in, accentuating the slim waistline. She was tall, lean, well shaped.

At last, he focused on Alondra's face: It was oval-shaped, almost long; it was highlighted by hair that hung below her shoulders. Darkness had crept into the room, but he knew that her hair was raven-colored. Don Flavio looked at the young woman's skin, olive-colored with dark brown tones around her temples and beneath the long, straight nose. Her mouth was like that of all of them, he thought: wide, thin-lipped, sensuous. Then he did what he feared he would do. He looked into Alondra's eyes: black, deeply set, almond-shaped, with long straight lashes. Suddenly, they became his own mother's eyes. Unable to sustain Alondra's gaze, the old man turned away. When he looked again, her eyes had become those of the hated Rarámuri who haunted Don Flavio. The stare was riveted on the old man accusingly, and he shut his eyes.

"Leave the room!"

His voice was a mix of rage and anguish. Alondra was not surprised nor offended; this scene had been repeated frequently during the last months. She had come to him only because Ursula, her grandmother, told her to do so. She left the room without speaking.

Don Flavio tried to control the tremor that had overtaken him. He stared at the pitcher on the tray for a long time before attempting to serve himself. When he did, his hand trembled as he poured the hot liquid, forcing him to take the mug in both hands. The steamy chocolate fragrance calmed him, and he glanced at the ceiling, following the coiling vapor. Suddenly he sat up. He bent his head, cocking his ear, straining to hear. In the beginning it was distant, an echo, barely audible, intensifying, growing louder, more powerful. Don Flavio then felt the thundering vibration as it pounded against the hardwood floor beneath him, and he recognized the dull clatter of hooves as a horse raced at full gallop on the packed earth of his hacienda.

The old man held his breath, and then he saw her. Isadora, his daughter, rode bareback at breakneck speed across the *llano*. Her hands clutched the beast's mane, her legs wrapped around its sides. The white cotton dress she wore clung to her body, swept up above her knees, exposing her legs and the boots he had given her. She was laughing in defiance of the wind that whipped her face. Her golden hair, the sun's rays trapped in the ringlets of its curls, swept around her head like an aura.

Don Flavio smiled, exposing yellowed, worn-out teeth. The trembling had left him and he felt serene. He loved conjuring the image of his daughter, especially as she rode the high-spirited mare he had given her when she had become eighteen. He sighed, reliving that day when she first rode the horse. Isadora could ride better than any of his ranch hands; she could become one with the animal.

Don Flavio closed his eyes, listening to the cascading music of her laughter and her call to him. On that morning, he had leapt on his horse and galloped to her side. Together they raced across the meadow until they reached the slope that marked the beginning of the Sierra Madre. He loved Isadora above all others, more than anything he possessed, more than himself. On that day, when they rode toward the sierra, he loved Isadora so much that his heart filled with joy.

The pounding hooves receded into the past but the old man kept his eyes closed. It had grown dark outside, and he could hear the soft rain against the windowpane. He sat in the gloom, mumbling to his daughter, trying to explain what he had done. His memories again took flight, soaring across the rainy Los Angeles sky, heading for Mexico. His life had two parts: before Isadora, and after her.

The Day of the Moon

In the beginning he was an ordinary boy. His father, Edmundo Betancourt, was a grocer who had settled in Arandas, Jalisco, having immigrated from somewhere in Spain. He never spoke of himself. As Flavio grew older, he heard others say that they suspected that his father was a deserter.

Flavio had a sister, Brígida, who was six years younger. Both had inherited their father's fair skin and blue eyes. His mother, on the other hand, was very dark. She was a native, and Flavio did not know why his father had married her. As he remembered it, his father hardly spoke to her. But her image clung to Flavio. Her face was long, her skin the color of mahogany, and her eyes oval-shaped with straight, long eyelashes. She always wore her hair, which was black and thick, in a braid tied at the nape of her neck.

Flavio could not remember her ever speaking, and she hardly came near her own children because their father had instructed her to tend to the chores of the house; he would be in charge of the boy and girl. Flavio had only two memories of his mother. The first was of once when he crept into the kitchen, where he watched her for a long time. She moved silently, first stoking the stove and then washing pots in the stone sink. Even though the place was gloomy with smoke, she was aware that the boy was there. He knew it because as she worked she looked over to the corner where he stood. She smiled at him. He remembered that clearly.

The second memory he had of his mother was of another time, when he was at his place waiting for breakfast. Brígida was sitting across from him, and their father had not yet come to the table. Flavio's mother came in to serve their milk. She was pouring his glass when suddenly she stopped, put down the pitcher, and took the boy's face in her hands. She held it so that he looked into her eyes. They were so black they glowed like silver, but they were not hard, they were soft. Her gesture lasted only a short while. The children's father came into the room, and she let go of Flavio's face.

Flavio always thought it strange that both Brígida and he came from a body that was so dark. Sometimes he wondered if she really was their mother. He did not want an Indian woman for a mother. But the servants would not let him forget who she was; even his father admitted that she was Flavio's mother. But he knew that he never loved the woman who bore him and that he never wanted to speak to her.

She died when Flavio was fifteen years old. By that time he had almost forgotten her. Flavio often thought that the beginning of his story was when he chose to blot his mother out of his memory. He told himself that there was nothing wrong in this, because even though he did not love his mother, he loved his sister. Years later he discovered that he was wrong: The only person he ever loved was his dear daughter.

Flavio left his father's home when he was eighteen because he did not want to be a grocer. He made his way north; if a man was to be successful, it had to be to the north. Finding the place in which he wanted to stay took several years. He worked on farms, on ranches, in towns, all the time getting farther away from the ordinary boy he once was.

When he got work at Hacienda Miraflores he felt lucky because the owner, Anastasio Ortega, was of a powerful family. Flavio liked to watch how the *Patrón* walked and wore his hat; and, without anyone noticing, Flavio began to imitate him. This went on until the day he beat Anastasio Ortega at cards.

Sitting in his armchair, old Don Flavio stared through the window reliving those moments. Even the smell of alcohol and rancid cigarette smoke filled his nostrils. On that night every sound had stopped in the cantina. The tinkling notes of the piano next to the bar dropped off. Loud laughter and horseplay abruptly stopped. Women, brightly painted and corseted, moved cautiously toward the card table. Men, sweaty and unwashed, turned away from half-empty shot glasses. One man stood up so unexpectedly that the woman sitting on his lap fell to the floor.

Chapter 2

Ciudad Creel, Chihuahua, 1906

"Amigo, cuidado. Be careful. Don Anastasio knows what he's doing. You might lose the whole thing, even your wages."

Celestino Santiago stooped over his friend's shoulder as he whispered, trying to counsel him against making the next move. Twenty-six-year old Flavio Betancourt knew what Celestino was talking about; the man sitting across the table was the *Patrón,* the ranch owner who paid him for breaking horses. He had a reputation for winning at cards.

Without responding, Flavio gazed into Celestino's face for a few seconds, as if his next move might be reflected in his eyes. Flavio scanned the copper-colored face, its long, beaked nose, the black, slanted eyes, broad cheekbones and protruding upper lip, the slack, drooping mustache that coiled nearly to his chin. Flavio then looked over to the dealer, scrutinizing him. The man's thin face betrayed nothing. He sat poised, holding the deck of cards securely between his hands. His eyes were so narrow that Flavio could barely make out the tiny pupils.

Shifting his attention, Flavio scanned the table, taking in the pile of silver pesos, ashtrays heaped with cigarette and cigar butts, empty beer and tequila bottles. The air was heavy with the blue haze of smoke. Part of the money piled in front of him came from five years of working and saving, and some of it had been won that night, but this was his entire holding. If he lost, he would have nothing; he would have to begin all over again.

Anastasio Ortega tried to smile at his ranch hand, but it was instead a sneer that spread out under his thick mustache. He was an experienced gambler, but he had been losing badly all night. As he waited, Anastasio reminded himself that he was a son of the landed gentry of Chihuahua. If he lost everything, there would still be more waiting for him at his father's door.

Ortega became aware, in the silence, that the table was now surrounded by the men who worked for him and by the women who slept with them. He thought of vultures. He looked over his left shoulder to make sure that his bodyguard stood behind him.

Flavio was taking time to place his bet, and for Anastasio the minutes dragged. Anastasio looked at his hand again and thought that it was almost unbeatable. He had been foolish to even think that his losing streak would hold. At any rate, he had made his move. Anastasio sniffed the air confidently when he sensed Flavio's hesitation. He tried to smile, but again it was only a grimace.

"I'll call. A thousand pesos. Everything."

As Flavio slid his coins towards the center of the table, he tipped over a glass; its contents dripped, spilling onto the floor. Anastasio was motionless.

"I've paid to see." Flavio's voice was steady, almost demanding. "What do you have?"

"Three queens and a pair of tens."

Anastasio spread his cards on the soiled green felt. The bright colors of profiled, flat-eyed queens, spades, diamonds, tens flashed through the haze. A hiss—half-whistle, half sigh—rolled off the lips of the curious spectators.

Without saying anything, Flavio put his cards on the table. Everyone shuffled forward, craning their necks, squeezing in as much as they could. Celestino closed his eyes, certain that Flavio's hand would not match Anastasio's, but he opened them when he heard a gasp. He gaped at the blues and blacks of four aces that seemed to leap from the table, alongside the devilish grin of the joker, *el comodín,* which mocked Anastasio Ortega.

There was silence for a few moments. What if Anastasio Ortega was armed? What if someone pulled a knife? Quietly, the onlookers began to creep for the doors, for the stairs, for anywhere that would remove them from risk. Only Celestino Santiago remained standing by Flavio Betancourt, as did Anastasio's bodyguard.

Neither man spoke; they seemed lashed onto the chairs that held them. It was Anastasio who moved first. He reached over and pushed the pile of coins toward Flavio, trying to make his voice calm, matter-of-fact.

"It's yours. You've won it."

This unexpected manner perplexed Flavio because he, too, was expecting a confrontation. He felt a growing suspicion as he cautiously pulled the money towards his chest. The pile of silver was more money than he had ever seen or possessed.

"You're a good loser?"

Anastasio smiled sardonically at Flavio but he kept silent for a long while.

"No, I'm not a good loser, and I take back what I just said. I haven't lost because I'm going to win it back. I have one more bet, and this time you're the one who will lose. Are you willing to play one more hand?"

Anastasio's voice was challenging, almost sarcastic. The bodyguard behind him put his hand on his shoulder, trying to convince him to stop, to leave the place. Anastasio shrugged off the hand as he glared at Betancourt. He reached into the inner pocket of his jacket and produced a document.

"It's the deed to my ranch. It includes my wife and four children. I bet all of it against that money that's in front of you."

Now it was Celestino who grabbed Flavio's shoulder as he whispered:

"Don't! You've won more money than you could make in five years. Don't risk it, Flavio. Besides, it will be the whole Ortega clan that you'll have to face if you win. Take your money and walk away from this."

"The hacienda? Your wife and children? Don Anastasio, you're trying to make a fool of me. You don't mean what you're saying." Flavio stood abruptly ready to leave, but Anastasio lunged from his chair, clamping Flavio back into the chair. The two men glared at one another.

"Have you never heard of such a bet? It happens frequently. Here it is, Betancourt, the opportunity of your life. Did you think that you would ever be in the position to own a ranch such as mine? Now *you* can be *Patrón*. Think of it! You make yourself the fool if you refuse."

Flavio relaxed in the seat. He had dreamed of being a land owner, he had secretly wished to be of the privileged few of these parts. Staring at the man who was his boss, he saw the mockery in his eyes. He pushed the pesos back toward the center of the table.

"A new deck!"

Anastasio's order to the dealer was crisp, urgent. The man silently went to a cabinet. The two gamblers glared at one another as the dealer removed the deck from its box, shuffled the cards, and indicated he was ready.

"Un albur."

Celestino began to breathe through his mouth when he heard Anastasio call for the play that narrowed the possibilities for the players. With *el albur*, the dealer cut the deck and dealt each gambler one card. The highest card won the bet. One card apiece, that was all; there were no discards, no fresh possibilities.

Flavio's mouth went dry. There was still time to decline, to take his money and return to work for Anastasio Ortega as if nothing had happened. Gambling was an everyday occurrence in Creel and the surrounding haciendas. But when he looked at his opponent, he deciphered fear in his eyes, and this made the difference for Flavio.

"De acuerdo. Un albur."

He agreed, thinking that his voice sounded thin, different. The dealer shuffled and reshuffled the cards. When it was time to cut the deck, he asked if both men agreed that he should do it. They nodded their permission. Anastasio got the first card, Betancourt the next one.

"*Señor* Ortega, please show your card."

The dealer's voice was taut, nervous. Anastasio turned over his card. It was the ten of spades.

"*Señor* Betancourt, please show your card."

The dealer's voice had escalated in pitch. Flavio's fingers trembled as he flipped over the card. It was *el comodín,* the joker again flashing its demonic grin. Anastasio's cheeks began to quiver as he rose to his feet. His voice now cracked under the weight of the insult he hurled at the winner.

"¡Eres el patrón, hijo de tu chingada madre!"

Flavio chose to respond calmly, and the tone of his voice startled even him: Although quiet, it was charged with haughtiness. He could now give orders to the man who, seconds before, had been his superior. Flavio liked his words and what he was feeling.

"The ranch and everything on it is now mine, but take your wife and children. I don't consider them part of the bet."

Flavio and Celestino walked out onto the muddy streets of Ciudad Creel in a deep silence which lasted for almost an hour. Each man cradled his thoughts as if they had been cards still clutched close to the chest. Celestino understood that they were no longer equal. Until then, they had been *compañeros,* taming horses, living in the common house shared by the Mestizos and Rarámuris. Now Flavio was *Patrón.*

On the next day, when he arrived at the hacienda to make sure that Anastasio Ortega had taken his wife and children off the property, Flavio had prepared himself to be hard. When he saw the woman and the children crying, he felt pity. He was almost ashamed of himself, but he pushed away his sentiments. He had won without cheating, without betrayal. It was legal and he had nothing to regret. He turned his back while Anastasio Ortega loaded his family onto a carriage and he did not look back. He never saw Anastasio Ortega again.

After winning the hacienda, Flavio concentrated on the house and its lands. Repairs were needed, additions had to be made. Mexico also was changing. The copper miners' uprising at Cananea was put down, but not forgotten. Don Porfirio, *el Presidente,* was in trouble. Everyone knew it. Those who clung to the old ways were going to be left behind.

Later on, when the war began, he was cautious. He sniffed the air and when the revolutionaries were on top, he was a revolutionary. When the *Federales* took the lead, he was a *Federal*. When the Zapatistas clamored for land for their Indians and *peones,* Flavio agreed, but he never said when he would give up the land. Depending upon who was victorious, Flavio was Carrancista, or Villista, or Obregonista. It did not matter. As long as they were on top, he was with them.

In the growing shadows of his room the old man wagged his head, approving of that distant memory, trying to convince his daughter of the righteousness of his actions. He knew that she was not in the room with him. Nonetheless, he saw her. The mass of golden curls formed an aura around Isadora's face, carving her out of the darkness. Don Flavio inhaled the damp air of Chihuahua and he reminded his daughter that it was a time when men seized and lost fortunes on a wager, at the whim of a Joker's grin. He wrinkled his brow as he held his gnarled hands over his puffy abdomen, hoping that she would understand his side of the story.

Chapter 3

Five years after Flavio gained ownership of the hacienda, Brígida Betancourt stepped off the train in Ciudad Creel to find her brother waiting for her. She had not seen him in nearly ten years. She was fatigued by the long trip. Even traveling with a woman companion, the distance between Jalisco and Chihuahua had seemed endless.

Don Porfirio Díaz had resigned the presidency in May of that year after the younger Franciso Madero had captured Ciudad Juárez. In June his forces marched into Mexico City, and Emiliano Zapata's army was organizing to formulate a plan at the end of that month. Brígida's train had run into stoppages and interruptions. The coaches were packed beyond capacity. Hordes of *peones,* most of them armed, clung to the roofs of the wagons, lugging their possessions and even their women and children.

"Welcome to Chihuahua. I hope your trip was not too unpleasant." Flavio's voice was low, and his smile told her that he knew what she had experienced.

"It was not too difficult."

As usual, Brígida found herself short of words; it always was a hardship for her to speak more than she thought necessary. She examined her brother and saw that he had grown taller since she had last seen him. His body had become muscular and his skin, naturally as white as hers, was tanned by the northern sun. When he removed his hat, she saw that his hair was blonder than she remembered, as was the handlebar mustache that shadowed his full upper lip.

Flavio also took time to inspect his sister. Her blue eyes sparkled as they had when she was a girl. The features of her face were elegant, finely chiseled, and when he slid his gaze down from her throat, he thought that she was somewhat tall for a woman.

"I know you'll be happy here."

Flavio bent over as he brushed her cheek with a kiss. She smiled in return, and he saw that her teeth were even and white. He was pleased because he intended that Brígida be the center of his hacienda until his marriage with Velia Carmelita Urrutia. After that, he would acquire a husband for her. It was encouraging to see that she was attractive, despite her having somewhat passed marriageable age.

The driver and two Rarámuri natives loaded the luggage and parcels onto a wagon while she and Flavio waited under a shaded porch. When the men were finished, the driver signaled that they were ready to leave. Flavio took his sister by the arm and helped her into a carriage. They rode in silence until they reached the gates of the hacienda. Flavio Betancourt had prospered over the past five years. He had expanded the horse ranch into a vast hacienda that spread out toward the skirts of the Sierra Madre on the west and downward along the Sierra Tarahumara. His land covered territory north almost to Ciudad Chihuahua and south nearly reaching Ciudad Creel. The Urique River watered the flat parts of Hacienda Miraflores before it disappeared into Urique Canyon.

The herds that Anastasio Ortega had gambled away had, under their new owner, multiplied into thousands of saddle horses and pack mules. Flavio Betancourt now socialized and did business with powerful families—the likes of the Terrazas, the Urrutias, the Reynosos, and even the Manriques. His stock was traded in markets and auctions reaching north as far as the copper mines of Cananea in Sonora and south to the silver mines of San Luis Potosí and Guanajuato. His *peones,* horsebreakers, and Rarámuri natives numbered in the scores. They were all his. He had made them grow. He had known how to deal with the armies of the Revolution that came and went through Chihuahua.

He looked at his sister out of the corner of his eye. Telling the driver to stop, Flavio stretched his arms wide, pointing to the buildings that loomed in front of them.

"This is your home. I've called it Casa Miraflores."

He jutted his chin in the direction of a mansion surrounded by an arched cloister. Other sheds and huts, some small, others larger, circled it, clinging to the pink residence like flowers under the shade of a huge tree. But Flavio's cocky gesture was cut off when he turned to face Brígida. She looked at him, and the boldness of her stare startled him; his self-confidence began to erode. He realized that she was not awed by him, nor by what she was seeing.

"You haven't asked about our father. Aren't you curious about him?" Brígida's tone of voice caught him off guard. It was cold, threatening, and he did not like it. He had grown used to being the only one to speak in such a tone.

"He's dead. What else do I need to know." It was Flavio's turn to be overbearing, his voice filled with ice. He frowned, disliking the direction their conversation was taking.

"You need to know that he took his life because we had fallen into poverty. You could have prevented that from happening."

He glared at his sister, realizing that he disliked her intensely at that moment. He wanted to tell her that she was there only because he needed the legitimacy of family. He resented Brígida's tone, her manner, and most of all the haughty look in her eyes. He decided that he would marry her off as soon as possible.

Flavio signaled the driver to head for the entrance. They fell into sullen silence until the carriage halted and he jumped from the vehicle without using the steps. Then he turned and extended his hand to Brígida, who stepped down with an affectation of aristocracy which surprised Flavio but which he calculated would be on his side in his negotiations for her marriage. That night as Flavio and Brígida were being served dinner, he went directly to the point.

"I'm to marry next month." He was peeling a pear. As he sliced off a wedge, he put it into his mouth with the blade of the knife. He waited until Brígida said something.

"Married? To whom?"

Her eyebrows had arched. Her expression said that she now understood why he had dragged her across hundreds of miles to his hacienda.

"Her name is Velia Carmelita Urrutia. Her family is influential in these parts."

"I see." Brígida was not eating; she was rubbing a water glass between her hands. "Do you love her?"

Again, the blunt way in which his sister probed into the privacy of his life irritated Flavio. He found being scrutinized by Brígida repugnant. He disliked being asked such questions, especially when they came from a woman, and that woman his sister.

"Don't you think that's my business?"

"You've answered my question. I supposed a more important question would be to wonder if she loves you. Eh?"

Brígida smiled, sarcasm stamped on her face. She looked as if she might burst out laughing. This was not the way Flavio had imagined his sister. He had assumed that she would be filled with gratitude and admiration for him. Instead he was faced with rudeness and impertinence. The young woman's face was a mask; something hard lurked behind it.

He fought the impulse to stand up and slap Brígida. Instead, he re-filled his wine glass and gulped it down. He knew now that her being in the same house with him would not work. He had thought that having her might bring to Casa Miraflores the civility and respectability demanded by a family such as the Urrutias. To the contrary, his sister would be nothing less than a constant annoyance, a disadvantage. Flavio understood that he had made a mistake. He glared at his sister through half-closed eyes, deciding to put her in place without losing time.

"I didn't bring you from Arandas so that you could mock me. I want you to understand that immediately."

He sat rigidly in the high-backed chair and pressed his body against it with such force that he heard the wooden frame squeak. He saw, however, that the look of sarcasm had only deepened around her eyes and mouth. His mind searched for a way to crush her boldness. "It's my intention that you marry as soon after me as possible. I—"

Flavio's words were cut off by his sister's laughter. Loud, cackling, vulgar, it came from the center of her body and echoed off the high ceiling of the chamber. She went on giggling until her face turned red and tears ran down her cheeks. He felt his nerves beginning to unravel. *She was laughing at him.* Flavio knew that he was losing control when he tasted a bitterness on his tongue.

As she went on with her merriment, he sprang to his feet, knocking the chair onto the floor. He banged the table with his clenched fist with such force that plates, glasses, and silverware crashed to the floor. Two women servants ran into the room, not knowing what to expect. They cowered when they saw Don Flavio, feet spread apart, his face purple with rage and his hair sticking out as if he had seen the devil.

"You'll hear from me tomorrow!"

He stalked out of the room, but not before Brígida had the last word, her voice still tinged with derision.

"You'll never marry me off! Never! Never!"

The next day, still in bed, she received a letter from Flavio. The servant who brought it to her was careful to knock at the door, open the shutters and windows, and bow in respect to the sister of the *Patrón*.

"*Buenos días, Niña.*"

"*Buenos días.*"

Brígida stared at the young woman as she moved, folding clothing and picking up the room. She was captivated by the Indian's graceful, quiet motions and the manner in which her bare feet slid on the polished hardwood floor.

"What is your name?"

"Ursula Santiago, *Niña.*"

She was a Rarámuri woman wearing the traditional cotton dress that reached nearly to her ankles. Her hair hung below her shoulders in two braids. She handed Brígida the sealed envelope and silently left the bedroom.

> *Brígida, You will marry the man that I select for you when I order you to do so. If you do not obey me, you will find yourself on the streets of Ciudad Creel.*

The note was not signed. Brígida laid back on the pillows for a long while, thinking, the note crumpled in her left hand. Then she smoothed the paper and re-read the words. She got out of bed, called the servant, and instructed her to bring hot water for her to bathe in. After she did this, she dressed, asked for a cup of chocolate, and she drank as she gazed out the window.

Brígida feared being destitute, but she dreaded being married even more. She had known from girlhood that she would do anything to keep from the condition that had turned her mother into a shadow. She had been very young when her mother had died, but Brígida remembered enough to see how her father disdained the woman who had given him pleasure. She was convinced that her mother had sickened and perished because of that abandonment, and she had determined then that she would never marry.

Brígida closed her eyes; she was shaky, unsure of what to do. She regretted having mocked her brother, but it had happened thoughtlessly. His conversation about marriage had taken her by surprise and unnerved her. It had clearly been a threat on his part and something inside of her had leapt, fought back, and it had come out sounding scornful. She thought of apologizing to Flavio, but something inside of her recoiled at the idea. She then considered conforming to his wishes and agreeing to marry, but she was sickened by the thought.

Brígida made her decision. She went to the desk at the far end of the bedroom, took a sheet of paper from a drawer and answered her brother.

I will never marry because I was not born to do so. If you cast me out, I will see to it that the scandal is so enormous that you will be rejected by the Urrutias and all other such families.

Flavio Betancourt was forced to allow his sister to remain in Casa Miraflores while he planned his wedding. He brought to the union holdings that, even though moderate, were among the most promising in Chihuahua. However, even though he was now wealthy, he was still a newcomer. No one forgot this, especially not Flavio.

On the other hand, Velia Carmelita Urrutia brought herself as the main prize of the marriage dowry. She was the only daughter of Don Plutarco and Doña Domitila, one of the most powerful families of the region, owners of silver and copper mines as well as vast territories housing more mineral wealth. Don Plutarco had been part of the turn-of-the-century mining boom in the Batopilas Canyon; the La Bufa veins, already of world fame by the time of the wedding, belonged to him.

It was an arranged marriage even though Flavio had fallen in love with Velia Carmelita when he had first seen her three years earlier, at a ball in honor of her coming out. At the time, she had hardly taken notice of the tall, blond man, but when her father told her of his plans, she agreed to marry. Her mother and father admired Flavio's aristocratic bearing, his ability in politics and war, and even though his holdings were dwarfed by the Urrutia wealth, he was suited for her.

Chapter 4

On the day of the wedding, garlanded carriages filed from the Urrutia mansion, heading for the church of Nuestra Señora de los Dolores, the mission church for the Samachique Rarámuri town that marked the beginning of the road to Batopilas. A long line of coaches accompanied the bride; they were filled with laughing girls feeling the thrill that one of their own age was about to be married. The young men of the surrounding families followed on purebred mounts. These men did their best to attract the attention of the girls, knowing that one of them more than likely would be his bride.

Flavio rode among these men. He was dressed in the northern fashion: black riding suit, fine boots, white tie and gloves, and a black Stetson hat. He felt tense but happy. He was marrying into a notable family, and he had the good fortune that the woman to be his wife was beautiful and, he told himself, he was luckier yet to be in love. This did not happen to many men.

Flavio's and Velia Carmelita's wedding day was the culminating point of days of celebration which had taken place at both residences: *rodeos, coleaderos, barbacoas, fandangos, verbenas.* Flavio had provided dozens of calves, chickens, venison, ducks, pigs and sheep for the meals of his ranch hands, and especially for *la indiada,* the Rarámuri people. He had held back nothing, giving his people days off and providing everyone with enough *mescal* and *cerveza* to last days. He had put up money for musicians and singers to entertain the throngs of men, women, and children who had come down from the sierras to help him celebrate his wedding. Long-distance foot racing, betting, and gambling drew dozens of Rarámuri to the hacienda. Singing and dancing in the surrounding fields preceded the wedding mass by days, and Flavio participated as much as he could by sitting by the bonfires at night, drinking *mescal,* and eating roasted lamb or pork wrapped in corn tortillas.

In charge of all of this was Celestino Santiago, the Rarámuri who had once been Flavio's friend but who now was the *caporal,* the head ranch hand. He had differed from many of the Rarámuri men by becoming a skilled horsebreaker, usually the job of mestizos. He was one of the few natives in those parts who was not a runner; he preferred horses, and it was chiefly because of his abilities that Flavio had made him his main overseer. Nor had he forgotten that Celestino had stood by his side when he won the hacienda in the card game.

Celestino had since married and usually lived with his wife and sons in the caves of the Copper Canyon, la Barranca del Cobre, but he bunked at the hacienda when he was most needed. The wedding was one of those occasions. On one of the nights of celebration Flavio noticed that Celestino had brought his children.

"These are your sons?"

The two boys hid behind their father. Flavio made faces, trying to tease them, but they shrank even further behind Celestino.

"*Sí, patrón,* and there's another one up in *la barranca* with his mother. We baptized him the other day."

As the two men spoke, shadows and light flickered from the campfire, casting Celestino's features into a mask. Flavio studied that face again, as he had done the night of the card game. He made a point of looking at the prominent cheekbones, slanted eyes, wide mouth with the protruding teeth, sparse mustache, and broad forehead.

"Another boy? I'm happy for you. Maybe soon I'll catch up with you. What did you call him?"

Flavio knew that he would hear a Christian name, but the true one would be held secret from him. Everyone was aware that the Rarámuri kept their true names to themselves.

"His name is Jerónimo."

As the celebrations went on, Flavio had teams of Rarámuri women come to the hacienda during the day to clean, move furniture, place new curtains, polish silver platters and goblets. He had a chamber prepared that was to be for Velia Carmelita and himself. He chose the one with the windows opening to the most impressive views of the sierras and meadows surrounding Hacienda Miraflores. He had women embroider linen with the initials *F* and *V* for their bed, and he commissioned dressmakers to make gowns for his new bride.

Flavio did not keep track of the money he was spending. Although on the other side of the residence his sister brooded, left out and uninvolved, he went ahead on his own, anxious and excited. The news had come that, with the entry of Francisco Madero into Mexico City, the Revolution was now a success. The war had ended and people could continue with their lives as usual. So Flavio was determined that his and Velia Carmelita's would be an unforgettable match.

Similar celebrations were happening at the Urrutia mansion, and the wedding ball, scheduled to take place after the mass in the main salon of Velia Carmelita's home, would be the highlight of the wedding.

As Flavio galloped toward the church that morning, he felt happy and grateful. He had even forgotten that Brígida was also part of the procession heading toward the mass, because she rode in a separate carriage far behind him.

When the musicians struck the first note of the wedding march, Flavio waited at the foot of the altar. His heart was beating so fast that he found it difficult to keep his hands from trembling. He looked up at the intricate niches, fluted pillars, gilded frames, and chubby-faced cherubim, then he breathed deeply, trying to steady his nerves. He forced himself to concentrate on the details of the church as he scanned the ornately carved altar loaded with white flowers, placed to accentuate the golden tabernacle. Above it loomed the image of a triumphant Christ with Mary, Mother of

Sorrows, at his side. The rest of the facade was taken up with the images of Jesuit saints, other holy figures, and angels with outstretched wings. Flavio closed his eyes, but the brilliance of the church penetrated the darkness behind his eyelids.

The organ's somber tones, combined with the silvery voices of violins, filled the nave of the church, bouncing off its baroque columns, stained-glass windows, and marbled images of Christ on the way to His crucifixion. The place was filled to capacity with gloved men in white ties and tails, and women dressed in brocades, lace, and broad-brimmed hats. The radiance of their jewelry matched the silver of the candelabra. It was through the center of this congregation that Velia Carmelita moved toward the altar on the arm of her father, Don Plutarco.

Flavio sucked in his breath when he caught sight of her: white gown, slim, corseted waist, uplifted breasts, high lace collar, diamonds hanging from her earlobes and intertwined in thick, auburn-colored hair; a gauzy veil proclaiming her virginity. When she reached the steps leading to the altar, he offered her his arm. Bride and groom climbed the three steps to kneel in front of the waiting priest and two altar boys. The music trailed until it stopped; someone in the back coughed, and this was echoed by another person clearing his throat.

"In nomine Patris, et Filii, et Spiritus Sancti. Amen."

The nuptial mass began, full of ritual and ceremony. People stood, knelt, or sat in imitation of the priest and altar boys. This was repeated over and again through the different parts of the mass. At the exchange of vows, everyone craned their necks, turning their ears in the direction of the altar, trying to see and hear what was happening. A few were able to glimpse Flavio putting the ring on Velia Carmelita's finger. Later others heard parts of her vows as the words floated up toward the gilded cupola that towered above the altar.

Brígida alone sat rigidly; she did not stand or kneel during the mass but kept her place, seemingly paralyzed and unmoving. When it began, she had stood along with the rest of the congregation, and because she was seated by the aisle, she was able to see Velia Carmelita closely as she walked by on her way toward Flavio. Brígida's eyes saw through the flimsy veil and captured the beauty of that face: olive-colored skin, round, full lips, Grecian nose, and hair the color of chestnuts.

Velia Carmelita's eyes were like none ever seen by Brígida. They were light brown and seemed to be gazing from heaven toward the altar. As she walked past her, Brígida examined the high, firm breasts outlined by the silk gown, and she was assaulted by an inexplicable impulse to reach out, put her hands on them, caress them, kiss them.

By the time Velia Carmelita reached Flavio, Brígida had been compelled to sit: The blood in her temples was pounding with such force as to make her dizzy, and she was afraid of falling. When she sat down, she closed her eyes, confused, not understanding the whirlwind of emotion that had overtaken her. She had never felt such sentiments: a mix of love, desire, happiness, wretchedness, tenderness and shame collided in her heart. Velia Carmelita's beauty had touched Brígida's soul as nothing else had in her life.

"Cor Jesu sacratissimum, miserere nobis."

The mass ended. The triumphant musical notes of the orchestra tore through the upper reaches of the church and the congregation stood, happy and relieved that the long ceremony had come to a close and that now the much anticipated ball would begin. Everyone crowded after the couple, trying to squeeze out the front portals of the church. They wanted to touch, embrace, express good wishes and congratulations to the bride and groom. Only Brígida remained seated, riveted and bewildered by the emotions she had experienced during the mass.

The celebration lasted until sunrise of the next day. Don Plutarco and Doña Domitila had left nothing undone to make the ball the most memorable in those parts. The food and drink was of the best, and the music was in the latest fashion from Vienna and Paris. Eligible men waltzed with young women, flirting, eyeing each other, enjoying the fiesta of the season. Flavio danced with

Velia Carmelita over and again because he wanted her to feel the desire that he was feeling. He smiled at her, made small talk, teased, squeezed her gloved hand. Yet instead of warming to him, she became stiffer and more remote with each hour.

On the other side of the hall, Brígida also danced because she was beautiful, and many of the men wanted to strike up a connection with the sister of Don Flavio Betancourt. She danced, but her mind was absorbed by Velia Carmelita. She constantly searched the crowded dance floor until she made out her brother and his new wife. Brígida wanted to go to her, put her arms around her, tell her how she felt. Instead she forced herself to dance with whoever asked her. It made no difference. Every one of those men was equally repugnant to her.

When it was time for Flavio and Velia Carmelita to retire, a hush came over the guests. She went first to her father, then to her mother. There were kisses and blessings: *Que Dios te bendiga, hija.* As the bride and groom disappeared down the corridor to the private chambers of the hacienda, the music struck up again and the fiesta continued. Only Brígida, once more, remained seated.

When they were in the room, Flavio coaxed Velia Carmelita to come to him. She did as he asked and sat down stiffly by him on the edge of the bed. He began to kiss her face, forehead, temples, the tip of her nose and then a soft brush on her lips. She pulled back.

"Please. Don't be afraid."

"Don Flavio . . ."

"I'm not Don Flavio. I'm your husband. Call me by my name."

He put his hand on her breast and she jerked back so violently that she nearly lost her balance. This excited Flavio more, so he pressed her down onto the bed, where they lay for a while. Then he began to unbutton her gown; she remained motionless until he was almost finished. Unexpectedly, she sprang from the bed and rushed toward the door, but Flavio was faster, and he caught her by the waist. He was so aroused by that time that he began to rip off her clothes.

Velia Carmelita struggled against him with as much force as she could, but Flavio overcame her. He fumbled and tore at her gown, then her underwear, with one hand, while he took his own clothing off with the other. It was awkward, hard, cruel, but he could not stop himself. She sobbed and pushed against him, but that excited him more and he wrestled her to the floor.

Flavio finally pinned Velia Carmelita to the floor, where he forced himself between her thighs and penetrated her. It was fast, without sentiment, without words. He climaxed in a burst of pleasure, but her whimpering told him that she had felt nothing but pain. When it was finished, he scrambled to his feet, hastily put on his clothes and left the room feeling ashamed and angry.

After that night, Flavio took Velia Carmelita to his hacienda, where he repeated what had happened on their wedding night many times, because she refused him each time. After a while, he became convinced that something was wrong with her and that she would never love him. So he entered Velia Carmelita's room, night after night, forcing himself on her until he impregnated her. After that, he left her alone.

Chapter 5

The year that followed the marriage was peaceful for Mexico. Francisco Madero was president and, although in the south Emiliano Zapata did not let up on his threat to unleash his people unless they received the land they had been promised, and in the north Francisco Villa also talked loudly about his *Division del Norte,* still, the nation went about its business.

During those months, Flavio brooded and spent most of his time with Celestino and the other hands, talking only to them and eating with them most of the time. He often traveled to Ciudad Creel and as far as Ciudad Chihuahua to close deals or to meet with associates who still were nervous about events in the nation's capital. Word had spread about a certain Victoriano Huerta, a general who had made a reputation as an Indian hunter decades earlier. He was an assassin, and rumor had it that he had wheedled his way too close to President Madero.

Flavio attended meetings and helped draft documents, plans, and manifestos, but that was his public life. Privately, he became more and more solitary. He had stopped going to Velia Carmelita's room when he discovered that she was pregnant, so he hardly saw her. Sometimes he joined her and Brígida at table, but whenever he did, he sat in morose silence. At those times, the only sounds to be heard were those of silverware scraping on china, or the gurgling of water poured into glasses. The two women followed Flavio's lead and neither spoke when he was present. He was aware, however, that their silence was aimed at him, knowing that they spent most of the day together and that they enjoyed each other's company. He had got this information from the servants, and it filled him with resentment because he could not understand why Velia Carmelita preferred his sister to him.

Despite the bits of gossip that he garnered from his workers, Flavio still did not know the full story. No one had told him that from the beginning, the two women had drifted toward each other. At first Brígida and Velia Carmelita had only chatted, telling each other of their childhood and adolescence, their pastimes and favorite things. Only they knew that each night, after Flavio had forced himself on Velia Carmelita, she secretly came to Brígida for comfort. At those times she got into bed with Brígida, who held her in her arms, soothing her, singing softly to her, until she fell asleep. The servants' prying eyes were not there the night when Velia Carmelita kissed Brígida. It was the first time, and it was a kiss that barely grazed her lips. This was followed by caresses, then a kiss in which their lips lingered, clinging to one another. It escaped everyone that after that, the two women became lovers.

What the servants *did* tell Flavio was that as the days became months, Velia Carmelita and Brígida had become inseparable. At times they embroidered, at others they played instruments. The servants informed him of the two women's singing, harmonizing, giggling when the notes fell flat. The *vaqueros* spread the word of how the *Patron's* wife and sister mounted horses and rode through *el llano* of Hacienda Miraflores for hours. Everyone saw that when Velia Carmelita began to show her pregnancy, she and Brígida rode in a small carriage, taking turns with the reins. Then, as she became heavy with the child, the two women gave that up and walked arm in arm through the corridors and patios of the house. What no one could report to Flavio, however, was that each day brought a new intensity to Brígida's and Velia Carmelita's love, a companionship in which they discovered a happiness neither had known before.

One evening, toward the end of November, Flavio joined his sister and wife for dinner. As usual, only the muffled coming and going of the servants broke the silence. At one point, when Flavio happened to look up, he saw the two women looking at each other, smiling. Joy was stamped on Brígida's face. Then he glanced at

Velia Carmelita and caught a similar expression. Rage welled up from his belly until it flooded his mouth, and he had to open it for fear of choking. But instead of the foul breath he had expected to come out, he heard himself speak. His voice was dry, incensed.

"Why are you smiling?"

He stared at his sister, who said nothing. Instead she answered his glare with an insolent shrug of the shoulders. Brígida hardly spoke to her brother, much less looked at him. This time, however, her eyes were filled with what Flavio thought was provocation.

"I asked you a question. What is making you smile?"

Velia Carmelita abruptly stood up to leave the room and Flavio saw that her abdomen had swelled since the last time that he had looked. He realized that he had allowed time to slip through his fingers, and he could not be sure if it had been weeks or even months since he had last been in her bedroom. Suddenly the rage that had filled him moments before melted into tenderness. He wanted to go to his wife, embrace her, tell her that he loved her and that he wanted the child above all things. He stood as he called out to her.

"Velia Carmelita . . ."

It was too late. She had slipped around the door and into the darkened corridor. When Flavio looked at Brígida, he saw that her eyes were now filled with apprehension. A look of protectiveness had invaded her face, hostile just a moment before.

He sat down, the palms of his hands flat against the surface of the table. Flavio was pressing so hard that the knuckles of his hands turned a bluish white. The only sound to be heard was the buzzing of a fly trapped amid the upper beams of the ceiling. Dread began to take shape in him, pushing away confusion and filling him with alarm. He looked up at Brígida; she was still sitting in her place. Her expression reflected her thoughts so clearly that Flavio was suddenly aware of the emotions hidden behind the skin masking her face. As he stared at his sister, he understood instantly what had happened between his sister and his wife during the past months. Brígida, undaunted, returned her brother's glare for a few moments, then calmly folded her napkin, placed it by the plate and wordlessly left the room.

Brígida went to Velia Carmelita's room, where she put her arms around her. They sat in darkness for a long time; neither of them spoke, and although they had done this many times, for Brígida it was the reason for her existence. Taking Velia Carmelita's face in her hands, Brígida kissed her lips, and she felt her kiss returned with a passion that equaled hers.

That night Flavio Betancourt decided to abandon Hacienda Miraflores. At daybreak, before leaving, he met Celestino Santiago in the patio between the mansion and stables.

"I'm leaving and I don't know how long I'll be away. I need someone to take care of the place."

Celestino kept silent as he peered at Flavio from under the wide brim of his sombrero. He shook his head.

"*No, señor.* It can't be me. I'm a Rarámuri, *un indio.* People will think you've gone crazy. They'll disregard your wishes. Pick someone else. Maybe somebody in town, or even in Chihuahua. If not from there, then one of your other *mestizo caporales* will do the job."

Flavio shook his head. Then he stooped and took out a packet of letters from the saddlebag he had put down on the ground.

"Look, Celestino, these are my orders to the magistrates in both places. They'll respect me and give you everything you need to keep the hacienda going. It won't be for long; or maybe it will. I don't know. You're the *patrón* now."

Celestino squinted his eyes and slowly shook his head. It would not work; someone like him could not be a *patrón.* But Flavio misinterpreted Celestino's gesture, certain that he knew why he was leaving. He was sure that everyone—horsebreakers, cooks, blacksmiths, dressmakers, housekeepers—knew that his wife and sister were lovers. He was convinced that they were laughing at him or feeling pity. Blood flushed his face. Disregarding Celestino, Flavio mounted his horse and rode away. It was the early dawn of one of the last days of November, 1912.

The Day of the Moon

Hacienda Miraflores did decline—not only because what Celestino Santiago had feared came true, but because shortly after Flavio left his hacienda, Mexico was again plunged into war. During February, 1913, the inevitable clash between Francisco Madero and General Victoriano Huerta happened. The cagey hunter of Indians ambushed and murdered Madero and his vice president, Pino Suárez. Days of indescribable violence followed in Mexico City. It was a time of assassinations, bombings, street-to-street shootouts, confusion, and disorder. For ten days, if anyone found it necessary to go out onto the streets, it had to be under the cover of a white flag. Even so, numerous people were found dead holding that sign of neutrality.

Those days were brought to a halt when Huerta was able to seize power. But to the north, Francisco Villa and his hordes—Yaquis, bandits, horse thieves, professors, lawyers, and idealists—were advancing towards Mexico City. Towns and cities fell under the rush, and when Villa captured Torreón in April of 1913, the nation became convinced that he was invincible.

To the south of the capital, a similar wave spilled over the land. Emiliano Zapata and his Zapotec and Mixtec Indians clamored for the lands that had gradually been taken from them since the arrival of the Spanish conquistadors. When Zapata told his men to get what was theirs, hardly an hacienda or ranch was left untouched. Deeds, land grants, maps, records, inventories were seized and burned. Any document or decree asserting that land passed on from one *hacendado* to his sons, and from them to their sons, was destroyed. The Zapatistas marched north toward the capital, clad in white cotton pants and sombreros with brims so broad as to hide their faces. With the fighters marched their women, their children, and most of the time even a burro or a cow. They advanced taking towns and cities, then losing them, and then regaining them. Years passed in the fighting.

Flavio drifted, not even paying heed to the towns and villages into which he wandered. He was a stranger everywhere, and he did nothing to befriend anyone. As he roamed aimlessly over sierras and stretches of desert, his loneliness hardened, encrusting his soul in bitterness.

In April of 1916, Francisco Villa was beaten by General Alvaro Obregón at the Battle of Celaya. The one-armed, calculating Obregón was an expert at organization. Villa directed charge after charge of his Dorados against the waiting guns of Obregón, and each time the Villistas were torn to pieces. The defeated Villista survivors limped back home, and the Obregonistas marched into the capital. The spinal cord of the Revolution was broken.

Flavio Betancourt had been caught unaware at Celaya because he was neither Villista nor Obregonista; he had wandered into the area without purpose. When the battle began he was a follower of Francisco Villa; by the time the killing ended, he was behind Alvaro Obregón. Flavio was wounded—once in the leg, then in the shoulder. Several horses were shot from under him, and when the slaughter was over, he decided to keep moving north until he reached Chihuahua and his hacienda.

It was early May when he dismounted in front of Casa Miraflores. The place was nearly in ruins; no one was in sight. The stables were empty, as were the corrals. Weeds had overrun the main patio. Many of the windows of the big house were shattered and chunks of masonry were missing. When Flavio realized that his hacienda had not been spared by the bloody tidal wave, he was struck by the realization that during his wandering he had never cared whether the place disappeared.

He walked slowly up the stairs and into the entrance hall. Everything seemed in place and clean here; the interior of the house belied its exterior. He stood for a few moments waiting for his eyes to adjust to the shadows of the hall, when his attention was caught by a child sitting at the bottom of the staircase. It was a girl. She had golden curls, blue eyes and she appeared to be about three years old. Flavio recognized himself in her features. He moved toward her and sat down beside her. They looked at each other for a long while.

"What is your name?"

"Isadora Betancourt. What is your name?"

"Flavio Betancourt. I'm your father."

He felt a stirring inside of him, a strange, new feeling. Flavio had thought of the child who would have been born after he left, but his despair had dispelled any curiosity about it during those years. But now, as he looked at Isadora, he wondered why he had not returned earlier.

Taking the girl by the hand, Flavio walked through the house. It was clean and orderly but empty; he felt the hollowness. He went to the kitchen, where he found two workers, a woman preparing something at the stove and a man grinding corn on a stone slab. Both were strangers to Flavio. They, too, looked at him, startled.

"I'm Don Flavio Betancourt. *El patrón.*"

Mouths open, the servants stared at him. He turned away, still holding Isadora by the hand. He walked through the gloomy corridors of the house, through the lower and upper levels. As he moved from one place to the other, he wondered about Velia Carmelita and Brígida. He decided not to check the bedrooms. He went out in search of someone who would recognize him.

"Allí está Don Celestino."

The girl's voice took Flavio by surprise. She was pointing. Walking toward him was Celestino. He was the same, unchanged by the years of the Revolution. He approached Flavio, shook his hand, nodded his head.

"Bienvenido, patrón."

As Celestino looked at him, he saw that Don Flavio's face and features had grown hard, almost coarse. He was heavier, and he smelled of tobacco and alcohol.

"I'm back."

Flavio knew that his words were flat, obvious, but he did not know how else or where to begin. He looked around and smiled artificially.

"This is where you and I parted a few years ago."

These, too, were empty words. He waited a while before he forced himself to bring up what he had been evading.

"Where is my wife?"

Celestino frowned. The wrinkle that cut downward from his hairline to his nose deepened; it was almost a crevice. He looked away for a moment, then returned his gaze to look at Flavio.

"She's dead, *patrón*. She died when the child was born."

He whispered so that Isadora could not hear him, and instead of pointing at the girl he used his eyes. Flavio felt strange, a coldness seemed to grip his stomach. It was not sadness; that emotion had long ago left him. Perhaps it was emptiness, he told himself. He stared at Celestino realizing that his glare was that of a fool; his look was wordlessly returned by Celestino. He waited, knowing that Flavio was in turmoil.

"It was better, *patrón*. Things weren't good."

Flavio did not ask Celestino what he meant, because he feared the response.

"What about my sister?"

"The women say she roams the house like a soul cast out of Purgatory. She never speaks. She only moans and weeps. Everyone knows, because when she cries out, her wailing fills the night. It frightens most of the women, and even some of us."

Celestino was still whispering, letting Flavio know that he did not want Isadora to hear. Then he put his face closer.

"Patrón, la señora Brígida está un poco tocada."

Hearing that something had gone wrong with his sister's mind made Flavio shudder, and he cursed himself for not returning sooner. He decided that he did not want to hear more about Brígida.

"Have we lost everything?"

"The livestock is gone but the lands are intact. We were lucky. The armies came from all sides, but all they took was what they could eat and what they could carry. We lost several girls."

Celestino waited patiently as Flavio kept silent for a time. By that time, Isadora was squatting on the ground, playing with a handful of pebbles.

"What about the child? Who takes care of her?"

"Different people. Some times it's the women in the kitchen, but most of the time she's with me, my wife Narcisa, and my boys. She lives on the mountain and sleeps in the cave with us."

Flavio frowned, imagining his daughter sleeping in a cave in the heights of the sierra. He looked down at the blond curls and found it almost impossible to see his daughter eating, playing, living with the brown tribe. But then his shock began to fade, and instead he felt thankful. He sucked in a deep breath of air, took Isadora's hand and turned toward the house.

"*Gracias,* Celestino. We'll start right away to put things together again. Tell Narcisa that I'm grateful for what she's done for my daughter. I'll talk with you in a while."

He turned away, taking Isadora to the house. There he left her in the kitchen, telling her to wait for him. Then he climbed the stairs to look for Brígida; he found her in what had been Velia Carmelita's bedroom. The curtains were drawn in, letting in just a little light. It took Flavio's eyes a few seconds to adjust to the gloom, but he soon saw his sister. She was crouching on the floor, her back against a corner, knees folded under her chin. Her face was buried in her lap, arms wrapped around her head. She wore a long black dress with sleeves that concealed her arms and most of her hands; it had a collar that wrapped itself up to her ears. Only Brígida's bare feet were visible.

The sight startled him for a moment, but then he moved toward the windows and flung one of the drapes aside. Light flooded in, jolting Brígida into rigid attention as her head jerked up to look at him. The declining sunlight washed over her face and body. She was emaciated, pale, dried out. Her hair, blond before, was disheveled and already streaked with faded gray strands. In that light, her eyes appeared transparent, nearly white, as if their pupils had been scrubbed of all color. Recognition, however, let Flavio know that Brígida had not lost her mind.

"You've come back."

"Yes."

"She died."

Brígida raised an arm and pointed at the bed. Flavio looked from the corner of his eye as he reached out to lift his sister from the floor. She refused his gesture and dropped her head back onto her knees.

"You've got to get up. People are saying that you're crazy."

"I *am* crazy."

"No, you're not."

"I said that I am insane! Leave me alone!"

"You must help me care for the child. There's only you and I. And you're a woman . . ."

"Get someone from the tribe."

Flavio stood looking down at her, uncertain of what to do. He tried to sound firm but to himself his own voice was weak, unconvincing.

"I'll throw you out if you don't do as I order. Now get on your feet, bathe, and dress yourself. We have much to do."

Brígida, curled and hunched in on herself, did not answer her brother, but he could hear that she was breathing heavily through her mouth. At last she spoke without raising her head; her voice was soft, but firm.

"You won't throw me out. I'm your sister, and it's my right to stay here."

Flavio closed his eyes in frustration. He was tired and he could not find the energy to fight. He left the room after a moment, in search of his daughter.

When she heard the door close, Brígida leaned her head against the wall. She was not insane, but her spirit had shattered. She inhabited two worlds, and she knew it. In one, she was with Velia Carmelita whose memory was so vivid for her that she could still taste her lips, smell the fragrance of her skin. The rooms and corridors of the hacienda echoed with her laughter and talk. When Brígida looked out of a window, she saw herself and her lover in a slow-moving carriage. If she listened carefully, she could hear the soft notes of the duets they sang. She felt Velia Carmelita: sitting next to her, lying in bed with her, caressing her face. She spoke to her.

The other side of her existence was empty. Velia Carmelita had vanished from it, and there was nothing in her place. At those times Brígida tasted the bitterness of unbearable solitude and the horror of facing a lifetime of loneliness. When she lived in this world Brígida wept, often moaning so loud that the servants heard, and they gossiped about it.

When her brother confronted her that morning, his presence only deepened the emptiness tormenting her. When he left the room, Brígida stood and walked to the window that opened to the sierras. Looking down, she saw Flavio approach Celestino.

The next day Brígida overheard a maid say that Celestino had brought back his sister, Ursula Santiago, who was seventeen years old, to care for Isadora Betancourt.

Old man Flavio remembered that day as he sat glaring at the Los Angeles night sky. He had wanted to rid himself of his sister Brígida, as he wanted to erase the memory of her relationship with his wife, but it was beyond his power. He snorted, chiding himself for having been a coward for so long.

Chapter 6

As the years dragged on, Brígida was seen only at table for meals, or during the night, when she wandered the corridors of the big house. She hardly spoke to anyone, which convinced the workers of the hacienda that she was a soul out of Purgatory—*como alma del purgatorio*.

During those years, Flavio concentrated his energies on reconstructing his holdings. It took years, but he did recoup almost all that had been lost during the Revolution. Many of the political ties that he had made during the Madero days survived. His allies had not forgotten that it had been Betancourt who had shown them how to weather the bad times.

Flavio was able to get his hands on added resources from the Urrutia family. Don Plutarco and Doña Domitila had died without any other heirs. The old man was killed when he was thrown from a horse. Doña Domitila's death happened shortly after. It was considered a mystery because she was not stricken by an illness her doctors could identify. In the kitchens and stables, it was said that sadness took her life. *Fue de tristeza* because it was sadness that overcame her inexplicably, little by little. Even though the Urrutia holdings had been dismantled by the Revolution, there was still some land left, much of it wooded. When Doña Domitila died, what was left of the family's wealth was passed on to Flavio Betancourt.

Flavio threw himself into work and business, but whenever he returned from his trips, he spent as much time as he could with Isadora. He had his daughter ride with him so that she would learn the routine of inspecting the livestock and of dealing with the men charged with their care, using every opportunity to instruct her on running the hacienda. Flavio was happy to see her confidence grow and her beauty increase each time he saw her. He loved her temperament, which was sunny, always ready to make him laugh.

However, his daughter was not receiving the education proper for a woman of her position, and this gnawed at Don Flavio. He had seen to it that she learned to read and write, but not much more. He took every opportunity to plant certain ideas in her, hoping that they would take root and guard her against making mistakes.

One morning as they rode, they came upon a bull mounting a heifer. Flavio, embarrassed, took the bridle of Isadora's horse to avoid the sight.

"Papá! Stop! Why are we going in the wrong direction?"

Flavio halted the horses and, knowing that he should take the occasion to teach Isadora a lesson, decided to touch on a delicate subject.

"*Hija,* what those animals were doing is natural; there's nothing wrong."

"Then why did we run away?"

"We did not run away. I want to speak to you about something. It's this: Unlike that bull and heifer, men and women are governed by rules that they must obey."

He looked at Isadora and saw that her head was cocked; she was listening intently. But Flavio did not know what else to say.

"Listen to me, Isadora. We humans beings, and women especially, are governed by barriers that they must never trespass. If they do, then there is trouble."

Flavio took in her expression and realized that Isadora had not understood his meaning. The girl's eyes told him that in her mind his words about women had little relation to what they had just witnessed with the bull and cow.

"Women especially? Why not men, Papá?"

"Because . . . Because God said it should be that way."

"God?"

Isadora's intelligence usually pleased Flavio, except in moments like these, when she seemed dissatisfied with a simple explanation. He decided to invent a parable.

"Let me tell you about the woman who decided that she wanted to be like a man . . ."

"Like a man?"

"What I mean is that she wanted to have authority like her husband. Well, one day she thought that she could do what he did, and she crossed over the forbidden line."

"The forbidden line?"

"Yes, yes, Isadora!"

Flavio's voice betrayed the irritation he was feeling. He paused for a moment; his horse snorted as it flicked flies from its rump with its tail.

"There is a boundary that a woman should never trespass; only her husband has that right. At any rate, as I was saying, that woman, the disobedient wife, was condemned to wander the Earth for all eternity, weeping and howling, because she went against her husband's commands."

There were other similar lessons later on, lessons in which he was careful to emphasize the differences in races: A white person, especially a white woman, should never mix her blood with a man of another race. When Isadora asked why not, he told her of the deformed child, half-animal, half-human that resulted from such a union, and how it was doomed to travel in a circus as a living example of what happens when men and women fall into such depravity. (When she asked him to explain what a man and a woman do to mix their blood, Flavio changed the subject.)

Going through those brief lessons did not dispel his concerns about her schooling, and no matter how much he resisted his fears, he was forced to remember that soon she would have to marry. He knew, also, that to be considered suitable, she would have to learn more than just reading and writing. She would have to be polished, prepared, as was expected of a woman of her class.

Flavio admitted that instead of seeing to it that she be properly instructed, he was allowing Isadora to grow up among the natives, almost as wild as they. Her closest friends were people of the sierra—women who knew only how to grind maize, weave cotton, and raise children. What worried Flavio even more was Isadora's close friendship with Celestino's three sons.

Once, by chance, he happened to be at the spot that the Santiago boys had designated as the end of a foot race. He saw four runners bolt into a full gallop, accelerating, gaining speed, kicking up billows of yellow dust that rose high above them as they approached him. He was shocked when he realized that Isadora was one of the four. They ran abreast, locked into place, neck and neck as their legs blurred with speed. Each runner was so intent upon lurching out front that no one noticed Don Flavio standing up ahead of them. He gawked at them, wide-eyed at what seemed to be a machine, driven by spinning legs, coming straight at him. He barely had time to jump to the side before the runners thundered past him, heading for a tree.

It was Isadora and Jerónimo, arms outstretched, who first reached the mark. The other two runners were clearly the losers. When Isadora and Jerónimo realized that they had won the race, they hugged, faces squeezed cheek to cheek, gasping for air, sweating and shouting. Jerónimo lifted Isadora, swinging her around and around as she laughed, mouth wide open. She held onto him, obviously elated to be a winner and to be in his arms, and she was so happy that she did not see her father standing a few paces away, glaring at her and at Jerónimo.

When she did notice Flavio she became very still and began to pull away from Jerónimo's arms. The three boys followed her eyes and froze, stifling their panting, trying to control their pounding hearts. They had been caught playing while they were supposed to be working: This was the thought that crossed the mind of the Santiago boys. Jerónimo had his arms around her, and her father had seen it: This was the thought that paralyzed Isadora.

Don Flavio looked sternly at his daughter, his mouth pinched, but he did not speak. With his eyes he commanded her to return to the house. He had nothing to say to the boys, who turned away and disappeared behind the stable. He brooded silently over the incident for days and nights. In the late summer of 1926, he made certain arrangements, and then he had a conversation with Isadora.

"You're going to Chihuahua in September."

Flavio was sitting at his place at the dinner table. He was dressed in a serge suit and wore the bow tie that by then had become his trademark. At the far end Brígida sat, dressed as always in a high-collared black dress. In the background, Ursula Santiago, Celestino's sister, silently moved about, seeing that plates were served and removed as necessary. Flavio was looking at his daughter, who was so busy eating that she did not realize that she was the person concerned. Ursula, who stood close by, nudged the girl.

"Chihuahua? *Me?*"

Isadora straightened her back and put down the fork that she had held in mid-air. Her mouth, cheeks puffed out, was filled with food.

"Yes. Chihuahua."

Flavio put a piece of meat into his mouth and took a sip of wine, but he kept his eyes on her.

"Papá, what for?"

"You need to be educated."

He glanced at Brígida, a rapid, furtive glimpse. He disliked making even eye contact with her. He noticed his sister's raised eyebrows. He looked away from her, suddenly realizing that although she never uttered words, it was through her eyes that Brígida spoke.

"But Papá," Isadora pressed, "I *am* educated. I've learned to read and how to write. Ask Father Pascual. He's the one who taught me."

"*Hija,* you need to know much, much more than just how to read a book or write a letter."

Isadora looked over her shoulder, searching for Ursula. When she caught sight of her, she looked at her apprehensively, and her expression begged Ursula to do something. Ursula instead picked up a pile of plates and disappeared behind the door leading to the kitchen. Isadora looked over at Brígida, and they exchanged a look that Flavio caught.

"Does this mean I have to live there?"

"Yes. At Convento de la Encarnación. All the fine young ladies of the region have been received there. I've investigated their record."

"Live there? In a convent?" Isadora's voice was now tinged with terror. "With nuns? With only girls?"

"Yes."

"I won't go, Papá. I won't."

Flavio put down the crust of bread he held, took the napkin that he had stuffed into his collar, wiped his mouth, and looked steadily at his daughter.

"Isadora, you'll go because I'm asking you to go. Years from now you'll thank me."

His voice was soft; it was not threatening. When he finished, he looked over at his sister and saw that she had grown very pale. Her expression was blank, and it said nothing to him.

Isadora left Hacienda Miraflores for the convent school in Chihuahua when she was fourteen years old. As she joined her father in the back seat of the touring automobile that now transported him on his trips, she was crying. He tried to comfort her, putting his arm around her shoulders, but he realized that she was trying to crane her neck to look out through the rear window, so he loosened his hold on her. When she looked out the window, Flavio did too. They both saw that receding into the distance were Ursula, Celestino, and his sons. This image stayed with Isadora during her four years at school, which ended in the spring of 1930.

Chapter 7

For Flavio, those years were empty. He traveled to see Isadora once a month, but he knew increasingly little of her friends, her thoughts, her life. He felt a separation growing between them with each visit. He counted the days and months until the end of Isadora's studies finally arrived. On that day he appeared at the convent door before any of the other parents. He was so early that he was asked to wait in the courtyard, where he and his driver stood by his car, listening to the hubbub of the students saying their good-byes. When the girls' chatter died down, he instructed his driver to load his daughter's things while he took leave of the nuns and other teachers. Soon he and Isadora were in his car, speeding south toward Hacienda Miraflores.

At first, they sat quietly, as if listening to the hum of the motor. From time to time, they were jostled when the car hit a bump in the road. Isadora was remembering the four years, which had passed by faster than she had expected, and Flavio was thinking that his daughter had blossomed into a stylish young woman. He gazed at the small felt hat that she wore cocked over one eye, the leather gloves and shoes to match, and he was happy that he had decided to part with her during the years of her education. She was, as he had hoped, transformed.

"Are there many of your friends that will soon be married?"

Isadora was thinking of her closest friends when Flavio's words broke into her thoughts. She sighed while she made a mental count.

"Yes, Papá. Blanca Peralta will marry in June. Isabel Morán and her cousin, Yolanda Lizardi, will marry in July. It's going to be a double wedding."

"The Lizardis are the bankers, aren't they?"

"Yes."

"Where will the weddings be?"

"In the capital. Probably in the cathedral. The fiestas will have to be in the Zócalo, since their families are so big. There must be thousands of them."

Isadora giggled at her exaggeration, and Flavio joined her. He liked chatting this way with his daughter, even though he knew it was silly. It was the opportunity to bring up a subject that was not frivolous.

"Have you thought of marrying?"

Her head snapped toward him. Her expression had taken a seriousness that contradicted the giddy disposition of moments before.

"Getting married was all anyone could talk about during the last months of the term. But since I don't know anyone, I can't say that I've thought about it for myself." Isadora looked out the window at the flat landscape blurring by as the car sped southbound. Flavio kept his gaze on her, studying her face and the movements of her body.

"There are several young men who would want to marry you, Isadora."

"Who, Papá?"

Flavio saw that her eyes clouded for a second, and that she appeared to be overcome by emotion, but it was momentary. When he responded he tried to make his voice sound gentle.

"Suitors worthy of you."

After this conversation, Isadora's marriage became the focus of Don Flavio's thoughts. He decided that her next birthday would be the time to gather potential suitors. Isadora's eighteenth birthday was a celebration that Flavio had planned for two years. Now that his daughter's future engrossed his thoughts, he plunged into organizing the fiesta. Despite his misgivings, Flavio had even approached Brígida to make her part of the festivities. He did this, not because he wanted it, but because he would have found it difficult to explain her absence to those who knew of her existence. There were too many embarrassing questions that would be asked.

As always she cast a pall on his household at a time when he wanted, above all things, to have his family appear perfect. To his displeasure, however, Brígida refused to appear at the fiesta.

As had happened before, Flavio decided to forget about his sister and instead concentrate on his daughter. He was satisfied with Isadora, seeing that she had matured into a warm, intelligent woman. He was happy that she was beautiful: Her hair had retained its blond, golden highlights; her eyes sparkled as they had when she was a child; she was well shaped and healthy. The schooling, which she had in the beginning resisted, eventually took hold, transforming Isadora. She was a suitable match for any family in the region, Flavio told himself.

He had observed changes in her with each vacation period. As the years passed, she became interested in pastimes more suitable than climbing mountainsides and competing in foot races with native boys. Flavio was especially relieved when he became convinced that Isadora no longer showed interest in Jerónimo Santiago. In fact, he saw that by the time she was nearing the end of her studies, she hardly remembered the boy.

Early on the day of the fiesta, Flavio went to Isadora's room. He had something special that he wanted to show her.

"*Buenos días, hija.*"

"*Buenos, Papá.*"

She was out of bed and about to dress. She appeared to be happy and ready for the celebrations.

"Put on something you can ride in. We're going to do something special before breakfast."

"What's more important than your morning chocolate, Papá?"

"Hurry. Come. It can't wait, and we have to be ahead of our guests. They'll soon begin to arrive."

Flavio straightened his bow tie as he gazed out the window, while Isadora went into the dressing room. He heard her moving shoes, lifting hangers, shaking out garments. He told himself that the day was perfect. As he craned his neck to look into the distance, he saw that the meadows were green from the last rain, and the far-off sierras were white with snow. Then, by a trick of the light, he caught his own reflection in the window. He had grown stout; his waistline had expanded. His face, no longer angular, was fleshy and puffy around the eyes. The blond tones of his hair had grayed, and the handlebar mustache he had worn for years was also gray, bushy; it hung over his lips, almost covering them.

"I'm ready."

He looked at his daughter because doing so filled him with energy, and he took whatever opportunity he could. She had put on a long, white cotton dress, heavy enough to withstand the brisk air, and she wore the boots that he had ordered from Nuevo León. They were fashioned in the northern style: calf-length; one-inch heels; and engraved with elaborate designs. They were made of cordovan, her favorite leather.

Just before going into the stables, Flavio stopped and put his hand on Isadora's shoulder, letting her know that she should wait. A few moments later he walked out leading his own horse alongside a mare which was a bridled chestnut-colored Arabian. Flavio's smile told it all. Without speaking, Isadora embraced her father. He could feel her heart beating, which made him well up with joy, and the force with which she held him told him that she loved him above all people.

Several men stood by watching, smiling, and as one of them approached with the saddle for the mare, Isadora leapt onto the animal and galloped away at such a pace that the man was left in the dust, not knowing what to do. Whooping and hollering broke out when the they saw her riding the barebacked horse. Flavio was so surprised that all he could do was open and close his mouth, as if gasping for air.

His daughter rode the horse across the plain at breakneck speed. Don Flavio saw how she clutched the beast's mane, her legs pressed to the mare's sides. The white cotton dress clung to Isadora's body as the wind swept it up above her knees exposing her legs and the maroon boots. He saw her laughing in defiance of the current that whipped her face. Her hair, the sun's rays trapped in the ringlets of its curls, swept around her head like an aura. Then she slowed down as if testing the mare. She cantered, circled, criss-crossed, moving her body in rhythm with that of the mare. She burst out laughing, and her laughter spiraled up above her head, cascading until it reached Flavio.

"Come, Papá! Come!"

He turned and grabbed the bridle of his horse, which was by now saddled, and sprang onto the animal. He galloped to her side, and together they raced across the meadow until they reached the slope that marked the beginning of the Sierra Madre. There they stopped, panting, gasping for air, laughing. Flavio looked at his daughter, knowing that he had done nothing in his life to deserve her.

Later on that day, the invited families arrived in canvass-topped touring cars, in Packards and other luxury vehicles. Knowing that many of the events would involve horses, some of the young men and women mounted thoroughbreds. As soon as Flavio and Isadora were able to greet as many guests as possible, the festivities began. There were competitions: roping calves, riding and fighting steers and young bulls. Because the fiesta had attracted dozens of people from the neighboring haciendas, and even from as far as the state capital, each of the games was a huge success. Waves of cheering and shouting filled the air. Food was served as well as drinks and sweets while they waited for the traditional high point of the fiesta, the foot race.

The competition was set to be run by ten Rarámuri men, aged fifteen and older, chosen from the neighboring haciendas. The prize for the winner was to be a horse, a gift from Isadora Betancourt's father. The length of the course was approximately thirty kilometers beginning at the far side of the Betancourt lands and ending outside the entrance to the main house.

Flavio had arranged stations from where his guests could view the race at its different stages. The best vantage point was the one at the end where the winner would be determined. It was there that he, Isadora, and his closest friends and associates were provided with seats sheltered against the sun by a canvass awning. As they awaited the outcome of the race, they were treated with refreshments and more to eat.

Flavio and Celestino met with the team at the starting point; both men wished the runners good luck. Ordinarily, these men would have been dressed in khaki pants and shirt, boots, wide brimmed hats, scarves around their necks to absorb sweat. But to run, the racers did away with those clothes, wearing only what was necessary to keep ahead of the wind: *huaraches,* loin cloths, and a headband woven with the colors of the hacienda.

El Patrón looked at his team, knowing that the runners had prepared rigorously for the race during the preceding days. But he was unaware that the Santiago boys were among the runners and that they had been with the holy man of the tribe, *el nahual,* for hours on the previous day, when he had rubbed their bodies with flat stones and special herbs. The brothers had even slept together after the shaman's blessing of the bones of a dead runner and after they had made signs of the cross, placing offerings of *tesguino* beer and peyote in front of the relic. The older married brothers had abstained from sex because of its weakening effects. None of them had taken food or drink from anyone except their families, fearing that an opponent might through such means cast an evil spirit on them.

Flavio finally focused his eyes until he saw the older Santiago sons. Then he flashed Celestino a smile, letting him know that one of them was bound to win the prize. After that he took time to scrutinize each of the racers. As he did, his gaze fastened on one of them; it was Celestino's third son, the youngest. He had forgotten his name by then, and knew only that he was known as El Rarámuri, because he was the fastest runner of his tribe.

Flavio had not seen him for some time, and he was startled to realize that he was no longer a boy; he had developed into a young man. Flavio narrowed his eyes as he studied El Rarámuri. His face was angular, and his eyes were slanted and accentuated by a beaked nose. His jaw had squared, and his mouth was wide and already shadowed by a thin, drooping mustache. Flavio lowered his eyes to examine the runner's body. His neck was tapered; his shoulders, chest and belly were muscular; his legs were straight and powerfully built.

When he had finished his examination, Flavio backed away, feeling strangely apprehensive. But shrugging off these thoughts as foolish, he raised his voice so that everyone could hear him. The runners were ready, and they stood waiting for the signal.

"*¡Muchachos! ¿Preparados?*"

"*Sí, patrón.*"

Flavio whirled a white handkerchief above his head several times giving the runners a chance to take their place. When he was certain that they were ready, he slashed his arm downward.

"*¡Empiecen!*"

The racers sprang forward at the signal and disappeared into a cloud of dust. Leaving Celestino behind, Flavio jumped into a waiting car and had the driver take him to the next viewing station, where he waited for the team to arrive. Once the runners thundered by, he again took the car to the next place, and he did this until he arrived at the end of the course where he found Isadora and the rest of the laughing, jabbering, drinking, eating guests. This route had taken him nearly three hours.

When Flavio's guests saw him they knew the race was ending, so they stopped whatever they were doing and concentrated on the place where the winner should appear; their silence made it possible to hear the runners approaching. In the beginning it was a dim sound, almost dull; it was the flapping of *huaraches* on clay. Then they began to feel a vibration beneath them, a tingling sensation that crept up their legs, coursed through their body, and compelled them to begin shouting. This coincided with the first glimpse of a cloud of dust, with one runner ahead of the others. As he came nearer, the crowd began shouting. It was an explosion of sound, filled with whistling and applause, because when the winner came close enough for them to see, they saw that he was one of the Santiago people.

Isadora was on her feet, cheering and waving a handkerchief. Her face was flushed with excitement. She stopped suddenly, however, when she saw that it was Jerónimo coming closer and closer. By the time he crossed the finishing line, she could only stare at him. She had not seen Jerónimo in years but she knew that it was the same boy who had played and climbed and run with her. She had not been prepared for the transformation. The hollering and cheering began to recede as she concentrated on him, feeling excitement overtake her. But she was shaken from her thoughts by her father, who had taken hold of her hand to get her attention.

"*Hija*, it's up to you to hand the prize to the winner."

Isadora laughed and followed her father to the winner, who stood waiting, sweating and still panting, trying to adjust to his normal breathing rhythm. When she got close to him, her eyes looked into his, but she saw that he had lowered his gaze to the ground. One of the helpers handed her the bridle, which she passed to Jerónimo.

Remembering that day made the old man squirm in his chair as he scanned the Los Angeles horizon. But he did not want to look out the window; he was afraid of the images he might see there. It made no difference. The ghost that haunted him had returned. Don Flavio heard the sound of *huaraches* flapping against dry canyon clay. It began remotely, then it came closer until it filled his room. His head jerked toward the window, to the apparition in the glass.

El Rarámuri, Jerónimo Santiago, was running toward him. The old man could see the rage stamped on the native's face. He came closer, closer, and the speed with which his body moved took away the old man's breath. Then Flavio, too, was in the race. He was running because the Indian was coming after him. Clinging to the armrests of the chair, his eyeballs on the verge of bursting, the old man panted, mouth wide open, gulping air so that his lungs would not collapse. He struggled to keep ahead of the long-distance runner, hoping to evade his grasp even if it meant that his heart would explode from the strain. Then the sound of *huaraches* stopped.

Suddenly the chase was over. El Rarámuri had disappeared, but Don Flavio sat in the chair, sweating, trying to understand what had happened. He shook his head to clear his mind.

Ursula Santiago did not wait for a reply after rapping repeatedly at his door; she walked into the darkened room. This time she did not ask if he wanted light. She simply groped her way to the bed and turned on a lamp on the nightstand.

"It's getting late, Don Flavio."

Ursula spoke as she turned down the bedspread and blankets. She puffed up the pillows and straightened a small crucifix that hung on the wall above the metal railing of the bed.

"It's still raining. It's going to be very muddy tomorrow."

She went on with her small talk, trying to draw the old man into conversation. After a while, she turned to look at him. He was deteriorating with each hour, she thought. His skin was turning yellow.

"Has Samuel come yet?" Don Flavio cut her short to ask for the grandson who had long since married and moved out of the house. His visits were not frequent, but still the old man asked for him.

"Not today, Don Flavio. Maybe tomorrow."

"Call my sister. I need to speak with her."

"*Señor,* remember that she's not with us anymore."

Ursula waited for a response, but the old man was quiet.

"Can I bring you something from the kitchen? *Pan dulce?* More chocolate?"

"No. Leave me."

Alone, Don Flavio went on with his memories.

Chapter 8

The servants of Casa Miraflores went about their work as Don Flavio sat at his desk smoking a cigar. Don Angel Pardo sat facing him. There was a pause in their conversation as they sat thinking. It was mid-December and there was a slight chill in the room. Flavio's eyes had narrowed and his mouth was pinched.

"It would be a good match, Don Flavio. I assure you. My son Eloy has expressed affection for your daughter, and I believe it has been returned."

Flavio stared at Don Angel, taking in his fleshy body. He was not a tall man, and the years had taken their toll. It was known that he was not used to riding or hunting, much less showing his workers how to do a job. And there in front of Don Flavio was the result: a squat, overweight man. But he was fair-skinned, and in Flavio's mind that compensated for Pardo's other physical flaws.

He looked away from Don Angel as he gazed out the window. Flavio was visualizing Eloy, who was more or less Isadora's age. He was dull and unattractive, Flavio admitted, but like everyone in the Pardo family, the young man was white. Isadora's children would no doubt inherit her color as well as their father's. Suddenly, Don Flavio tensed and frowned; his mother's brown face had unexpectedly flashed through his memory. The image lasted only seconds before he brushed it aside.

"I would first have to speak to my daughter about this proposal, Don Angel. I wouldn't force her into anything. And, I will add frankly, I haven't heard her mention your son. Perhaps she's not even noticed him."

"Ah, but Don Flavio, don't you remember how they danced without interruption at her birthday ball? Surely, you must have noticed. Everyone was gossiping about it, delighted at what a wonderful couple they made. Truly, there's no doubt in my mind that the match was made, as the saying goes, in heaven."

"Umm."

Beyond this grunt, Flavio did not respond to what the other man had said. He had noticed that Isadora had danced mostly with Eloy Pardo that night; how could anything like that escape him? But Isadora had not mentioned the young man afterward.

Flavio studied his fingernails as he reflected. He had much more wealth than Pardo, so the reason for Don Angel's enthusiasm for a match was obvious. On the other hand, the Pardos had lineage and family history, unlike the Betancourts, who were still considered outsiders by some families.

"I'll speak to her," Flavio said curtly. And when he saw that the other man was about to say something, he cut him off. "I have never forced my daughter to do anything. As I've said, I'll speak to her, and if she accepts, well then, it's her decision."

"But Don Flavio, surely you must have influence over your daughter. What father doesn't? I am here because I have already brought this issue to Eloy's attention, and after—well . . . after much conversation and—well . . . persuasion, he agreed with me that it would be the match of the year."

Flavio, who had begun to leave his chair, slumped back into it on hearing Don Angel's words. He frowned, looking intensely at the other man.

"What do you mean? Do I understand you to say that you had to *convince* your son to marry my daughter? Is that it?" Flavio did not try to hide the irritation he felt at the thought of Don Angel even hinting that his son was doing Isadora a favor in marrying her. His daughter had much more money, more education, more elegance of person than the Pardo family could offer.

"Ah, no, no, Don Flavio! A thousand pardons if that is the impression I've given you. Eloy is in love with Isadora, believe me. He speaks of her constantly, he yearns for her, he hardly eats . . ."

Flavio held up his hand, palm turned toward the man, interrupting his chatter. He was incensed, and he wanted only to end the conversation. But something urged him to take hold of himself and explore the possibility of a union between the two families. There was much to gain from such a marriage.

That evening, Flavio and Isadora spoke about the Pardo marriage proposal. When Flavio tried to ferret out her feelings regarding Eloy, Isadora was evasive, changing the subject each time he mentioned it. He allowed a few days to pass and again he brought up the question.

"Papá, I've thought of it, and I think it will be a good idea for me to marry Eloy. I like him. I like the way he is, and he dances well."

"He *dances* well!"

Flavio's voice was sarcastic, but inwardly he was surprised that Isadora had agreed so easily to marry. Secretly he had hoped that she would ask for more time, resist, argue—even threaten. Her attitude disappointed him, but then he imagined that her mother must have agreed to marry him in the same way. The thought of Velia Carmelita disturbed him. He had not thought of his wife in years. Remembering her also annoyed him because it forced him to think about Brígida.

Isadora married Eloy Pardo one year later. Flavio had a home constructed for the couple on his land, not far from Casa Miraflores. Ursula Santiago, filling the role of mother, moved in with Isadora. Soon Isadora told Flavio that she was pregnant. Flavio was happy and, for the time being, he was able to forget the thoughts that nagged at him during those days. One was that Jerónimo Santiago lurked around sullen and moody, until one day (to Don Flavio's silent relief) he simply disappeared. The other worry, more important to him, was that Eloy was already showing signs of straying from Isadora. He spent nights away from their home, fueling rumors that the new husband was a womanizer. Don Flavio tried to silence the gossip, but it grew each day.

Isadora had a son, and she named him Samuel. When Flavio first took him in his arms, he felt immense joy, especially when he saw that the child had inherited his mother's looks. His happiness faded, however, when word reached him that Eloy had run away with one of the servants, a woman who left behind four children and a husband.

After Eloy abandoned Isadora, the years crept by for Don Flavio. During this time Flavio suffered, blaming himself for his daughter's failed marriage and knowing that she was alone. She did not speak of the matter, but Don Flavio was afraid. He did know the reasons, but he feared for her. His fear increased when he heard one day a rumor that Jerónimo Santiago had returned.

When Samuel was five years old, talk about Isadora began, quietly at first, then escalating, becoming enormous and beyond even Don Flavio's power to control.

At first, he did not believe what his eyes and ears told him. She was his daughter, the person he loved above all else, the one to whom he had given everything. But it was the truth. Soon he was convinced that what those tongues were spreading from house to house, from hut to hut, from stable to mine shaft, from the *llano* up to the canyons, and even to the caves, was true. Those gossips said that Isadora was now Jerónimo Santiago's woman, that she slept with him, that she showed herself by his side, holding his arm.

Don Flavio finally confronted Isadora. She did not even try to deny what the rumors were saying. She admitted that she was Jerónimo's concubine and that she was pregnant with his child. After that, she left. She disappeared, taking Samuel with her, but Flavio knew that she had fled to the caves up in the sierra.

Shortly after Isadora's flight, Flavio collapsed. He was assaulted by a recurrent high fever, vomiting and delirium. His illness lasted days, and when he emerged from it, his spirit was paralyzed. He was unable to think or to move. He would not leave his room because he was ashamed and humiliated by his daughter's actions. When food was brought, he refused to open his door. When someone knocked, he kept silent. He neither bathed nor shaved, and when each day turned to night, he kept vigil during the dark night until the first rays of light penetrated the gloom of his lair.

Flavio did not know how many days had passed before his mind cleared. When he was finally lucid, he began to hatch his plan. He determined that not only would El Rarámuri pay, but his father, his mother, brothers, uncles, aunts, the whole tribe would suffer with tears and anguish. Flavio took his time, thinking, calculating day and night.

First, he decided, he would allow time to pass. Flavio knew that the tribe would expect him to get rid of El Rarámuri and the rest of his family, run each one of those devils off Hacienda Miraflores. But he would do the opposite; he would do nothing because that would confuse them. He would wait until they thought nothing was going to happen, and *then* he would strike. After that he would fold his arms and watch as they sunk into grief and starvation.

It took Flavio a longer time to devise the next phase of his strategy because it involved El Rarámuri and Celestino. His first impulse was to have both son and father eliminated. Flavio knew that it would be simple, that his authority would not be challenged, especially in light of the offense he had suffered. He decided, however, that killing them was not enough, that it was too easy, too kind, too quick. Flavio thought of castrating Jerónimo, leaving him to limp through life, neither man nor woman. But the idea of his lingering presence sickened Flavio.

When it came to what to do with Celestino, Flavio's stomach tightened. What would cause him to suffer the same pain that he, Flavio, was enduring? In what manner could he create the same amount of torture for Celestino, a torment that would last as long as he lived? When the answer came to him, he reproached himself for not having seen it from the beginning. Both punishments were linked: By killing the son, the father would then be left behind to suffer the same loss and outrage that he, Flavio, was experiencing. With this calculation, Don Flavio saw that his plan was set. But he resolved to practice patience. He thought of Isadora's pregnancy, deciding to wait a year before putting his plan into action, even though each hour was torturous for him.

After finalizing the details of the plan to his satisfaction, Flavio bathed, shaved, dressed and emerged from his bedroom. As he walked through the passages and corridors of the hacienda, he was aware of staring, startled servant eyes. He had looked in the mirror and realized that he had lost weight, that his face had aged, paled and become wrinkled. Flavio understood that when the eyes of the Rarámuri servants looked at him, they were filled with a mix of curiosity and fear; they were waiting for his fury to be unleashed. But he did nothing, taking satisfaction in knowing that this frightened them even more, heightened their anxiety, increased their fears of what would happen now that El Rarámuri and Isadora were living together.

The time to implement his scheme arrived. On that day, Don Flavio nervously fingered his bow tie as he stood at the window with his back to the man, a stranger to those parts. He had been hired, at Betancourt's bidding, by a contact in Los Mochis. Flavio spoke first, his words cautious.

"I don't answer questions."

"I don't ask any."

Betancourt whipped his head toward the man, surprised by the sharpness of the reply as well as the coldness of the voice. When Don Flavio looked him over, he saw that the man's appearance masked his words and voice: wire-rimmed glasses; shortsighted eyes; round, pink face; tiny, carefully trimmed mustache; double-breasted serge suit; straw hat nestled daintily on his lap. He looked like a schoolteacher, or even a banker, Flavio told himself.

"What are your terms?"

"Five thousand. In gold. No paper. Fifty percent now, the rest after the project is completed. "

"What are your weapons?"

"The ones you wish."

"When?

"Whenever you say."

The rapid exchange weakened Flavio's knees. He took a seat facing the small man. He scrutinized the assassin's features, his body, the way he sat. Flavio had decided to have Jerónimo Santiago taken out of Isadora's life, and although he had analyzed, questioned, sometimes even doubted his decision, in the end Flavio found no other way.

His mind darted back, reliving the bitter confrontation between himself and Isadora. He admitted that it had been he who had provoked the clash with his daughter when he became convinced that she was indeed the woman of El Rarámuri. At the time Flavio had been certain that he would be able to change her mind, to prevail by using his authority if necessary. But Isadora was rebellious, unbending, and instead of trying to hide the truth, she flaunted it to his face.

Months had passed since then. Now, facing the man who would be Jerónimo's executioner, Flavio inexplicably began to waver. He had thought that he was unconditionally committed to the plan that he had hatched, but the sight of this assassin seated in front of him began to unnerve him. He had taken part in bloodshed during the Revolution—what man had not, he asked himself. But he had never ordered the death of any man.

He looked at the small man and thought he saw an amused expression on his face. His eyebrows had arched and his mouth had rounded to a tiny circle, emphasizing his pencil-line mustache. Flavio lowered his eyes, trying to hide the emotions within him. He wanted to appear hard, determined.

His mind calculated: Isadora had been bewitched by Jerónimo, and she was set on living among his people as if she were one of them. Of this Flavio had no doubt. Nothing short of the man's elimination would take her from his side because she was now beyond reason. By her own admission, she was carrying a child and in time everyone would know who had spawned the creature. As for his grandson Samuel, there were only two ways: Either he would stay with his mother and become a primitive like the people surrounding him, or return to Flavio to face a life of mockery and humiliation because of what his mother had done.

Putting together these considerations renewed Flavio's resolve. But then he was assailed by a new apprehension: What about Isadora? She would certainly know that it was he who had ordered her lover's death. How would she react? Would she hate him? Would she choose to live among those people in a cave—even without El Rarámuri? But these thoughts could not now change Flavio's mind. He was certain that he had no alternative. He could not stand by and watch his daughter mix with those people; he could not allow the intolerable offense to go without punishment.

Flavio sat upright, tense, unmoving. Without realizing it, he had spread his hands palm down on the desk. He was sweating so much that a foggy outline of his fingers was left upon the polished surface when he removed his hands. Putting aside his fear regarding Isadora's reactions, he reconfirmed his decision. He stood, walked to the closet where he kept cash, and returned with a leather purse in his hands. He handed it to the small man.

"Count it."

"No need, *Señor* Betancourt. You have a fine reputation. Please tell me who we are talking about, when you want the assignment taken care of, and by what means."

Flavio forced himself to sit down again. He laid out Jerónimo Santiago's name and description, the place to find him, when and how it should be carried out.

"I don't want firearms used. It will attract attention."

The small round-faced man nodded amiably, a salesman taking an order. When he saw that Don Flavio had finished, he got to his feet without speaking, shook hands with him and walked to the door. Before leaving he glanced back and said, "I understand your hesitation, *Señor* Betancourt. It's not easy to kill. Believe me, I know."

A few days later, the small round-faced man blended in with the shrubs and trees as he waited for Jerónimo Santiago. He was flanked by two men whose names he did not know. And they, too, did not know his name. They hid from sight in a wooded area. The hired killer had spent several days following El Rarámuri, memorizing his routes, times, habits. He knew that his prey no longer worked for Hacienda Miraflores, but it was not difficult to gather the necessary information. When he was satisfied that he had mastered Jerónimo's comings and goings, he struck.

It was mid-day when Jerónimo crouched to drink from a creek. As he cupped water into his hands, he heard something behind him. He turned as two men rushed at him. Jerónimo had expected this from the beginning and, although afraid, he was not surprised. He kicked at one of them and lashed out at the other with his fist. His blows landed on target, giving him enough time to dash through trees that were close by. He ran, but soon the boots he wore began to hold him back. He stopped abruptly, just long enough to yank them off. Barefooted, he gained speed and his pursuers fell back until he could no longer hear them. But he did not let up on his pace, heading up toward the *barranca*.

Jerónimo ran, sure-footed, and the rhythm of his feet increased his energy. His feet blurred over the ground as he picked up speed, outdistancing the attackers. He knew that only another one such as he, one of his brothers, could reach him or keep up with him. He ran, confident, knowing that he would soon be with his people and Isadora.

Unexpectedly, a man leapt onto the path in front of him, nearly colliding with Jerónimo, but keeping the distance needed to raise his arm. The man brought down his weapon. It happened so suddenly that Jerónimo did not see where the first slash of the machete came from, but it caught him in the right forearm. The force of the blow, intensified by the momentum of his run, sent him reeling backwards. As he was falling back, he had time to see the glint of another blade as it made its way toward him. This one sliced his left thigh, nearly severing his leg. Blinding pain flashed through his body, convulsing it, and Jerónimo quivered, rolling on the dusty clay, his blood mixing with the dirt. Before darkness overcame him, he had time to see a round face. Its spectacles caught the glimmer of the declining sun and its round lips signaled someone to aim for Jerónimo's throat.

Years had passed since that day, but the memory still haunted Don Flavio who sat in his chair, scarecely breathing. He stared straight ahead at the watery window as he remembered El Rarámuri's head, its dead eyeballs glaring at him. The old man relived the assassination and Isadora's attempt to kill him afterwards. He clutched at the armrests of the chair, trying to relax his body, but the memory of her hatred bore down on him. Some impulse compelled him to peer into one of the corners of the room. He narrowed his eyes; folds of parched skin hung over them, making it difficult for him to see, but, certain that she was there, he began to cry.

"Ahh! Ahh!"

The old man was groaning so loudly that Ursula rushed into his bedroom without knocking. The lamp she had turned on was not enough to light the room; it was so dim she bumped noisily into a chair.

"*Por Dios, Don Flavio, ¿qué pasa?*"

He did not answer. Ursula finally made him out, hunched over in the chair. He was almost curled over, arms hugging his stomach, as he went on moaning. She tried to straighten him up, but he pushed against her. She looked around, searching, as if the cure for his pain were somewhere in the room. Ursula heard a noise and saw that Alondra, clad in a nightgown, had come in.

"*El viejo está enfermo,*" Ursula whispered. "I think we should call Doctor Canseco. What do you think?"

"*Abuela,* you know how he gets when we do that. He gets crazy."

"What are you two whispering about?" Don Flavio spoke up, his voice thin and raspy, but steady. "Leave me. It's passed." When the women did not move, he repeated his words. "Leave me. Please."

Ursula and Alondra looked at one another, surprised. Neither could remember Don Flavio ever being polite. After a few seconds, Ursula shrugged and jerked her head toward the door. They left the room without a word.

The old man, eyes closed, pressed on his belly with both hands. Sharp pains shot from one side of his abdomen to the other. He leaned his head back and returned to his memories. Beyond the window, rain was still falling. Don Flavio's frail body shuddered, his eyes on the window, which flashed with reflections from headlights of passing cars.

The old man again doubled over in the chair. The pain in his gut was too severe, too intolerable. Saliva trickled from his flaccid lips. He tried to straighten his body, but could not; his stomach was clamped, as in a vise.

"Ahh!"

Ursula and Alondra rushed back into the room when they heard the old man whimpering. They opened the door and found him on the floor, on his side hugging his knees to his stomach. His face was twisted in pain; the moaning turned to howling, and the howling escalated with each second.

The women got down next to him, trying to soothe him, trying to get him to stop the wailing, but Don Flavio wept, mouth open, groaning and crying out to Isadora. He called her, but there was no reply. He convulsed even more until pain overwhelmed him, plunging him into unconsciousness, where his spirit still wrestled with the vision of his daughter, locked in a cell.

Isadora Betancourt

Chapter 9

Jalisco, Mexico, 1939

Isadora Betancourt stirred from the drug-induced sleep in which she had been plunged for days. Sprawled out across the rear seat, she was jostled back and forth as the car lumbered over cobblestones and potholes. When she was able at last to lift herself up, she saw her father's craggy silhouette up front beside the driver. She craned her neck and squinted, but her vision blurred as she twisted to peer through the rear window. All she could make out were the bushes that came into view under the reflection of the tail lights of the Packard.

Isadora tried to speak, but the roof of her mouth and her tongue were parched. She opened her lips; no sound came out. Slowly, her mind began to clear as the vehicle rumbled along the tight, curving road. She tried to think, but all she could recall after the shooting was being locked in a room; for how long, she didn't know. She remembered vague images: her father and another man dragging her into a car. This confused her—she was certain that she had killed her father. How could he have survived? How much time had passed?

Her last clear memory was of her father's house, where they had argued. After that, there was darkness, thick and impenetrable as that now enveloping her. The pupils of her eyes distended, trying to focus. She thought of Samuel and of Alondra, but a drugged fog wiped out all other images.

"Where are we going?" she croaked.

Don Flavio twisted his neck to glance sideways at his daughter. Terror suddenly flooded her; she was beginning to understand.

Isadora could see the loose, wobbly skin of his lower jaw; its layers hung over the starched collar of his shirt, which was held together by a bow tie. His mouth was set rigidly, and in the darkness she made out the glint of his faded blue eyes.

"Where are we going?"

Without thinking, her panicked hands lunged at the door. No matter how many times she pushed the handle up, down, it would not open; it had been locked from the outside.

She began to flail her legs wildly in the air. When her bare feet did not land on the padded back of the seat, several of the blows found a mark. One landed squarely in the driver's right ear. He hunched over the steering wheel and grunted with pain. The next barrage grazed her father's cheek, but then he twisted around in his seat and was able to grasp both her ankles in a tight grip. His fists gripped her so tightly that she let out a moan. The car halted abruptly.

As the driver waited before iron doors for the arrival of a gate-keeper, there was silence except for the whirr of the car engine and the heavy breathing of its three passengers.

Isadora stopped struggling, and Don Flavio let go of her legs. She pressed her face against the car window to read the words inscribed on the wall that loomed above them. *Sanatorio de San Juan. Zapopan, Jalisco.* Through the front windshield, as her eyes distended in fright, she saw the curving façade of the asylum.

No, it was a convent. Perhaps even a church.

But as the car approached the building, Isadora began to hear a woman shrieking in the distance. She tilted her head and turned her ears in the direction of the screaming. Brígida had described such a place to her once, a place where men hid away disobedient women. At first, the insane screaming seemed to be far off. It began to draw closer until it was almost on top of her.

Then she knew. Isadora's hands jerked up to find her mouth wide open with terror. She tried to clasp her hands over that wailing, gaping hole, but she had lost control over her body.

The large front doors of the sanitarium were yanked open and four men ran down the steep stairway. Isadora caught sight of their uniforms as the rear door of the car was unlocked. She lunged in the opposite direction, trying to avoid their groping hands. She pounded at the closed window with her fists, and when the glass shattered, she did not mind the shards as they penetrated her wrists and forearms.

She had been wearing a nightgown and thin robe, and these ripped apart as she was dragged from the car, but she was oblivious to her nakedness and to the pain inflicted on her breasts, shoulders, and abdomen by those pulling and wrenching hands. She continued to jerk her arms and legs violently as she screamed. With a strength that caught her restrainers by surprise, she wiggled and contorted her body until she pulled herself from their grip. Feeling herself free, she raced, stumbling and tripping, up the stairway and deep into the inner courtyard of the asylum.

The columns of the cloister loomed in front of her. Its potted ferns and geraniums glistened like black monsters in that hour before dawn. She ran around the plants, stubbing her toes and cutting her bare feet against the sharp tiled floor. She crashed into a top-heavy planter that blocked her way, sending it smashing to the floor; dirt and fronds lashed up at her. After circling the courtyard frantically several times, panting and out of breath, she ran headlong and fell into a fountain that she had not seen.

The men finally yanked her, gasping and stupefied, from the cold water and held on to her. Isadora heard one man breathing hard through his mouth as he grasped her left arm and plunged a needle into it, unloading the contents of a syringe. Her last sensations before drifting into unconsciousness were of water streaming out of her nose and of tile cutting into her knees.

She could hear voices, but her body was paralyzed and she could not speak. She was lying on a hard surface and covered by something that felt like a sheet. Although her eyes were shut, the light of an overhanging lamp filtered in; whirling white and black spheres drifted by in the void beneath her eyelids.

"Señor Betancourt, we'll have to put your daughter through a series of tests before any conclusions can be reached."

Isadora's ears strained to hear a response, but there was only silence.

"What I mean, Don Flavio, is that we can't just keep her here without the strongest evidence that she is, indeed, demented. Remember, please, that this sanitarium is only for the most extreme cases. If your daughter has been showing signs of melancholy, or any other symptoms, this doesn't mean that she has lost her mind."

Isadora struggled to move but she could not—not a finger, or a toe, or an elbow. She wondered why it was that she could hear and yet not move. After several minutes, she detected her father's heavy breathing.

"Doctor Alférez, she is demented; she tried to kill me. I'm afraid you'll have to take my word for it. She inherited it from her mother, believe me. She, too, lost her mind, but God was good to her. He took her to Him."

Her father's lies began to steady Isadora. She remembered what had happened. She had learned of Jerónimo's murder. She was glad that she had tried to kill her father.

"But—"

"This stranger is no longer my daughter. She died some time ago, I tell you. In her place we have this woman who has shown her demented condition in acts of depravity and violence."

Jerónimo's face penetrated the darkness. She thought of Alondra. Then she stopped being afraid. Isadora felt a finger peeling the eyelid from her left eye. A pinpointed shaft of light inundated the pupil, and then the lid clamped back in place as the finger moved away. She heard a deep sigh.

"Still, Don Flavio—forgive me, for there is no offense intended—but I cannot take only your word. We are obliged to—"

The voice halted abruptly and there was rustling or shuffling of what sounded like paper. There was movement in the room. A window opened, and she felt a gust of air against her face.

"You will get this on a monthly basis, doctor. It will increase with each year of her life. I see also that you are in need of new equipment; this table should be replaced by a more modern one. Be assured that you will guarantee the improvement of your institution."

There was more silence, then the click of an opening and shutting door. Fear shot through her again, compelling her to scream, but the howl echoed only in her mind; her mouth was frozen shut.

Isadora understood that she was abandoned. She realized that she would be isolated for the rest of her life and that it had been her father who had condemned her.

Chapter 10

Isadora Bentacourt's earliest recollection was of being curious about *Tía* Brígida. After that, it was Jerónimo Santiago who filled almost every moment of her childhood. Even when she was with her father, even when they ate together or rode out to the *llano,* her mind was usually filled with thoughts of her aunt or the Rarámuri boy.

One night, when Isadora was twelve years old, she heard some-one singing, or maybe it was sighing. Although she had been in a deep sleep, the lilting sound awoke her. She slipped out of bed and crept slowly down the corridor. As she moved, she looked around, then up. The shadows that clung to the vaulted ceilings like giant black birds scared her, as did the elongated windows along one side of the hallway. They seemed to be pointed eyes that followed her. All of this frightened her, but she wanted to discover what it was that she was hearing.

"*¡Ay, Dios!*"

Isadora was so close to *Tía* Brígida's room now that she could make out words that seeped from underneath the door. She stopped for a moment, undecided, wanting to run back to the safety of her room, but curiosity held her back. Then she heard more. This time it was a name.

"Velia Carmelita!"

Brígida's voice was soft. Isadora thought it sounded almost like the beginning of a song, and she felt her fear melting away. She moved as close to the door as she could and pressed an ear to the carved panel.

"Velia Carmelita!"

There it was again! Isadora had not been mistaken: her aunt was calling out her mother's name. Brígida's voice was so beautiful that the girl could not help herself when she put her hand on the bronze handle and turned it. The door opened almost without a push; the vast bedroom loomed in front of her. A pale light flooded the place, and Isadora saw Brígida sitting on the edge of her bed. Now she heard her voice clearly, but she still could not make out whether Brígida was singing or crying.

The girl hesitated for a few seconds, then began to inch toward her aunt. Brígida suddenly became quiet and the faint swish of Isadora's bare feet filled the room. Brígida jerked around. This frightened the girl so much that she ran out of the room. In her white nightgown, Isadora's flight formed a streak of light in the gloom until she disappeared from sight.

When she reached her room, she was breathing heavily from the strain of running and from fright. She jumped back into bed and covered her head with the blanket, giggling and crying at the same time. She felt sorry that she had run; she wished that she had stayed to hear her aunt's song. As sleep overcame her, Isadora thought that she would have liked for *Tía* Brígida to hold her in her arms.

Early next morning, Isadora rode out with her father, as they did nearly every day. That morning, however, she made up her mind that she would not listen to her father's parables, nor about the rules and barriers that governed women.

"Papá, why does Tía Brígida act funny?"

Flavio abruptly halted his horse, taking the bridle of her mount at the same time.

"What do you mean?"

"Well, she sighs a lot, and she sings. Don't you hear her? I think it happens nearly every night."

He sucked air through his teeth. Now Brígida was affecting his daughter. He knew now that he could no longer put off the subject.

"Because she's crazy."

"Crazy? How?"

Isadora was puzzled. She frowned because she did not see the connection. Trying to be patient, Flavio pursed his lips, but he could not help the scowl that made him look angry. He did not want to speak about his sister, even if it concerned Isadora.

"When someone has everything—food, clothing, a fine house, servants, anything she wants in the world—and still passes her days and nights acting like a fool, that's a crazy woman. Don't you think it's time for our cup of chocolate?" He pressed his spurs into his horse and galloped away.

Isadora stayed behind a few moments, considering what her father had said, then she followed him. While they were eating, they chatted, but although Brígida was not part of their talk, both were thinking of her.

Isadora would not be put off. After breakfast she went to the kitchen to look for Ursula. She finally found her outside, at the rear of the house, where she was ordering flour, rice, wine, and other things from a traveling merchant. The girl waited until Ursula was finished.

"Ursula, why does *Tía* Brígida act like she does?"

The older woman looked at Isadora. For ten years she had watched her grow from a child of three, and during that time she had come to love her. Ursula had not married; she had taken Isadora as her daughter. Now one of the questions that she had known would be asked one day had been asked. She turned away as she poured water into a jug. "How do you mean?"

"At night she sings and hums and walks through the corridors."

"That's not so strange."

"It isn't?"

"No. She sleeps during the day."

Isadora wrinkled her forehead and put her hand on Ursula's shoulder. She wanted her attention.

"Why does she call out my mother's name?"

Ursula put down the jug, wiped her hands on her apron and looked at the girl. She was like her father. Her eyes, her hair, her face, her developing body. *This*, Ursula told herself, *makes her like*

Brígida as well. But as she looked hard at Isadora, she saw what she had seen in her since she was a child. Somewhere around the edges of her forehead, the corners of her lips, the slope of her cheeks— there, if anyone looked and remembered, was Velia Carmelita. Ursula knew, because she remembered Don Flavio's wife, even if she was yet very young when the woman died. She wrapped her hands in the apron and tilted her head. Her eyes squinted in the morning sun.

"Well, *niña*, I'm not sure, but I think it's because she loved your mother very much."

"But . . ."

"When you love someone and that person dies, a part of your spirit goes with her. It is a sadness that comes to take the place of what used to be yours."

When Ursula heard her own words, she realized that she was speaking without really knowing of what she spoke. She had as yet not lost someone she loved, someone like Isadora.

"But she sings, Ursula. People sing when they're happy, not sad."

"Sometimes we sing when we're sad. We do this especially in our dreams."

Having said this, Ursula freed her hands from the apron, patted down a few strands of hair that had come loose in the breeze, and returned to the kitchen. She left Isadora alone, but when she looked back, she saw that the girl was still standing where she had left her.

That day, Isadora decided to face her *Tía* Brígida. She did not wait until nighttime because she was afraid of losing her nerve; darkness frightened her. So she waited until after the meal, when almost everyone in the hacienda was taking a siesta and there would be no one watching, not even her father.

Making an effort to be brave, Isadora headed for Brígida's bedroom. She even took off her shoes, so that there would not be any noise. This time, as she walked through the corridor, everything seemed different. The windows weren't elongated, peeping eyes; they just let in the afternoon sun. The high ceilings did not conceal ugly birds, but seemed to give shelter, protection.

When she reached Brígida's door, Isadora knocked softly. There was no response, so she rapped again, louder this time. As she pressed an ear to the panel, she was startled when the door opened unexpectedly. Brígida stood facing the girl; she was dressed in a full-length black dress with a collar that reached to her chin; and the sleeves were so long, only her white, tapered hands showed.

"*Tía . . .*"

Isadora was near her aunt nearly every evening at dinner. This was, however, the first time that she had ever faced her alone, in her room, away from her father and the servants. Isadora knew intuitively that if her father were to find out, she would be punished.

As she stared up at her aunt, she realized for the first time that Brígida's dress was old-fashioned, that she was tall and very thin. She also noticed that her face was not hard, as it usually was at table. It was not like the plaster that covered the walls, after all, and although Brígida said nothing with her lips, Isadora saw that she was speaking with her eyes.

"Come in, Isadora."

The girl walked past her aunt, timidly at first, then with more confidence as she neared the center of the chamber. She looked around and saw photographs, some so small that she could not make out who was in them. Others were yellowed or even covered with a purple tint. What most caught Isadora's attention was that there were pictures everywhere: on shelves, walls, chests, tables, even scattered on the floor.

"*Tía,* that was me last night." Isadora blurted out the first thing that entered her mind. "I'm sorry if I frightened you. Forgive me, please."

"I know that it was you. Come, sit here by the window with me."

She pointed at a low bench beneath the window. As they sat, Isadora saw that her aunt was looking at her intently. After a few moments, Brígida took Isadora's chin in her hands and moved the young face slowly from one side to the other, looking, scrutinizing. Isadora was surprised to feel the warmth of Brígida's hands; she had imagined that they would be cold, like the ice that clogged up on puddles sometimes during winter.

Then Brígida folded her hands in her lap without speaking. Isadora was remembering why she had come to her aunt in the first place, but she was afraid of asking the question. She fumbled with a fold in her skirt, pretending to smooth it out, only to crumple it again. Several minutes went by, still Brígida said nothing; she merely gazed at Isadora, who finally decided to speak. Her face took on a serious expression.

"*Tía*, do people sing when they're sad?"

Inwardly Isadora scolded herself; *this* was not the question she wanted to ask! But it was too late.

"Yes."

The girl smiled weakly, breathed in hard, and tried again. "Ursula says that you loved my mother. Did you?"

Isadora did not take her eyes from Brígida's. She thought that her aunt's look was soft, serene.

"Yes. I loved her. I still love her above all things."

The girl was taken aback for a moment. Her aunt's response was simple, yet there was something about it that bewildered Isadora. She flashed a smile, wrinkling her nose and forehead. She felt happy that she had asked the question, although she would not understand the answer until years later, until she had loved and lost Jerónimo Santiago. But for the moment, Isadora felt at ease with Brígida. She decided that her aunt was not crazy, after all. Isadora wiggled on the seat, edging closer.

"What were you like when you were a little girl?"

Brígida shrugged her shoulders and moved her head from side to side. She shifted in the seat, thinking.

"Well, I looked like you."

"Did you have a mother and a father?"

"Of course. Everyone does."

"I mean . . . what were they like?"

"Well, my father was from Spain. He had a grocery."

"Where?"

"He owned a grocery store in Arandas."

"Where's that?"

"Far from here."

Isadora saw that her hurried questions were annoying her aunt, so she decided to keep quiet for a few minutes. If Brígida asked her to leave, she would; if not, Isadora had more questions. After a while, she felt confident enough to ask for more information.

"What about your mother?"

Brígida cocked her head to one side and narrowed her eyes. She appeared to be remembering, summoning images and places.

"My mother was an Indian."

"An Indian!" Isadora's eyes widened and her mouth dropped open.

"Yes, my mother was an Indian woman. Do you find that hard to believe?"

"You mean she was *brown*? Like the Rarámuri women?"

"Yes."

Isadora fell silent: She was shocked.

"If your mother was an Indian, then that means that since Papá is your brother, his mother was the same Indian woman. Or maybe—"

"We had the same mother, Isadora."

"Then, that means that she was my grandmother."

"Yes."

"She was brown? *Really* brown?"

"Like a chestnut."

"Then why are the three of us so white, *Tía?*"

"I don't know. We just are."

Isadora, astounded, slouched against the wall. The curtains floated in the afternoon breeze, whipping some of the photographs from their place. The image of a brown woman drifted by in her imagination. She saw her dressed like the Rarámuri: long, white cotton, embroidered with flowers and butterflies. She longed to know her.

"Why doesn't Papá talk about her?"

"Because he's ashamed."

Isadora did not ask about this; she knew the answer. Her father's many examples and warnings echoed in her mind.

"Where is she now?"

"She died."

"Of what?"

"Of sadness."

Isadora's face whipped up to meet her aunt's eyes, but she saw that they were calm. She was captivated by the thought of being the grandchild of an Indian woman. *Maybe in time,* she told herself, *my skin will change and become brown.* This idea thrilled her so much that she wanted Brígida to tell her more. *Maybe a change of skin has happened before in the family.* Isadora knew then that she did not want to leave, she wanted to linger with her aunt.

"I want you to teach me the song you were singing."

"What do you think your father will say when he hears you singing a song that I've taught you?"

"I won't tell him that you taught it to me."

"But he knows everything."

"Then I won't sing it in front of him."

Brígida smiled, and Isadora was startled because this time she knew that here was something she had never seen; she could not remember her aunt ever smiling. She returned the expression, and for a while aunt and niece were silent. By then, the late afternoon sun was casting long shadows on the old furniture and on the hardwood floor.

Brígida began to hum, and the girl, moving closer to her on the seat, echoed the melody, because it lilted and because she liked it. She wanted to sing with her aunt, especially when she heard that her voice was full, rich and warm. After that day, *Tía* Brígida and Isadora became secret friends.

Isadora's other secret was her life with the Santiago family. She could not remember when it had begun, but she was happy going up to the *barranca* to stay, sleep, and eat with the Santiagos in their cave. Whenever her father was away, she took a backpack and trekked up the canyon with Jacobo, the oldest boy, in the lead. After him came Justino, and then followed Jerónimo, the youngest, who was a little older than Isadora. The two youngest children walked side by side most of the time.

She had known Celestino from the beginning. His wife Narcisa came into Isadora's memory later on. She remembered her as being very small, but that when she let out her cackle, the laughter echoed off the rocky walls of their dwelling. Isadora liked being with Narcisa because she could take off her shoes whenever she wanted, and she could sit on the ground, and use her fingers instead of a fork when she ate.

Whenever Isadora joined the Santiago family, she became one of them. Everyone forgot that she had blue eyes and hair the color of gold. They gave her a new name, and she became so much like the Rarámuri that she even dressed like the women of the tribe when she was with them. Isadora was still small when she joined in the running; the women raced among themselves as well. As the years passed, she became so skilled at racing that she was able to compete with Jerónimo and his brothers.

Isadora was happy during the tribal fiestas, when they danced the *dutuburi* around a bonfire nearly all night, and she ate food that was never served at home. She had fun watching the grown-ups jump around, flailing their arms in celebration, especially after they passed a gourd from person to person. Whatever they drank made them very happy. She enjoyed the ceremony of the cross most of all, because it was then that the dancing and chanting took its most beautiful form. For the Rarámuri, Narcisa had told Isadora, the cross was a saint, not a symbol, a spiritual being that needed peyote and *copal* to keep their people from sickness and death.

Isadora and Jerónimo were together whenever her father went away, or when she was not taking lessons from Father Pascual.

Jerónimo taught her how to tie a string on a lizard and pretend it was a horse; how to take hold of a bee without being stung; how to climb a tree to its highest limb. But it was his way of walking and smiling that she liked most.

As they grew, things began to change between Isadora and Jerónimo. At first they only looked at one another shyly; at other times they observed each other secretly. She saw that his body was growing: He was getting longer, his arms were getting stringy, with veins that outlined muscles that she had not seen before. His jaw was squaring; it was losing its roundness, and his nose was taking the shape of a beak.

Her own body was developing as well. It had begun with the frightening experience of waking one morning to find her inner thighs smeared with a paste that looked like chocolate. When she screamed out, it was Ursula who ran to her side and calmed her, telling her that it was her time, that she was now a woman. After this, her breasts began to swell and her waist to shrink. Deep inside of her, in the center of her body, she felt a strange sensation when she thought of Jerónimo, and she knew that he felt something, too.

Isadora told *Tía* Brígida about Jerónimo. She began slowly, cautiously, taking days to speak up because she was unsure of what her aunt would say or think. After a while, however, she saw that Brígida was interested and listened carefully.

"He's taught me many things, *Tía*."

"What things?"

"How to run and catch lizards—"

Isadora stopped, realized abruptly that Brígida was about to laugh at her. But she was wrong; her aunt did not laugh. Instead she looked concerned, so Isadora decided to tell her what had happened the last time she was up in the *barranca*.

"When I sleep up there, Narcisa puts me on a blanket next to the fire. The other night I was almost asleep when I felt something, and I opened my eyes a little. There, next to me, was Jerónimo, and he was looking at me. He has strange eyes, especially when there's not too much light. They glow, like a cat's, but I'm not afraid because I like them."

"He was next to you?" Her aunt brought Isadora back to what she wanted to tell.

"Yes."

"And?"

"And we just looked at each other. It was very strange."

Isadora stopped speaking; she was tracing an invisible picture on the seat of the chair with her finger. Brígida was silent, but she showed the girl that she was waiting.

"Then he took my hand and held it."

"What did you do?"

"Nothing. I left it there. I liked the feeling of his hand."

Isadora was on the brink of telling her aunt what had happened next, but decided to keep it a secret. She did not tell of how Jerónimo moved so close to her that she felt the heat of his body and that parts of his body throbbed. She hid from Brígida that she, too, had edged as close to him as possible, and that she had allowed him to put his fingers between her thighs. She yearned to tell her aunt that she had slid her hands downward on him and that, as she cupped her hand over the mound it discovered, she had felt something move.

Brígida sighed, stood, then walked over to the photographs. She absent-mindedly traced her finger over one of them, thinking of something else. Then she looked over at Isadora.

"What's the matter, *Tía*?"

"You know, Isadora, there are certain things that are forbidden."

The girl stiffened, thinking that her aunt had read her thoughts, that her secret was not a secret, after all.

"*Tía*, are you going to tell Papá what I've just told you?"

"No."

"Going to the *barranca* is forbidden for me, isn't it?"

"No."

Isadora's apprehension was quickly turning into impatience; her aunt seemed now to be saying only one word. She was beginning to regret having told her about the incident, when Brígida returned to her place next to Isadora.

"What I mean is that we are forbidden to love certain people."

"Are you saying that I shouldn't love Jerónimo?"

"No."

There it was again! Isadora wanted more; she wanted her aunt to speak out what she meant.

"What are you saying, *Tía?*"

"I am saying that you are forbidden to love him. I am saying at the same time that even when a woman is forbidden to love someone, it doesn't mean that she *should* not love, or that she *will* not love."

Isadora cocked her head to one side and closed her eyes, trying to decipher the fine distinctions being made by her aunt. It was muddled and too complicated for her. Brígida's riddle scared her, especially because she sensed that her aunt was talking about herself.

"*Tía*, have you ever done something that was forbidden?"

"Yes."

Isadora felt elated at hearing her aunt's affirmation. Although she did not know what she had done, it explained why she now spent her life as she did. She decided that she loved *Tía* Brígida more now that she knew that she had done something that others forbade.

As the summer passed, Isadora mulled over her aunt's words, trying to unravel their meaning. During that time, she and Jerónimo were together almost constantly, until the autumn of that year, when her father told her that she must go away to study. On that day, Isadora went to her room and sat in the dark until she was certain that her father had gone to bed. Then she made her way to Brígida, who was waiting for her.

Isadora did not say anything to her aunt. Instead she sat on the floor next to her and put her head in her lap, where she stayed for a long while. She cried, but she did it quietly, as she felt her aunt's hands on her head.

"Your father has seen you with the boy."

Brígida's words astounded Isadora; they were precise, certain, without doubt. The girl raised her head to look at her aunt.

"Did he tell you?"

"We never speak. You know that."

"Then how do you know?"

"Why else would he send you away? He loves you above all things, you know."

"If he loves me, why is he sending me away?"

"Because he's afraid of what you and the Rarámuri boy will do, and this is stronger in him than his love for you."

Isadora put her head back on Brígida's lap. She was considering, trying to understand what it was that her father feared. She, too, felt afraid, but for this she knew the reason: She did not want to be away from *Tía* Brígida, or Ursula, or the Santiago family. She would have to think more, and maybe she would be able to make out why this was happening to her.

Isadora Betancourt's four years at the convent school went by quickly. During the first weeks, when she was homesick and lonely, she disliked everything and missed Casa Miraflores intensely, but soon she made friends among her fellow students and the nuns. After that, she enjoyed being a student. She also liked the girls' joking and pastimes, and she threw herself into the fun.

Her time at school was shortened by summer breaks, when she returned to Hacienda Miraflores. She enjoyed those times spent riding through the *llano,* watching the men at work, meeting her father's associates. She would pass most of the early evenings in the kitchen with Ursula, helping her organize meals and doing other chores. At those times the two women chatted, laughed, and told each other the news of the day. After dinner, Isadora would find her way to Brígida's room.

When her first year at school had ended, Isadora came home eager to see Jerónimo and his brothers, as well as Celestino and Narcisa. But no matter how much she searched for him, she could rarely find him, and whenever she did see him, he would stop whatever he was doing to go somewhere else. Isadora soon became convinced that he was avoiding her, that he did not want to see her.

Isadora did not understand Jerónimo's behavior until she realized that it was because her father almost always watched her—that he was by her side whenever she left the house, keeping his eyes on her. She knew that El Rarámuri was the target of Flavio's vigilance. That was why Jerónimo kept away. Isadora then pretended to have forgotten him during those years at school.

On the day her father came for her at the end of her studies, Isadora was nervous. She had grown used to being away from his sharp eyes and questions. But most of all, she was tense because she knew that he had plans for her, including marriage. She was not surprised when he broached the subject almost as soon as they were in the car heading home. Although he tried to sound casual, Isadora knew that her father was preparing her for the match that he would make.

As they spoke, Isadora looked at the desert unfolding on each side of the road, but Flavio's questions made her think of men and women mating. She remembered her experiences with Jerónimo: touching, caressing, but no more than that. She had wanted more, and she knew that he had felt the same desire, but they had never gone beyond what their hands touched. They had never even kissed.

This thought made her think hard about her father. There were so many questions that she wanted to ask him about her mother, and about what it was like when they first lay together. No matter how much she tried, Isadora could not imagine her father and mother coupling, and so she longed to ask him about it, but she was too afraid.

During her last year at school, sex had been the favorite topic among the girls. They waited until the lights were turned out in the dormitory, then they jumped from their cots and gathered, heads under blankets, to giggle and talk about what a man does to a woman on the night of their wedding. Some of the girls had heard terrible things, like the one of the man whose private part was so long and hard that when he inserted it into the bride, he nearly ripped her apart. Others told stories they had heard from older sisters and friends who had married.

Isadora joined her roommates most of the times, but never had anything to say; she only listened. She wondered about Jerónimo and what it would be like if he were to do such things to her. Isadora usually put this thought aside, knowing that loving Jerónimo was forbidden—not only by her father but by all of the people she knew. This reflection then turned her mind to her father, and why he had remained alone after her mother died. Isadora also had had questions about Brígida. Why had she never married? Had anyone ever touched *her* body or kissed *her* mouth? As the car sped toward Hacienda Miraflores, Isadora thought of these things, deciding that, unlike *Tía* Brígida, she would have to marry. And since that was inescapable, she would have to face whatever came with it.

On the night of her birthday fiesta, Isadora danced with the young man who would become her husband. She felt nothing for him. She thought only of Jerónimo. But she pretended to the others and even to herself, thinking that if she could pretend once, she could do it again. She tried to put Jerónimo out of her mind. But that night, when Isadora was in bed, she wanted Jerónimo. She even dreamed that they were together in a cave, arms and legs entangled.

Isadora's wedding did not take place until Don Flavio had a house built and furnished for her; he chose a place close to the main house. Once the project was completed, he set the date for her to marry. The ceremony took place in 1931, when she was nineteen years old. She felt neither joy nor sadness; there was only a strange sensation that clung to her stomach and throat. She decided not to have anything to do with the preparations, allowing her father to make all the arrangements, to decide who would be invited and what would be the entertainment.

During those months, Isadora spent her time writing letters to school friends and chatting with Ursula in the kitchen. Sometimes she sat gazing out of a window, her eyes blank and her body listless. At other times she rode through the *llano*, but she did this without the exhilaration that she had once experienced. It was as if she were searching the vast plain for something, for someone who never appeared.

On one of those days Isadora, lost in thought, let her horse slow to a canter, then to a walk, until it stopped, content to munch on a clump of grass. She had not even noticed that she had come to a standstill when she was startled out of her absorption by the clopping of hooves. Twisting in the saddle, she saw her father approaching on his horse. He reined in brusquely, making her own mount spin around nervously, pawing at the ground.

"*Hija*, I've been looking for you."

Isadora stared at him without answering. A distance had been growing between them since she had agreed to marry Eloy Pardo. It was a separation that even she could not explain, and she no longer felt the affection for her father that she had when she was a child. Somehow, that had slipped away. In its place was a shadow, something that deepened and widened each time he approached her, spoke to her, looked at her. It was a sensation that was like fear, she told herself, an apprehension that gripped her nerves and made her head ache. Now, realizing that he had taken the time to ride out to meet her, the feeling became more intense, and she tried to guess what had brought him to her. Something important had happened.

"What's wrong, Papá?"

"Wrong? Nothing. What makes you think that?"

Flavio smiled, but his smile was strained. He, too, had sensed the gap that was widening between Isadora and himself, and it made him irritable: Brígida might be influencing her. And it was because of this fear that he had decided to speak to her. Taking the bridle of Isadora's horse, he dismounted and helped her to do the same. Then he walked her over to a clump of trees, where they sat down. The sun was beginning to slope downward, smearing the western sky with lavender and orange streaks.

"It's hard for a father to speak to his daughter as I must, Isadora. The truth is, however, that since you don't have a mother—and it's a mother that should do this—it is my responsibility."

"If you're going to explain how babies are made, don't bother, Papá. That's what schoolgirls gossip about when the nuns are out of the room."

Isadora heard her voice; it was harsh and sarcastic, and it surprised her. She looked at her father and, even though the brim of his hat shaded his eyes, she saw that he was momentarily stunned.

"Oh? And do they gossip about how they like to keep their legs clamped shut when they're supposed to open them to their husbands?"

Now it was his turn to be taken aback, by his own words. When he heard himself he felt a rush of embarrassment, especially when he saw Isadora's mouth fall open. But it was too late for him to retreat, so he went on because this was the very conversation he had wanted to have with her. The fact that it had unexpectedly taken a crude, raw turn only helped him come out with his concern.

"You're a woman now, Isadora, and it's your obligation to allow your husband to do what is his responsibility. That's why women are put in this world, and that's what you're going to do! You must not resist, do you understand me?"

Isadora did not respond, but disgust was evident all over her face. Flavio perceived this, and his voice escalated, rasping like falling gravel. He was no longer held back by politeness, modesty, or even consideration for his daughter. Flavio felt himself dragged backwards by bitter memory, reminding him that he had forced himself on a woman. Moved by these thoughts, he struck abruptly at the other canker that had secretly corroded his soul.

"Have you ever had relations with another woman?" Flavio's voice was filled with bitterness as he relived his anguish on discovering that Velia Carmelita and Brígida were lovers. Even more than

The Day of the Moon

outrage and jealousy, he now felt suffocated by an overwhelming anger, which he could not and would never recognize for what it was: envy. He did realize now what he had ignored before: His wife had loved Brígida and not him. After all these years, Flavio still felt the humiliation.

Isadora got to her feet but did not take her eyes off her father's face. She was quiet for a while before she answered.

"At school, some girls slept together, they touched each other and kissed. I have not done that, but I don't know what will happen in my life."

She turned, leaped on the horse, and left Flavio, still squatting on the ground, glaring at her as she rode away. She was trembling, and the sensation in her throat intensified so much that later at dinner she hardly spoke.

On the night of her wedding, as the dancing was at its peak, Don Flavio tapped Eloy on the shoulder, took Isadora by the hand and escorted them toward the corridor. There he raised his hand in blessing and signaled that it was time for them to go to their chamber. Eloy bowed his head, as expected, but Isadora glared at her father. She looked into his eyes with such intensity that he had to look away, unable to sustain the emotion in her eyes.

She walked rapidly, almost tripping on the hem of her gown; Eloy nearly had to run to keep up with her. When he closed the door, he clicked on a lamp and gawked at her.

"Turn off the light."

"No light?"

"No."

Eloy did as Isadora wanted. He turned off the light and waited for his eyes to adjust to the shadows. He was shocked when he made out that she was taking off her clothes. Garment by garment, she shed everything until she stood in front of him completely naked.

"You do the same."

Eloy was unprepared for this behavior from his bride. He had anticipated squeamishness, exaggerated modesty, even resistance—but now he was faced with her telling him to take off his clothes. He began with his white tie, then the cufflinks. He was slow; his fingers trembled and he could not manage the buttons.

Isadora stood looking at Eloy as he pulled off shoes and socks, shirt and trousers, and all the rest. She was shivering, not from cold but from a mix of disgust and fear. She was thinking of the stories her schoolmates had fabricated about this moment.

When Eloy penetrated Isadora, the pain was so excruciating for her that she let out a low moan despite her intention to not make a sound. His grunting, sweating, and especially the rancid smell that trickled from his body, sickened her. When he was finished, he rolled over and began to snore.

Weeks after that night, Isadora told her father that she was pregnant. He grinned and squared his shoulders as if it had been his own doing, and that night he got drunk with the ranch hands, dancing with every servant girl that he could reach. Eloy slept with Isadora every night until her abdomen began to swell. Afterward, he hardly appeared in her room, and soon it became the gossip of the hacienda that he was having relations with a woman who did the laundry. One day, Eloy disappeared without a word.

Locked in the isolation of the asylum, these recollections bore down on Isadora as she felt her back ache from the hardness of the slab on which she lay. Suddenly, a rough hand seized her chin. It moved her face from one side to the other, as if examining it. She tried to open her eyes, but could not. Her eyelids, her lips, the tips of her fingers and toes, every part of her was heavy and beyond her strength to budge.

She had difficulty sorting her thoughts. Brígida's image blurred with the white of the uniforms that held her prisoner. Then she saw Ursula, arms outstretched, trying to reach her. After this, Isadora heard a voice droning, its slurred words penetrating the thick fog that had gripped her brain. *One more injection,* it said; *Just to placate her,* it insisted; *Just to be on the safe side,* it repeated.

Parts of Isadora's body were beginning to gain sensation and she could wiggle her toes, turn her feet from one side to the other, flex her knees and thighs. The rest of her body was stiff, unfeeling. She longed to scream out so that someone might come to help her.

She looked for Jerónimo, but remembered: He was dead. She called out to her children and thought that they, too, were dead. Then her mind turned, straightened, reminding her that they were not dead, that Ursula had sworn never to abandon them. She vowed to Isadora to die rather than leave them. This thought calmed her, and she told herself that soon she would leave the trap she was in. Soon she would return for her children.

Coarse hands were now propping her up. Isadora felt the cold plaster of the wall against her naked back. She discovered that she could now move her legs and her arms and even swivel her head from side to side. She heard voices. They mumbled, but she caught some of the words.

"She's coming out of it."

"Don't be too sure. Hold her, she might bolt again."

"Should I get another needle?"

"No. We've got the jacket."

Isadora kept her eyes closed, fearing that anything she did might cause another injection to be plunged into her. She pretended not to hear or know what was happening to her. Instead she concentrated on her body. Pain streaked up and down her legs and arms. Her back ached as if it had been wrenched, and her breasts throbbed painfully.

She was kept in a straitjacket for days, until the nurses were sure they had pacified her. After that, she was allowed to walk in the patio of the asylum, but only under close watch. Even after months had passed, the staff was still uneasy. They were cautious, remembering the problems she had caused when she arrived.

Isadora did not speak to anyone. She ate little, and whenever she could she sat on a stone bench in a corner of the cloister to stare at the fountain that she remembered from the first night. Her mind filled with thoughts and memories. Her father's image drifted in and out of her consciousness, but as soon as it appeared, she pushed it away. She thought of Eloy and she again experienced the relief she had felt when told that he was gone. She conjured Ursula's face and the feeling of safety she had always given her. Brígida sat on the edge of her bed, motionless, an enigma, surrounded by photographs and memories. Then the cycle of Isadora's memories made a full turn when her thoughts returned to that day when Jerónimo had come back into her life.

Chapter 11

When Eloy deserted her, Isadora was relieved. She was glad not to have him near. Her life became flat and routine; nonetheless, the dullness of it brought her peace. She moved back into her father's house, where she ate and spoke to him, but never talked about herself or her feelings. The rift between them that had taken shape before her marriage had widened and not even the birth of Samuel helped.

Jerónimo had vanished at the time of her wedding, and Celestino would say nothing about his son. Isadora thought often of them and Narcisa, and at times wanted to go up to the *barranca*. She never did. She lost touch with the Santiago family.

When Samuel was five years old, Jerónimo returned to Hacienda Miraflores. Isadora, in the kitchen, overheard two of the servant girls giggling. She thought that she heard his name mentioned, but the place was so large that she could not be sure. When Ursula returned from the rear of the house, arms loaded with onions, Isadora went to her. Her voice was low, almost a whisper.

"What are those two girls talking about?"

Ursula, taken by surprise, dropped the onions on the cutting board, wiped her hands on her apron and looked over at the two women standing near the stove, gossiping. She turned to Isadora, puzzled and impatient.

"I don't know, *niña*. I've been outside."

Ursula pointed with her chin. She was grumpy and showed even more irritation when Isadora put her finger to her lips, letting her know that she should lower her voice.

"Go ask them," Isadora ordered.

"What?"

"*Go ask them.*"

"*Niña . . .*"

"Go!"

Ursula shrugged her shoulders and rolled her eyes, but she shuffled to the other side of the kitchen and, unnoticed, edged her way closer to the girls, pretending to check the contents of a pot. She fussed with the lid, then stirred the coals as if making sure there was enough wood to finish cooking what was simmering, then with a rag wiped a wet spot off the counter. When she returned to where Isadora was waiting, Ursula's face was stamped with a smug expression.

"*Niña*, El Rarámuri is back! They're saying that he went as far north as Texas, where he's been these past few years; that he worked there; that he made a lot of money; that he learned their language and even how to drive an automobile; that he made many friends, especially women. They say he picked up strange customs. He's returned to visit Narcisa. She is sick."

Isadora's eyes widened silently as Ursula breathlessly rattled off what she had heard. Yet she was not sure that she believed her. She frowned, trying to imagine Jerónimo among the gringos, talking like them and even thinking like them. When she saw that Ursula was about to move on to her next chore, she grabbed her arm. Isadora's voice was low, husky. Her eyes had narrowed to slits.

"Ursula, are you telling me the truth?"

"*Niña!*"

"How could those girls have said so much in so little time?"

Offended by Isadora's distrust, Ursula puckered her lips and looked down at the onions without answering. Isadora realized that she had hurt her, but she repeated her question. This time her tone was softened.

"I didn't mean to say that I don't believe you, Ursula. It's just so much information, and you were close to them for only a few moments."

"*Bueno, niña.* All I can say is that these modern girls talk very fast."

Ursula smiled broadly, showing that the offense had melted away. She moved over to where the onions were and began to peel and dice them. Isadora went to a window, sat on the sill and reflected on what she had just heard.

After that day, she made sure to ride out to the stables, to the *llano,* and even to where the sierra slopes toward the *barranca.* She did this every day, uncertain of exactly why she was doing it. All she knew was that she was driven by a nervous, unsettled feeling. On one of her visits to Brígida, Isadora told her of her daily rides.

"Has he returned?"

Her aunt's question jarred Isadora, although it did not surprise her. She had long before grown used to her aunt's ways. When she answered, she heard her own voice; it was soft, almost a whisper.

"Yes."

Brígida continued to silently gaze at her hands, which she held in her lap. Isadora took the moment to look around at the dozens of photographs. She smiled, remembering her first impression of her aunt's bedroom. Then she looked at her again. Brígida had aged. Her face had become more angular than ever, and it had a pinched expression. She still wore turn-of-the-century dresses, always black.

"*Tía,* I want to see him."

When Isadora heard herself, she unthinkingly put her hand to her mouth. But after a few moments, she thought that it was good to be honest with Brígida. Why else had she come to see her that evening? Isadora took a deep breath. "Yes. I want to see him. I hear that he's been in the United States, and people are saying that he's changed."

Brígida shifted in her chair and let out a sigh; it was frail, like her. Head cocked, she looked at Isadora, questioning, wondering.

"I'm sure he's met many women," Isadora said, then paused as she rubbed her fingers against the armrest of the chair. "Maybe he's even married. What do you think?"

Finally, Brígida chose to speak. She pursed her lips as if gathering saliva or clearing something off her teeth. "How can I think anything about Jerónimo? I haven't seen him in years. If you need to know this about him, Isadora, you'll have to ask him yourself. Also, you should not depend on gossip. It's hardly ever the truth."

"Do you think it's wrong to look for him?"

"Only if it's so in your heart."

"I'm still married and—"

"There's something more important than being married."

Brígida cut off Isadora, leaving her not knowing what to say. She frowned, inwardly repeating what her aunt had just said, turning it over in her mind. She remembered one of their conversations years before, when she was still a child.

"The forbidden?"

"Yes."

Isadora leaned her head against the back of the chair. She thought that she understood Brígida's meaning, but something made her unsure.

"If I were not married, Jerónimo would still be forbidden to me?"

"Yes."

Closing her eyes, Isadora was now certain that she understood. It was not because she was married, and therefore bound by the laws of God and by everything that surrounded her. Jerónimo was forbidden because he was a Rarámuri. She sat up in the chair, stiff and tense.

"*Tía,* have you ever done what was forbidden?"

"When you were a little girl, you asked me that question, and I answered that yes, I had done what was forbidden."

"I remember."

"And now you want to know what that was."

"Yes."

"I loved your mother."

Isadora looked at her aunt with disappointment. Brígida was merely telling her what she had known for years, and she did not see what could be forbidden about such an affection. Her aunt let minutes pass before she spoke again.

"Fuimos amantes."

Now Isadora did sit up, eyebrows raised, eyes rounded and bright with emotion. *We were lovers.* As Brígida's words seeped into her brain, they drew forth in reply an echo: the question Don Flavio had asked Isadora before her wedding. *Have you ever had relations with another woman?* In a few moments, it came together: her father's hatred of his sister, his disdain for her mother's memory, his possessive care of her every move.

Isadora's mind moved from thought to thought. She wondered if at the center of her father's torment was a void, an anguish over something he had never had. This made her realize that she, too, had never been loved as Brígida must have loved her mother. Eloy had not loved her, and Isadora had not loved him either. She pondered all of this for a long while. Her eyes roamed the room, its walls, its pictures, the fading light filtering through the window. Then she relaxed into the chair and looked into Brígida's eyes.

"I'm glad. Yes, I'm very glad."

When she left the room, Isadora walked for a while through the house, simply looking at its chambers and hallways, and as she did she thought of Brígida and her mother. Then she headed for the kitchen, where her son Samuel preferred to eat. She sat next to him, stroked his forehead, thinking of what would have been of her aunt's life had Velia Carmelita lived. After that day, Isadora wandered farther out on her horse until at last she found Jerónimo. It was October, 1937, a time in which the *llano* began its seasonal slumber and the days were short.

Jerónimo had just walked out of the stable, where he had been grooming horses, and he turned at the sound of an approaching horse. Isadora was mounted, looking down at him as he stood there. He was so surprised that all he could do was stare at her, a rope dangling in his hands.

"¡Hola, Jerónimo!"

She dismounted. The horse snorted, pawing the earth, moving its hindquarters from side to side. Without thinking, Jerónimo took the bridle from her hands; but since she kept quiet, he felt forced to say something.

"*¡Hola, Niña Isadora!*"

His voice was soft and he smiled, exposing even, white teeth. His complexion was mahogany-colored. Isadora thought that his skin had become rougher, richer than before. He stood erect and, even though of medium height, he was taller than Isadora. He was dressed in khaki, heeled boots, and a sombrero with a brim that shaded his eyes.

"No longer a *niña.*" Isadora laughed quietly. He smiled, but his body was tense, and his eyes were bright with nervousness and surprise. He fumbled with the bridle, shifting his weight from one foot to the other.

"Have you been on the hacienda for long?"

"*Sí.*"

"I haven't seen you until now."

"No."

"Why haven't you come by to say hello?"

Jerónimo stared at Isadora. He wanted to run, but he could not. He wanted to speak, but he could not do that either. He wished that he could speak the words that were in his heart, but his tongue would not obey him. As if hearing his thoughts, Isadora spoke for him.

"We used to be friends. We used to do so many things together, but it's as if that hadn't happened. And I don't know why."

Isadora's voice was charged with emotion; it had lost its playful tone of a moment earlier. Jerónimo's body relaxed as if her voice were a warm, soothing fluid coursing through his veins. He dropped the bridle and took her arm, steering her to a place to the side of the stable where they could sit.

"I am happy to see you, *niña.*"

"I'm not a—"

"I know you're not a child, but that's how I call you in here." Jerónimo pointed to his chest. The nervousness that had overcome him when Isadora surprised him was melting away, and instead he felt the joy he had always experienced when he was with her. She smiled at him and nodded.

"Where did you go?"

"Up there, to Texas. I worked on a ranch like this one. It's not too different from here. The horses are the same."

Isadora stared at Jerónimo, absorbing his voice, his looks, into her skin. Her heart was beating intensely, and she felt the same stirring as on the night of her eighteenth birthday fiesta, when she had desired him in her bed.

"Why did you go?"

Jerónimo looked away from her, and she saw his jaw twitch. His lips pursed nervously, and his eyes seemed riveted on to the tip of his boots. Suddenly, he jerked his face up toward her and looked into her eyes. He was smiling.

"Remember the last race we ran together? The time you and I beat my brothers? I've never forgotten. It was the best race I've ever run."

Isadora knew that he was trying to distract her from her question. She remembered that race because it, too, had been wonderful for her. But she returned to the subject.

"Jerónimo, please tell me why you left Miraflores."

"Because you married, *niña*, and because I thought I was going to die of sadness."

"Are you angry at me because I married?"

"No. Women in my tribe marry who they're told to. It's more or less the same for women everywhere." He paused for a moment. "It was the sadness that made me go."

"My husband went away. Did you know that? He left me soon after we were married."

Jerónimo mumbled something under his breath, but Isadora could not make out the words. After this, they kept quiet. Evening was approaching and several of the workers were picking up gear and belongings as they prepared to make their way home. Muffled sounds drifted in the air: doors opening and shutting, horses snorting, the crowing of a rooster. In the bushes, crickets were beginning their song, and somewhere in the distance a *tecolote* owl prepared for its night watch.

"You have a son."

Jerónimo's words startled Isadora; she did not know what meaning was in them. The idea that he resented Samuel flashed through her mind.

"Yes. What about it?"

"Nothing. I'm glad."

Isadora sensed that Jerónimo was mouthing words, not saying what he felt or thought. She thought abuptly that they had lost too much time, years even, not to speak what was on their minds, and hearts, immediately.

"Jerónimo, I've loved you ever since I can remember and I know that you love me."

His face showed shock and elation at once, as if he were two men, each going in a different direction. His breathing became agitated, and he clenched and loosened his fists. He cocked his head to one side as he looked at Isadora. Then raising his hand, he put his index finger on her lips. His touch was soft, and she took hold of his hand and kissed it.

"*Niña*, we can't do this."

"Why? Because I'm married? Eloy has gone. He'll never return."

"It's not that. Think . . ."

"Is it my son? I love him in a different way!"

"You know why." Jerónimo had recovered from the wave of emotion he had felt hearing Isadora's declaration of love, as well as the sensation of her lips on his hands. He looked at her steadily, but she had slouched back and was sucking in air through her teeth in exasperation. "It's impossible for someone like me to love someone like you."

"Impossible?"

"I mean that I shouldn't."

Brígida's words returned to Isadora. In front of her also was the unseen barrier her father had repeatedly forbidden her to transgress.

Isadora felt anger growing within her: rage against her father who warned of invisible boundaries; irritation against her aunt who played with words; impatience with Jerónimo who circled the truth.

"Why don't you say it as it is: You *won't* love me because it's forbidden. That's what you mean, Jerónimo. Because you're a Rarámuri and I am who I am. Because you and your family come from a cave and I from here."

They fell silent after her outburst, but Isadora's words dangled in the waning light.

"What are we going to do, Isadora?"

Jerónimo closed his eyes, waiting for her answer. His body betrayed surrender, mixed with fear. With his eyes still shut, he reached out, groping for Isadora, who took his hand in hers. She moved closer to him and put her face next to his.

"I've tried to listen and do whatever Papá has asked of me, but now I can't. I want to be with you."

Darkness covered Hacienda Miraflores as Isadora and Jerónimo made their way toward the *llano*. No one saw them when they lay on a grassy place under a clump of trees. There were no witnesses when she took off her clothes, nor when he took off his. Don Flavio, sipping his early evening chocolate as he sat in his armchair, thought of the past day's business as his daughter was transported by joy and pleasure to a world she had never experienced. Not even Isadora and Jerónimo could have imagined the happiness they now felt as they embraced, becoming one with each other and with the ageless sierras and *barrancas* that sheltered them.

After that night, Isadora and Jerónimo met each evening at dusk to make love under the trees. Every time was more intense, longer, less cautious, less silent. She began to abandon discretion when she was with others, laughing loudly in the corridors of her father's house, in the kitchen, joking with the maids, and teasing Samuel. Jerónimo also became more assured after separating from Isadora each night. Instead of walking with a normal step, he strutted. He grew reckless, insisting on riding the wildest horses. He smiled incessantly, without apparent reason.

Their ecstasy went on for weeks before people began to talk. In the beginning, there were whispers, insinuating questions, hints, sometimes assertions. Soon eyes exchanged meaningful glances whenever Isadora or Jerónimo came near. Pursed lips communicated silent messages. Raised eyebrows affirmed the unmentionable. After a time, maids, cooks, seamstresses, washerwomen, ropers, *vaqueros,* loggers, mestizos and *indios,* were all gossiping, and they murmured about nothing else except El Rarámuri and the daughter of the *Patrón.*

Finally, Jerónimo and Isadora were struck by the reality that swirled around them. Their secret was not a secret: What they did, when they did it, and why they did it was on the tongue of every worker on the hacienda.

One night, Isadora and Jerónimo met at a different place, where, with contempt and fear, they spoke of what was happening around them on the hacienda.

"I'm going to him. I'm his daughter and he should know it from me."

"I'll come with you. He must hear me say that I love you."

"No! He won't even allow you in the house."

Jerónimo stared at Isadora, knowing that she spoke the truth. "When will you speak to him?"

"Tonight."

That evening after dinner, Isadora rapped at the door of her father's den; she felt her knees weakening and her heart beating. He was seated at his desk. The green lampshade cast sharp, lime-colored tones on his face. She realized at once that he already knew why she was there.

Flavio's jaw was clamped shut as he glared at Isadora, but she moved closer to him despite his intimidating manner. She was inwardly shuddering but convinced that she could not run away as her body was urging. She had to face him with the truth.

"Papá, I—"

"Your *son* is only five years old. Have you thought about *him*? And what your actions will do to *him*?"

Isadora was taken by surprise. She had not expected him to hurl Samuel in her face. "Samuel will understand."

"When you've abandoned him! He'll understand?"

"I'll not abandon him! He'll come with me!"

"Where? To those vermin-infested caves?"

Isadora felt that rage was about to engulf her, cut off her breathing. She feared losing control over herself, so she held back the words she was thinking.

"Tell me that this filthy gossip is a lie. Tell me that you are not the concubine of a savage, that you haven't defiled yourself and me. Tell me that you haven't forgotten all I've taught you. Tell me this, Isadora, and everything will be as if nothing had happened."

A clock ticked on the mantelpiece. A horse whinnied in the gloom of the night. Isadora thought of the hearth in Narcisa's cave.

"Papá, I love him. I have his child inside of me and I intend to live with him the rest of my life. Nothing will stop me from doing this."

Isadora turned to leave, but when her hand was on the doorknob, she heard her father's bootheels slam down on the hardwood floor, and she turned to look at him. The light behind him radiated a glow around him, a silhouette, and she imagined that he had grown, because he looked like a giant. His legs were spread apart and his hands were hooked into his belt.

"Isadora, I won't allow you to insult me in this manner."

She turned away from him to go to Jerónimo, who had been waiting where they always met. When she found him, they sat in silence. The realization that Don Flavio was aware of their relationship, that he was in a position to control their lives, and that he would be exempt from punishment no matter what actions he took, all this filled them with apprehension.

"We'll leave this place and go to Texas." Jerónimo nodded his own head up and down several times, confirming his own idea. His mouth was pinched and his forehead furrowed. When Isadora did not respond, he looked at her. She was staring at him.

"Texas! What will we do there?"

"I know where I can work and we can live without being afraid. We must go as far away from him as we can. If we stay in Mexico, he'll follow and hurt us."

Isadora was quiet, but Jerónimo saw that her hands were coiled into fists and her body had stiffened. He waited for her to speak.

"We belong here, we were born on this land. Why should we go to a strange place?"

"Because he'll come after us if we don't, Isadora."

"What about Celestino and Narcisa?"

"They will suffer more when Don Flavio hurts us."

She did not say anything, but her head shook in wordless denial. Her breathing become loud, agitated, and she nervously pressed her knees one against the other.

"Your father won't rest until he makes us pay for what we've done."

"No! You're wrong!"

Isadora's voice was shrill, defensive. Her face showed the anxiety she was feeling as Jerónimo pressed her with talk of her father's reprisal.

"Isadora."

"He's angry, that's all. But he would not hurt me. I know, because I'm what he loves most. Let's give him time, Jerónimo. You'll see that I'm right. In a few months, when our child is born, he'll celebrate just as he did when Samuel was born. And then everything will be as usual. Soon he'll consider you his son."

"You're the one who is wrong! Let's not take a chance. We can return if we think—or if he lets us know—that he has given up planning to punish us. Isadora, think of the child. Think of *yourself*."

Exasperated, Jerónimo's voice had escalated, matching Isadora's testiness. But then they fell into silence, both of them wrestling with what they imagined would happen. It was Jerónimo who yielded. He looked at Isadora; he was calculating, figuring. Then he nodded, at first slowly, then with more energy.

"Maybe you're right, *niña*. Maybe he won't hurt us. Maybe we can go on living here. We'll go up to the *barranca*, with my family."

Next day before sunrise, Isadora waited in the stable; Samuel, sleepy and grumpy, was with her. When Jerónimo arrived, they left Hacienda Miraflores and began the climb up to the caves of the Rarámuri. A few days later, Ursula Santiago packed her belongings and she, too, left the hacienda and made her way back to her people.

Isadora pressed her forehead against the damp windowpane. She straightened her head and stared at the wire mesh embedded in the glass. How much force would be needed to break through that net? She closed her eyes and felt her eyeballs burning. Then she opened them and focused on the park surrounding the asylum.

It was the end of the day; darkness had wrapped itself around the high arches and recesses of the building. Isadora concentrated on the fog creeping in from the marshes of Zapopan, snaking its way beneath bushes, and clinging to the drooping stalks of tall grass. The trees loomed against the sky; their branches hung low against the soggy ground, and she heard them weeping.

Isadora traced a line on the clouded glass with her finger, then she wrote her name. Next to it she etched a *J*, then an *A*. She jerked away from the window and paced the cell, moving from one wall to the other, back and forth, until she stopped at the cot where she slept. She sat on its edge, feeling the crossbar press against her buttocks.

She got back on her feet and returned to the window. The fog had risen, almost reaching the lower branches of the trees. She craned her neck and saw the moon rising in the eastern sky. The thought flashed through Isadora's mind that the phosphorescent white sphere glowed like a skull circled by a transparent halo.

After staring at the moon for a few moments, she remembered that the Rarámuri believe the dead return to meet with the spirits of those who are alive—to those who lie dreaming during the moonlit night.

Chapter 12

"They call it the Day of the Moon."

Isadora and Jerónimo lay on a grassy embankment, away from the cave they inhabited. His gaze was fixed on the sky as it turned shades of red and orange toward the west and lavender in the east. As she reclined on her side, her head on his outstretched arm, she outlined his profile with her finger.

Jerónimo and Isadora had grown more and more worried at what was happening around them, and today they had been trying to distract themselves. They could no longer deny the antagonism of the tribe. It was a resentment that Jerónimo had not anticipated when he brought Isadora and Samuel to live among his people. He had known that there would be surprise and even gossip, but he had not expected the undercurrents of bitterness that welled up each day.

Another source of uneasiness was Don Flavio's silence and inertia. He was behaving as if nothing had happened, as if Isadora's abandoning Hacienda Miraflores and her flight with Jerónimo had not been an affront to his honor. When Jerónimo left the hacienda with Isadora he was able to find work on a nearby ranch. Each day, when he went down to the *llano*, he listened to the rumors that eventually reached him: The *Patrón* of Miraflores was sick. He could not even leave his room. But then, as time passed, Don Flavio was seen riding his horse, crossing one side of his land to the other, yet no change in his behavior was detected by anyone, no matter how closely he was watched. This filled everybody with anxiety. It was unnatural that the father of a white woman did nothing when she ran off with one of their own. Instead, there was a strange calm in Don Flavio, and the tribe suspected that something dreadful was about to happen to them.

That evening, hoping to distract her, Jerónimo began speaking of Rarámuri beliefs. Isadora listened carefully, although much of what he told her was not new to her. As he talked about the cross, she remembered how it was thought of as a saint by the Rarámuri—an actual being, deserving of homage and reverence. She knew also that peyote was considered a god and often called Tata, father, by the old ones, the *huehues,* of the tribe. As a child she had experienced the processions, the dances, the chants; and all along Isadora had felt that even though different from what she had learned from the nuns, the beliefs of Jerónimo's people did not contradict her own way of thinking. But now Jerónimo's words caught Isadora's attention. *They call it the Day of the Moon.* She drew her hand away from his face and lifted her head, balancing herself on her elbow.

"That's beautiful, but what does it mean?"

"The ancient ones believe that while we sleep, our souls join the spirits of the dead, and that together they work hard—harder yet than during the day, when we walk about in sunlight. They also believe that during the night, when we're sleeping, we do wonderful, mysterious things with those who have gone to the other side of the sierras. They say that it is at this time that we make new songs and poems, and that we discover who we love. This is what is meant by the Day of the Moon. It happens, they say, every night when we're dreaming."

"I had never heard that before," Isadora said as she looked into Jerónimo's eyes. "But you say *they* as if you don't believe in the Day of the Moon. I think I could believe in it."

He smiled and shrugged. "Well, maybe. What I mean is that I don't know. Maybe when I'm old I'll see things as the ancient ones do." He looked up at her, his eyes shining. "Do you believe everything that you're told?"

"Not everything. But don't you think that our spirit does something when we're sleeping? I do. I ask myself, Where does my soul go? Does it look for something, for someone?"

"Maybe. I'm not sure."

"It's beautiful to think that we'll meet again after we die, Jerónimo. And what better time than during a dream, when the moon gives us another day to work, to sing, to love."

Isadora now sat up, captivated by the notion. Jerónimo, still stretched out on the ground, crossed his arms behind his head and looked at her silhouette as the last glimmer of light cast tones of silver and green on her. His eyes traced the curve of her forehead and nose. Then his gaze slid down to her lips, chin, throat, breasts. He paused at her bulging abdomen; it was swollen with his child. This thought forced his mind back to that which had been making them grow more apprehensive each day. He shook his head as if to shake off an insect; and he sat up, put the palm of his hand on her stomach, and kissed her. It was growing dark now, so they got up and made their way toward their cave.

As they walked, they put aside the night's talk, and returned to what had been troubling them for weeks. Don Flavio's stillness baffled them, the antagonism of the tribe hurt them—and there was also Samuel, who had become despondent as the weeks melted into months. Unlike Isadora, who had dwelled in the caves whenever she could as a child, he could not get used to living there; sleeping on a mat on the ground, eating maize and beans and squash almost every day. He wanted to see his grandfather and keep him company in the stables as he used to before he was taken to the cave. He missed his comfortable room and having servants. Most of all, he resented that his mother slept with El Rarámuri.

Isadora had attempted to soothe Samuel by talking to him, taking him on walks, singing to him. At first, she had told him that his grandfather had gone away, but when she saw that the boy did not believe her, she decided to tell him the truth: Jerónimo was now her husband, and his father. When Samuel heard this, he became even more disconcerted, and he refused to speak, even to her. Not even

Ursula could comfort the boy, no matter how many times she tried. Through this all, Jerónimo had tried to make friends with him, but he was rejected by the boy.

Jerónimo and Isadora spoke about Samuel as they walked, pausing, moving cautiously in the waning westerly light. After a while their conversation returned to the reaction of the tribe to Isadora's presence. Resentment had become apparent when the two had first walked through the plaza of the communal village. People stopped to stare at them. Those on the way to the marketplace paused to get a better look. The talkers cut off what they were saying to gawk at the unlikely sight crossing the cobblestone plaza. The black-robed priest who had just emerged from the darkened portico of the church blinked and took a second look, convinced that his eyes were indeed failing him. A small cluster of old hags stared first at the young Rarámuri, then at the white woman, then at the boy child, then at one another, their wrinkled lips pursed in disbelief, their tiny eyes bright with curiosity.

What at first was an oddity soon became the only topic of conversation and gossip. After a few days, interest became apprehension, and finally the presence of the white woman and her child became a source of fear for most of these people. The men who trekked down the sierra to work each day, especially those paid by Don Flavio Betancourt, asked each other what would happen once the *Patrón* found out where his daughter was living. Those who were not peons for Hacienda Miraflores either sympathized or heckled Don Flavio's workers about how they would soon have to find new work.

For the women of the tribe, what Jerónimo Santiago had done was a calamitous offense. Although it was the *huehues* who dictated the laws of the people, the women made the decisions that counted. They were the custodians of the family and the traditions that bound it. They were the ones who jealously safeguarded who married whom, which households would come together, and what would become of the children from those unions. As they ground the maize, wove wool, dyed cloth, gathered wood, helped the sick and the pregnant, and especially as they gathered water at the well, it was the women who decided what was approved and what was forbidden within the tribe. When Jerónimo Santiago arrived with a white woman by his side, and she with another's child, tribal women flocked together; they gathered in small groups, finally they crammed into caves in large assemblies. The son of Celestino and Narcisa Santiago had somehow snatched away their right to decide. Such behavior could not be tolerated.

Those who secretly observed the lovers were convinced that Isadora and Jerónimo mocked the tribe with their constant smiling, chatting, and laughing. When her bulging abdomen became obvious, the men and women of the tribe found it intolerable. It was wrong for one of their own to mix with the offspring of the white *patrón*. Only evil would come of it. So it was that they pressed the *huehues* to convene and put an end to the danger that loomed for the tribe.

Celestino and Narcisa also talked of what to do. When Jerónimo appeared with Isadora and her son, they were not surprised, thinking that it was another of the visits she had been making since she was a child. But when Jerónimo announced that he was leaving the family dwelling to set up one of his own, it became evident that their son intended to make her his woman, to sleep with her. Narcisa and Celestino, and even their other sons, became alarmed, frightened. Don Flavio was capable of destroying their lives.

Celestino knew that his years of service to Don Flavio would evaporate. They meant nothing. He would become merely the *indio* in the eyes of the *Patrón*. His family would become the enemy, his cave dwelling the site of Isadora's violation, and they would all be ruined. As weeks had passed and Don Flavio did nothing, the lull only frightened him more.

On the other hand, Celestino and Narcisa could not forget that Jerónimo was a good son, and that Isadora was also a good woman; that they had known and cared for her since she was a child. Mother and father wrestled with their apprehensions, as well as with the gossip that had engulfed them. They knew they would soon have to decide between what the tribe determined and what their son had chosen to do.

When Isadora and Jerónimo made their way into their cave that night, they found Narcisa and Celestino waiting for them. As Jerónimo stoked the fire, the others squatted on the earthen floor. Flames leapt up from the hearth, casting shadows on their faces. Only the crackling of the burning twigs broke the silence. Isadora looked around, observing the faces of Jerónimo's mother and father.

Celestino's face was a mask carved in mahogany. His forehead was seamed by a deep crevice that started at his hairline and crept down to meet his long, beaked nose. Isadora looked closer and saw that his eyes were half-closed; slanted slits resting above high cheekbones.

Narcisa sat cross-legged, hands resting in her lap. Her still raven-colored hair was parted in the middle and slicked back into tight, thick braids; their blackness was dappled with specks of silver cast by the dancing flames. Isadora was struck by the thought that she had never looked closely at Narcisa's face. What she now saw was a beautiful picture: almond-shaped eyes cast beneath a high forehead, a short nose, and round, full lips. She wondered if this was what her own grandmother had looked like.

"The *huehues* have agreed to come together to consider what you have done."

Celestino's voice broke the silence, muting the snapping sounds of the fire. He did not utter his son's name but he looked only at him.

"What do you think, *tata?*" Jerónimo, too, looked only at his father. The younger man sat cross-legged, his back straight and stiff, betraying the tension that gripped his body.

Celestino wagged his head from side to side. His lips were pursed and he furrowed his forehead, deepening its crease; in the gloom of the cave it looked like the cut of a knife.

Narcisa spoke instead: "It's not only what your father thinks but what we all feel and talk about, *hijo,* that has to be considered.

"*Niña,* we've known you since you were a child." Narcisa continued, scanning those sitting around the fire. "You're good—we have nothing to say against you. But you are of another people, another blood, and we should not mix. It's against what our tribe holds most holy. This is why the Rarámuri have survived while the others perished."

"But Narcisa, Jerónimo's and my blood have already mixed." Isadora put her hands, fingers outstretched, palms down, on her belly. Then she added: "My grandmother was of your people."

Even Jerónimo's head jerked toward her. He had never heard Isadora say such a thing. His mother and father gawked in astonishment at Isadora. It was Narcisa who finally broke the trance.

"What do you mean? She could not have been of the Rarámuri. Of that we are certain."

"No, not of your people. She was of the tribes of Jalisco. She was a Cora Indian. My grandfather married her, and together they had my father and his sister, Doña Brígida."

Celestino, disconcerted, turned to Jerónimo, who remained speechless. Then all three turned to look at Isadora, unabashedly scrutinizing on her appearance. If there was a brown grandmother, why was Isadora's hair golden? How could her eyes be blue? Why was her body so long, so angular? Celestino sighed, unable to say anything further about Isadora's grandmother. He found it too unbelievable to give it more thought.

"The *huehues* are going to meet tomorrow night. They have asked me to be present."

"*Tata,* I'll be there too."

"I'll be there also."

Narcisa's words were emphatic, firm. It was not the tradition for a woman to sit in on the council of the elders, but she had resolved to be present, and Jerónimo and Celestino knew that she was beyond changing her mind. Isadora shut her eyes, knowing that even though she was at the center of the storm, her presence at the meeting would not be tolerated.

A pall of apprehension hung over the tribe the next day. The priest sensed something brewing, but no matter who he asked, where he looked, how much he listened, he met only silence. He was sure it had something to do with the Betancourt woman. He decided to remain in the rectory that night, in case he was needed.

The council was to take place when the moon began to rise, but the early evening stillness of the community was broken before the appointed time by the shouting of angry men and women. Everyone rushed to the plaza, attracted by the commotion. As the throng grew, the priest emerged from his house. The furor escalated until one man stood on the central fountain to gain height.

"Don Flavio has recovered from his illness. We're sure that he's going to take away our work!"

Celestino and Narcisa, Jerónimo and Isadora, stood motionless. What everyone had expected for weeks had finally occurred. Now the worst was sure to happen; without work, the probability of starvation loomed before the tribe. Isadora felt her knees weakening. Even though the dark was gathering, she detected fear, shock, and rancor in the eyes of the men and women. She even thought that their stares were aimed at her abdomen, at her child, and she jerked her hands in front of it.

"What are we going to do?"

"We'll starve without work!"

"It's happened before when we had to eat lizards and weeds!"

Fear flashed from one person to the other. They mumbled, shook their heads, jabbed their clenched fists at one another in the night air. Children began to cry, and soon even the adults' voices were tinged with tears.

"It's *their* fault!"

The crowd turned to glare at the clustered Santiago family, standing at its fringes. Jerónimo stepped in front of Isadora to shield her.

"People, take hold of your senses!"

The priest's voice rang out, and Narcisa seized the courage to run to the fountain at plaza's center.

"Have you been run off Hacienda Miraflores? Has it really happened?"

"No . . . Not yet . . ." A voice trailed into the night, and Narcisa turned, making sure that she faced most of the upturned faces.

"Then, why are we acting like frightened beasts? We won't starve!" Her voice was so shrill that it commanded silence while she moved from where she was and climbed to the highest step of the fountain. "We won't starve! But even if we are exiled from Hacienda Miraflores, other *patrones* will give us work. And if they don't, we'll march all the way to Creel, or to Los Mochis, or even to the capital. No! We won't starve!"

"You talk that way because you want us to forget what your son has done!"

Everyone turned to see who had uttered their unspoken thought.

"Who said that?"

No one stepped forward. Only stars now lit the dark sky, and in the east the moon had begun its nightly voyage to the other side of the horizon. A breeze whistled through the crevices and niches of the sierra. Narcisa held her ground on top of the fountain.

"We will find work, I tell you!"

A wave of grumbling and murmuring rose from the people as they swayed from side to the other. They exchanged glances, wagged heads, sighed. After a few minutes, some muttered that Narcisa was probably right. They would first wait to see if they did lose their work. After that, they would decide what to do. Besides, this was not the first time a *patrón* interfered in their lives, and it was not the first time that they had to hold their ground.

One by one, or in families, people gradually returned to their dwellings. A few hours later, word spread that the council of the *huehues* had been canceled until it was known what was to become of the workers. That night Jerónimo and Isadora hardly slept, but they huddled close to one another, whispering, caressing, soothing one another. He begged her to sleep, but when he saw that her eyes refused to close, he cradled her in his arms.

After that night, the men and women of the tribe returned to work at Hacienda Miraflores. Although some were suspicious, in time most of the Rarámuri fears were placated. The men tended the fields and herds of the *ranchería*, and the women tended to the kitchens, laundries, and bedrooms of the *Patrón*. A pall of apprehension nevertheless still lingered over the tribe until the day that Jerónimo found work elsewhere. When he returned to the sierra, word spread that he was again going to be able to contribute to the commune. With that, the last shreds of fear and the expectation of revenge melted away. Weeks became months until the day came when most of the Rarámuri were convinced that Don Flavio's fury must have been dissipated by his severe illness. Sometimes, they told each other, the spirits of evil invade a man, crippling him, making it impossible for him to behave as everyone would expect. Everyone thought this except the Santiago family.

During those days, Samuel became Isadora's growing worry. His silence, now complicated by his refusal to eat, made her fear for his health. She told him stories, remembering how he used to love her imaginings. Jerónimo took him on explorations, showing him plants and birds. Nothing, however, could dispel Samuel's sadness. He would say only that he wanted to return to his grandfather's hacienda. As he grew thinner, Isadora decided that it would be best if she sent him to her father. She cried when she made this decision. She did not want to let go, but her eyes told her that Samuel could not live among the Rarámuri.

It was Ursula who took the boy back to Hacienda Miraflores. When she returned, she brought back news of the hacienda: The *Patrón* looked very ill; he had aged, and now he looked like an old man. He had not shown signs that he even recognized Ursula. He did embrace Samuel, kiss and bless him, but that was all. There was no fury, no threats, no shouts.

Samuel's absence made Isadora feel lost, and sometimes she took comfort in speaking to Narcisa. The women often crouched near the hearth, talking, and listening to one another. On one of those occasions, Isadora let her uncertainties slip through.

"I think that what I'm doing is wrong."

Narcisa, head cocked to one side, looked at the younger woman. Her round face expressed a mix of emotions. *"Niña,* it is done. Perhaps these days were determined before you and my son were born. No one knows. What I do know is that there's a new child coming. That is what should point to the future."

"My father is capable of doing good things, Narcisa, but he's also able to do terrible ones. I've humiliated and offended him, I know, but I could not help it."

Narcisa was quiet for some minutes, she was deep in thought. She stoked the fire and rubbed her hands, palm against palm.

"Perhaps your father will one day see that some spirits are made for one another. Remember, Celestino and I were also angry at you. We feared what happens when blood is mixed, when two paths are forged into one. But you now see that we've changed. Give him time, *niña.* It could be that he'll take you back."

"At first I thought that way too. I even persuaded Jerónimo to bring me here instead of going to another land. But as time passes, I'm beginning to think that my father is incapable of understanding. I've turned my back on all that he taught me. I've given up the home he has provided, as well as the privilege. He's cast me out, Narcisa, and perhaps he'll never take me back."

"He's incapable of accepting that you've mixed your blood with ours?"

"I think so."

"As I said, the Rarámuri are that way also. There are some, especially among the *huehues,* who say that to mix our blood with that of others will bring evil."

After a while, Narcisa began to hum, as she sometimes did when she was meditating. At last she said, "Tell me about your grandmother. The brown one."

Isadora, sitting cross-legged and placidly running her hands over her swollen abdomen, nodded. She wrinkled her forehead after a moment of reflection.

"I don't know very much, only what *Tía* Brígida has told me. It's strange, because that grandmother is almost like a shadow for my aunt, and for me. What my aunt remembers is a woman, who was a native, who was always in the kitchen, and who never spoke. That's all."

"That means that your father must also have a memory of her. Has he ever spoken to you about her?"

"Never. Never."

"How did Doña Brígida know that the woman was her mother?"

"I think that it was her father, my grandfather, who acknowledged it. Or maybe it was the other servants who gossiped about it. I can't be sure, Narcisa."

"Then how can you be certain of it?"

"Because my heart tells me that it's the truth."

Isadora's pregnancy ran its course, and just before the birth of her child she and Narcisa followed the ways of the women of the Rarámuri. First, the village *nahual* was summoned to the Santiago cave, where many of the tribeswomen were gathered, squeezing in around the hearth. Isadora knelt in front of the holy man so that he could cure her of any evil that might have been wished on her or her child.

The *nahual* raised his sacred staffs over her head, pointing them first toward the east, where the sun and moon rise, then toward the west, where they set. He then thrust his staffs toward the north, where the gods are born, and to the south, where they dwell in the kingdom of the dead after they are finished with their mission. As he did this, he rasped his wands, chanting and murmuring sacred incantations. When this ceremony was completed, the holy man raised his outstretched arms, holding his hands palms down, over Isadora's head. Again he sang out a litany—this time to cut the invisible thread that bound the child in her womb to heaven.

After the curing ceremony, Narcisa and Isadora trekked to a place hidden in the sierra, where they found a tree with a branch strong enough to hold Isadora's weight and low enough for her to grasp. Then they gathered grass and soft bushes, and beneath the branch they built a nest large enough to cradle an infant. Now Isadora was ready to give birth.

A few days later, Narcisa came to the cave for Isadora because she had seen signs that her time had come. They set out for the place they had prepared for the birth of the child. They took gourds filled with water and bread packed into a *morral* bag to sustain them as they waited for the baby to make its way out of Isadora's womb.

They did not wait long. Isadora began her labor shortly after they arrived at the site. The sun was dipping in the west; nighttime was beginning. With Narcisa's help, Isadora removed her dress and underclothes. Naked, she clung to the branch with her legs straddling the grassy cradle. Pain shot through her body, covering her with sweat. Her breath came in spurts, and saliva dribbled from her open mouth in silvery strands. As Isadora's strength began to diminish, Narcisa stood behind her and put her arms around her, bracing her, holding her beneath her breasts.

Through all of this, both women were silent, until a blinding flash of pain convulsed Isadora's body, and blackness shrouded her eyes for a few seconds. Then she heard the wail of the babe, and as she looked down she was able to see the child sliding from between her thighs. Narcisa had circled around and was on her haunches, arms stretched out, ready to take the child. When it was in her hands, she looked up at Isadora.

"It's a girl child."

Narcisa's voice was filled with music. Isadora slouched down to her knees, then on to one side, balancing herself on an elbow. She lifted her free hand and ran it over the sleek black hair of the child who had just emerged from her body. She was oblivious of her own body, and her pain was forgotten in the wonderment of seeing that the girl's skin was coppery brown and glistened like a chestnut in the light of the rising sun. Isadora's heart filled with joy at the mystery that such a child should have come from her body.

After Narcisa wiped the child of its covering of mucus, she cut and bound the umbilical cord. Then she put the girl in her mother's arms. Isadora was still naked, and the sensation of the child's skin against her own made her pulse race. She closed her eyes and felt that her heart would burst of the joy that was flooding it. Although elated, Narcisa had not forgotten her duties. She wrapped the umbilical cord in a cloth; there was yet another ceremony to perform once back at the cave.

Isadora rested, reclining with the child still on her breast. In a few hours she and Narcisa would begin their return to the village. For a moment she doubted that she would have the strength, but she reminded herself that this was the way of all the women of the tribe.

She slept. In her dreams she was choosing the child's name. Jerónimo and she had agreed that if the baby were to be a boy, he would name him; if a girl, the child would bear a name of Isadora's choosing. In her dreams, names danced in front of her. *Rosa, Violeta, Lidia, Iris.* Flowers took shape in Isadora's reverie followed by their names. But after she awoke, she remembered. The girl would be named after the bird that sings sweetly and flies to unknown distances.

"Her name will be Alondra."

Four days later, as is the custom of the Rarámuri, the fiesta in celebration of the birth of a girl child took place in the village center. It was also vital, however, to have the priest baptize the child in the Catholic manner.

On the day of the baptism, everyone came together before sunset. The men wore ornamental sarapes that they wrapped around their body, concealing the loincloths they would later reveal. The women wore long cotton dresses, embroidered with flowers, butterflies, and other intricate designs. Jerónimo, with the child in his arms, made his way through the crowd toward the facade of the church to the baptismal font. He was followed by Isadora, Narcisa, Celestino, Jerónimo's brothers, and their wives and children, as well as Ursula. The priest, vested in an alb and stole, waited for them with a prayer book in his hands.

"*In nomine Patris, et Filii, et Spiritus Sancti, Amen.*"

He traced a broad cross in the air with his right hand. Everyone followed him, making the sign of the cross on forehead, breast, and both shoulders. Then they kissed their fingers held in a cross. The men had removed their sombreros, and the women had covered their heads with shawls. The quiet of the early evening was broken only by the breeze that swept down from the highest levels of the *barranca*.

"Who are the *padrinos?*"

"Here we are, *Padre.*"

Celestino and Narcisa stepped forward when the priest asked for the godparents. His head was bowed, but she looked into the priest's eyes.

"What will the child's name be?"

"Alondra, *Padre.*"

It was Isadora who spoke, and she too looked into the priest's eyes. He returned her gaze, letting her know that he was aware of her sins of infidelity to her marriage vows, of being El Rarámuri's concubine, of betrayal of the education given her by nuns and, worst of all, of disrespect for her father. She did not look away; she steadily returned his gaze, and he understood her meaning.

"It can not be just Alondra. The baptismal rite demands the name of a saint."

"María Alondra."

"So be it."

The priest's voice was sharp, brittle, but he understood that he could not change all the ways of the people to whom he was supposed to minister. They would call the child what they wished.

He motioned to Narcisa, who now held Alondra, to bring the child to the font, where he poured holy water over her head. When the chill of the water saturated the baby's hair, she let out a squeal that made those that heard it smile. The priest went on with the ritual and sacramental prayers, rejecting Satan and all his works. He emphasized the meaning of the words by pausing and nodding his head. He then made the sign of the cross over the child's head. The ceremony was over. He turned and disappeared into the church.

As soon as he was out of sight, the fiesta began. The men took off the sarapes and stepped forward, showing their breechcloths. From among them the *nahual,* followed by the *huehues,* came forward; a large circle formed around them. The holy man held the sacred rods over the baby's head, again held by her father, chanting and dancing as the tribe joined in the rhythm.

From the crowd the Santiago men, women and children stepped forward, then knelt in front of the *nahual,* waiting for his blessing. He made the sign of the cross several times with incense as he approached Isadora, who was also kneeling. With water which he had taken in his mouth, he blew a cross on her head, thus ensuring her fertility in the future.

Throughout these rites, the Rarámuri swayed and stomped. The flapping sound of bare feet against the cobblestones added to the tempo of the dance. Jerónimo, the only one not kneeling, also moved in rhythm, turning slowly, facing the cardinal points of the universe, lifting Alondra high over his head as he faced each direction.

The people hummed as the *nahual* lit a fire in the center of the circle, plucked a twig from the flames, and burned a bit of the child's hair. One of the *huehues* handed him four lighted pitch-pine sticks; with these he traced more signs of the cross into the mountain air.

After this, everyone feasted on goat meat, *tesguino* beer, and peyote consecrated by the *nahual.* La Chirimía, a group of musicians who pounded on drums, rattled seed gourds, puffed upon flutes, and scraped at tinny violins, provided a rhythm that engulfed the people's talk and laughter. The people of the tribe sat on the ground for hours, eating, drinking, and many times getting to their feet to perform a quick, fiery dance.

As evening turned into night, everyone was transformed by the beer and peyote, until they were ready to dance the *dutuburi*: The men formed a circle, and began to sway to the beat of drums, flutes and rattling gourds. Then the women formed an outer circle, gyrating in the opposite direction. In the center, Jerónimo, with Alondra in his arms, danced joyfully in celebration of this new child who had been born into the Rarámuri. The rest of the Santiago men then joined him, honoring their brother. Isadora, her eyes fixed on Jerónimo, her head giddy with *tesguino* beer, danced and laughed. She had never been so happy. Later on in the cave, as she fell asleep, Isadora was at last able to put aside the fears with which she wrestled. It was better to believe in what happened during the moonlit night.

Chapter 13

Three weeks later, Isadora sat waiting for Jerónimo in a hollow overlooking the path from the plain up to the village center. The sun was setting, and she enjoyed the soft breeze at her back, ruffling her hair forward. She gazed at the sky, taking in the shades of lavender that blended with orange and pink hues. Above her the sky was still a deep blue dotted by white clouds that scurried toward the horizon, as if being sucked in by the setting sun. She craned her neck in the opposite direction: The moon was new, a transparent crescent.

She looked down to the sweep of the plain below. She knew where her father's land began and ended; much of what she was looking at belonged to Hacienda Miraflores. The image of herself, still a girl, riding by her father's side, flashed through her mind. The memory shook her heart, as if a slight tremor had moved the earth beneath her. She sighed, scanning the distance, taking pleasure from the vastness and beauty of the land. To the north, in the convent school where she had spent her adolescence, other girls were learning and listening, just as she had done. To the west, the ocean rolled with its endless tides and ebbs.

Suddenly, Eloy flashed before her eyes, and Isadora jerked back, startled by the forgotten and unexpected memory. She thought it strange that she should think of him; she hadn't in years. She chuckled, wondering what Narcisa would say to this. Was his spirit trying to reach her? Maybe he was dead. She shook her head, trying to clear it of the foolish thoughts going on inside. Then Eloy's face moved aside, making way for that of Samuel, reminding her of the void left in her heart by his absence. Would he understand when he grew to be a man? She forced herself to think of something else.

She put her thoughts aside when her attention was caught by a dark speck on the flat land below that moved in her direction. She squinted, trying to focus her eyes on the object approaching her. She sat up when it became clear that it was a Rarámuri runner. He was alone, and not playing at racing; he was pressing himself to his limits of speed. She got to her feet, sensing that the boy carried important news, something out of the ordinary. In minutes, she saw that he had reached the beginning of the ascent and that soon he would be winding past her.

As the runner rushed up the path, his feet pounded the earth, lifting small billows of dust that trailed behind him. Isadora jumped out onto the pathway, knowing that soon the runner would be where she stood; she wanted to know the reason for his haste. When the boy was close enough to see her, however, he stopped so abruptly that he nearly lost his balance. He wheeled to the side and took another way, deliberately changing his direction.

The runner's evasion frightened her, and something compelled her to swing around to look down to the plain. She cupped her hands over her eyes and made out a group of men carting something heavy that made them struggle with its weight. It was now growing dark, but she could still make out the figures. One, two, three, four, five men. As they came closer to her, she saw that it was a bundle they carried, something with the shape of an animal. But the Rarámuri did not wrap what they had hunted.

She trotted toward the men, gaining speed despite the flapping of her long dress and its tangling between her legs. She was breathing hard, open-mouthed, taking large gulps of air as she made her way down the hill toward the approaching group. Her feet were bare, and though callused, they began to hurt her. Bushes scraped against her legs and arms, slashing, making them bleed, but Isadora was oblivious. The drumming in her head had now become thunderous. When she finally reached the men, she stopped, her chest heaving and her face encrusted with dust.

Two of the men facing her were Jerónimo's brothers. She caught the expression in their eyes. She looked to the others and when they turned their faces, avoiding her look, Isadora knew the truth. She did not have to look at the blood-stained sarape to know whose body was within it.

It was almost dark, and only the upper reaches of the sierra were still showing the last of daylight. No one said anything. They stood as if frozen, as if their bodies were paralyzed. Isadora felt that the air in her lungs had drained, and that her insides were collapsing. The roar in her head grew louder. She stared at the form outlined on the blanket; it was saturated with blood and mud, and she feared that Jerónimo had been mutilated, hacked, dismembered.

"Undo it!"

When she mouthed the order, her voice was unrecognizable. Those of the men who knew her were startled by its harshness and its gravelly tone. It was almost the voice of a man.

"*Niña,* no . . ."

"Undo it!"

The men looked at one another, unsure of what to do, but they understood that Isadora would not move until they obeyed her. They were still reeling from what they had seen, but they did as she commanded. One of them stepped forward and peeled away the cloth, uncovering the mangled remains. Isadora's body reeled backward, as if shoved by an invisible force, but she regained her balance in an instant. She stared at what had been the man whom she had loved since childhood, the man who had given her happiness beyond her imagination.

"Where is his head?"

No one answered. They heard each other breathing through nostrils clogged with dust and sweat. Isadora looked at them, then knelt by the body to make certain that she was not mistaken. She got to her feet again.

"Where is it?"

"It was gone when we found him. The assassins took it with them."

"Assassins? There were more than one?"

"Yes. One man could not have done this. It was two or more of them."

Isadora rolled her eyes from side to side, realizing that only her father could have ordered Jerónimo's murder in that manner. He had been attacked and torn apart by jackals. And it had been she who had demanded that they stay with the tribe. If she and Jerónimo had escaped to another place this would not have happened. She could not scream or cry out. Her throat had closed. She could not even get down on the ground. Her bones had locked; her body was stiff, unbending. At last, silence, she turned in the direction of the sierra to lead the cortege and what was left of her lover up the slope.

By the time Isadora and the others arrived at the village center, Celestino and Narcisa were waiting. They already knew that their son was dead. Their faces were masks: eyes shut to slits, mouths drooping like upside-down crescents. They stood erect, wordless. There was a throng of people behind them. The silence was complete; the only sound was that of the wind snaking through the crevices and cracks of the *barranca*.

Jerónimo's brothers laid down his remains on the cobblestones, but no one moved until the priest and the *nahual* approached, shoulder to shoulder. The face of the priest betrayed his shock. The face of the holy man was expressionless. Both ministers went to the body, and each began to perform the ritual of his belief.

"*Pater noster . . .*"

"*Tata Hakuli . . .*"

The incantations of the holy men spiralled toward heaven, the priest making the sign of the cross with his right hand, time after time, the *nahual* thrusting his sacred rods toward the cardinal points of the universe. The mourners surrounding them spontaneously followed the chanting of the *nahual,* humming mixing with their muffled wailing. Isadora remained silent. Her throat had constricted so severely that it had blocked saliva from wetting her mouth, and tears from flowing through her eyes. She stared at the two ministers as if they were phantoms, and she felt suddenly filled with the desire to be close to Jerónimo. She moved forward and knelt next to the bundle, despite the Rarámuri custom requiring a widow to keep her distance.

On her knees, Isadora rocked back and forth, swaying with the mournful tones of the grievers. She put her hands on the bloodied mound, trying to pray, but all the invocations she had learned to recite during her lifetime had dried up. Instead, all she could feel was scorching hatred for her father. She forced herself to look around at Jerónimo's family to see if they hated her for causing this calamity. They continued to stand, eyes closed, as if in a trance.

Hours passed while the grievers wailed and lamented, but none collapsed or even knelt. Instead, they remained on their feet, their faces upturned toward a sky now black, lit only by a canopy of stars and a young moon that inched its way toward its cradle.

The priest moved over to Celestino, then to Narcisa. He whispered and patted them on the shoulder, all the while nodding and shaking his head. Isadora knew what he was counseling: Their sons must not be allowed to attempt to take revenge; Don Flavio would be waiting for them. The Santiagos would end up losing all three sons. Through this, Narcisa and Celestino stood unmoving, not flinching even a facial muscle.

When the moon was nearly above them, the men who had discovered Jerónimo again picked up his remains. Hoisting their burden onto their shoulders, they began the trek leading higher up the sierra, to where a bier had by then been constructed for the cremation of the body. Isadora, Narcisa, Celestino and Jerónimo's brothers followed. After them came Ursula with Alondra. Next came the children of the Santiago family, then the priest and the *nahual,* and finally the entire tribe.

They trekked upward in darkness, lighted only by pine pitch torches held by some of the men. It was a slow climb, dangerous because of the sheer cliffs on which the mourners crept. The throng, led by Jerónimo's remains, scaled the heights of the sierra to the rhythm of incantations uttered by the priest and the *nahual,* and to the dull shuffling of bare feet on the rocky surface of the mountain.

Isadora walked stiffly. Love collided with hatred; the memory of Jerónimo crashed into the image of Don Flavio. The face of her lover became overshadowed by the gigantic silhouette of her father. So lost in thought was Isadora that she did not realize when the cortege arrived at its destination and the body was laid on the pyre. Before her unseeing eyes, pitch was smeared at the base of the bier, and flame was thrust into it. Isadora's mind returned only when the pyramid was engulfed by fire and the bundle that had been Jerónimo exploded in a ball of blue-red flames. Then she was keenly aware of what was happening. She heard the crackling of logs and bone. She smelled the stench of pitch and burning flesh.

The tribe returned to the village center to begin the rituals that would usher Jerónimo's spirit into the kingdom of the dead. Isadora knew the ceremonies: three days of food, drink, peyote, and uninterrupted talk about the one who had just begun the trip to the underbelly of the world, where he would dwell with the gods. There would be dancing as well as weeping. When the days of mourning came to an end, the Rarámuri would be satisfied that they had done all they could to accompany Jerónimo on his trip to join the others who had gone before him. When the men and women of the tribe returned to their caves after the three-day ritual, they knew that Jerónimo would be with them each night, when it was the day of the moon.

During those three days, Isadora did as she was expected to do as a widow, and she remained in seclusion without food or water. She accepted this obligation because what she desired was to be alone. Alondra was cared for; she slept with Ursula. During those days of abstinence and nights of insomnia, Isadora's mind drifted in a mist of her life's memories, especially of those times she had spent with Jerónimo. She saw him as a boy, running, his hair a blur of black feathers waving behind his head. Then he appeared to her on a horse; he was now an adolescent, with the shadow of a sparse mustache over his smiling lips. Then she saw him on the day of her birthday race, when looking at him had aroused her. After that she relived their love, their year together, and Alondra. These memories took a full circle and returned to the present, to the sight of his mutilated body.

Isadora was bewildered by the mystery of Jerónimo's life with her. He had been with her until his last morning. They had eaten, laughed, spoken, embraced, lain together. She had felt, seen, and heard him. She shuddered, thinking that in a matter of seconds his existence had been snuffed out. Where did he go? Where was he? Was he watching her, sitting next to her in the gloom? She wanted to believe that he would return to her during her nighttime dreams, when the moon appeared, but her mind rejected such a possibility. The loss of Jerónimo loomed in front of Isadora, filling the cave, leaving her anguished and enraged because he and she had been robbed, cheated of life. It was at this point that her thoughts returned to her father.

Isadora began to plan what she would do at the end of the mourning period. She became obsessed with the scheme, perfecting it as she repeated it over and again, constructing and reconstructing every step, every move, every detail. Her intentions were confirmed when Ursula informed her that Jerónimo's brothers had been tied to trees so that they would not attempt to kill Don Flavio, and that Celestino had succumbed to a strange spirit that kept him crouching, huddled against a wall in their cave, paralyzed and mute.

When the mourning days were over, the tribe returned to its ways and Isadora prepared to leave. Ursula was with her, following as Isadora moved about in the cave.

"Where are you going, *niña?*"

"You know where. Come here."

Isadora took Ursula by the arm, bringing her to sit next to her. When they sat side by side, Isadora whispered in a husky voice. "If I don't return, swear to me that you will care for Alondra and Samuel. That you will do so until you die."

"If Jerónimo's brothers have been forbidden to do it, why should you? You'll bring a curse on your head and that of your children."

"I'm already cursed."

"No! You must live. That is your obligation. It is your father who is cursed by the blood on his hands. Do you want the same for yourself?"

Ursula's words nearly unnerved Isadora, who moments earlier was committed to revenge. But the thought of a lifetime without Jerónimo flooded her, making her return to her resolve.

"Are you going to swear or not?"

"I swear. But . . ."

Isadora stood up and helped Ursula to her feet. It was early morning, and the fire in the hearth had died out, but light was trailing in from the entrance to the cave. Isadora looked around, remembering, wondering if she would ever return to the place where she had loved and known happiness.

"I'll return soon, *vieja*. Remember, you've taken an oath to care for my children."

Isadora took nothing with her except a gourd of water. She wore the long dress of the tribeswomen, a shawl, and *huaraches*. As Isadora made her way out, Ursula took her in her arms. It was an embrace that lasted only a few seconds.

Once on the pathway down toward the plain, Isadora walked briskly, then trotted, accelerating her speed until she was running. She was sure-footed. She had not eaten or slept; a spirit had possessed her body, energizing it. She was a Rarámuri distance runner now; her feet were those of the deer. Isadora ran knowing that her strength would hold and that she would reach her destination by sundown.

She was not surprised that, when she walked by the stables of her father's hacienda, no one stopped her. No one ran to tell Don Flavio of what they had seen; they simply went back to what they were doing. She was not suspicious when no one said anything as she walked into the house, going through its rooms and corridors, past Brígida's locked door, heading for her father's den. Isadora felt calm, knowing that Samuel would be in the kitchen at that time, away from what was about to happen. She knew also that all the workers were waiting for her to appear sooner or later.

She opened the familiar door, taking a few seconds to run her fingers over its ornate carvings. Once inside the huge room, she saw that it was empty. She looked up at the high, dark ceiling, then she turned her head towards the desk where she had last confronted him. She closed the door behind her. She did not need light. She went to the desk, opened a drawer, withdrew the key and went to the cabinet. It was easy to open its paneled doors. She removed the Remington revolver, checked that it was loaded, and waited, standing in a darkened corner with the weapon clutched in both hands.

The clock on the mantelpiece marked the minutes before Don Flavio entered the room to take his evening chocolate. He was freshly bathed, shaved, and wearing a Stetson hat, as was his custom. He sat at the desk, lit the green-shaded lamp and waited, staring at the darkened window. He seemed lost in thought.

"Papá."

Don Flavio's body recoiled at the sound of Isadora's voice. He swiveled the chair he was sitting in with such force that it nearly capsized. He faced the corner from where he had heard his daughter's voice, but he saw only darkness.

"Papá."

Isadora repeated the word; it was dry, raspy, cutting, like the edge of a rusty knife. When she raised the revolver, holding it stiffly in both hands, Don Flavio finally made her out. His face was stamped with horror and relief. He swung his arms up to shield his face. The first blast sounded out. A second shot followed. The reverberations bounced off the wood-paneled walls, slamming into the stuccoed ceiling. Then another shot rang out, filling the room with the stench of burnt gunpowder.

Isadora flung the revolver at her father's body, which was now sprawled out, face down on the floor. As she turned to leave, she saw a pool of blood seeping from him onto the polished hardwood. She dashed out through the corridor, past the elongated windows now blackened by the night, past the rooms of her childhood, through sitting rooms and chambers, out of Casa Miraflores, to head up to the *barranca*. But as she darted through the last archway, arms grasped her, entangling her, lifting her, taking away control of her legs and arms.

"*¡Dios Santo!*"

"She's killed her father!"

"Get the doctor!"

"Run! Hot water! Bandages! Quickly!"

"Don Flavio is dying!"

The cell was dark. It was lit only by moonlight that spilled in through the wire-netted window in a square. As she sat on the edge of the cot, Isadora felt heat welling up into her throat, flooding her mouth. She knew that what she was tasting were tears of hatred. They had squeezed into her mouth because her eyes had refused to shed them. She tried to calculate how much time had passed since her father had murdered Jerónimo. Was it days? Weeks? It could have been months, even years.

The iron door swung open, flooding the cell with yellowish light from the corridor lamps. Two white jackets loomed in front of Isadora.

"Not in bed yet?"

"Get into bed. Why do you give us so much trouble?"

"What day is it?"

"What?"

"Please tell me what month and year it is."

"Well! Well! Well! And what else would the great lady want? A personal servant, maybe?"

The door slammed, leaving her in the dark, but she was able to hear mocking laughter and words that drifted back to her. "Tried to escape three times, and she expects special treatment!"

Once she had gotten as far north as Nuevo León before being caught. But now she did not know even the day or month or year. The only thing that she knew was that her father had lived; he had survived three shots. At first he had kept her a prisoner in her bedroom at Miraflores, with a guard to prevent anyone—especially Brígida—from communicating with her. What no one ever imagined then was that Isadora was to be kept in an asylum for the insane. Her father's intention, from the beginning, was to leave her there for the rest of her life.

Úrsula Santiago

Chapter 14

Los Angeles, 1965

¡Buenos días! I'm happy to see you. Please, come in. Sit here by me. I hope that you don't mind sitting in the kitchen. It's where I'm comfortable, and no one will disturb us here. Let me serve you a *cafecito*. Black with a little sugar is best. I know you'll enjoy it. I know you have questions. A little coffee makes it all go down better. You saw for yourself; Alondra and I were up most of the night with Don Flavio. He's dying, but he's doing it little by little. Doctor Canseco is with him now.

And look at this rain! Everyone says it never rains in Los Angeles, but it's been raining for days. It's a soft rain, slow and damp, and it makes my fingers ache. It's not like the summer storms that come to the *barranca,* when the rain falls in torrents, filling the canyons and rivers. Up there, one can see fat, gray clouds swelling up, and you know that it's about to rain. Then comes the sudden storm, with thunder and lightning that flashes across black skies. Tata Dios speaks, and the Rarámuri listen. Afterward, the sky becomes blue, and the sierra glistens. But that's the way it is where I was born; here it is different.

Please don't get impatient; we'll get to your questions in a moment. You know that I am Ursula Santiago—that is why you want to speak to me. You're right, these eyes have seen more than anyone would suspect. Tata Dios has placed me in certain places where I've seen and heard what others have missed.

Now, you'll have to help me. You say that too much has been left out. I agree, but I can assure you that it's no one's fault. It was the way of the family. They seemed to understand each other without saying words. Believe me, many times I was left to wonder what was happening between father, daughter, and aunt.

Doña Brígida was the worst one. She was as silent as an uninhabited cave. I ought to know, because I first met her on the day after she arrived at Casa Miraflores, when I delivered a letter from her brother. And after that it was my duty to make her bed, clean her room, and help her with her bath and other needs.

In all those years, she hardly spoke, but I learned about her by looking at her photographs. Like everybody else, I thought she was crazy. But after a while, when I started concentrating on the pictures that she had placed all around her, I realized that if you looked at them in a certain way, you would understand that they were telling a story—her story. One of those photographs has stayed in my memory. In it was a man dressed in a black suit. At his side were two children, a girl and a boy. The man was a stranger to me, but the children were Doña Brígida and Don Flavio. The most interesting part of that faded picture was that behind them, wearing an apron, just like the one I have on, was a young woman and, like me, she was an *india*. Anyone could tell from her face, hair and color, even though the photograph had yellowed.

As I was . . . *Sí,* I think you have reason to say that. For example, the story begins in Mexico, but here we sit in Los Angeles. Why did they abandon Hacienda Miraflores? Why did Don Flavio drag the children along with him? You were led to believe that he hated Alondra, and yet, here she is, as real as you and I.

¡Ay! ¡Ay! ¡Ay! You ask many questions, and you say you have even more! *¡Dios Santo!* Very well. There is only one thing I cannot tell you: what happened to *Niña* Isadora. Let's go step by step with what I do know. If you get hungry, tell me; I'll make you some *quesadillas.* Bitterness slides down better with a bit of tortilla and *chile.*

When *Niña* put Alondra in my charge and descended to the *llano*, I knew what for. I was afraid for her, because Don Flavio has always been a *zorro* . . . yes, yes . . . a fox. It's almost impossible to fool him. We knew that his not doing anything after his daughter ran away was a trap. So after a few hours I decided to follow . . . No, I left Alondra with Narcisa.

Everything was in turmoil at Casa Miraflores. There was shouting, and people ran around getting hot water and bandages and medicines. I got there in time to see a *vaquero* mount his horse and gallop away as if a demon were pulling at his hair. He was on his way to get the doctor. Everyone was repeating the story: *Niña* Isadora had shot her father, but he was still alive. Like the wolf wounded by the hunter, he lived to strike back.

I made my way to the kitchen and stayed there, listening, looking. No one noticed me because they were all scared; all they could do was gossip about the *Patrón:* Would he live? What would happen to his daughter? What would happen to *them?* I decided to stay, and no one even asked why I was there. So I cooked and washed dishes and slept in the stables until I knew what was happening. After dark, I roamed the corridors, trying to find out about *Niña* Isadora.

I discovered that she was in her old bedroom and that she was a prisoner. As soon as the servants had lifted Don Flavio from the pool of blood that was drowning him, he spoke: *Put her in her room. A guard at the door. No food, only water, until I say so.* Those were his words. I know because that's all anyone could talk about for days. *¡Ay!* You can imagine. I wanted to help her, reach her, soothe her, but it was impossible. In the meantime, several doctors came to Don Flavio's bed, and they were able to save him. *El diablo guarda a los suyos.* What? Oh, excuse me. The devil takes care of his own.

As he recuperated, Don Flavio made *Niña* more of a prisoner. He had boards nailed over the windows of her room. No women were allowed to go near; only men guarded her and went in and out with food and water. Those of us in the kitchen saw that *Niña* hardly ate. He kept her that way until he got back on his feet. I don't remember how long that was, maybe weeks, maybe months.

One morning, before the sun was up, I walked into the kitchen to find everyone babbling. *Niña* Isadora had been *taken away.* Her room was empty, its door wide open, all the furniture taken out.

The boards had been pulled down from the windows. Not even curtains. I ran to see for myself. It must have happened during the night. I never saw *Niña* Isadora again. That terrible thing happened in December, when we should have been celebrating her twenty-seventh birthday.

Once, putting my fear to the side, I even asked the driver of Don Flavio's car where he had taken her, but he only stared at me. But I knew that he had been part of something terrible, because I saw him and the doctor whispering, wagging their heads, pointing fingers at each other.

Then one night I waited until it was completely dark, when only the light of the moon cut though the shadows. I crept into the main hall of Casa Miraflores and up the staircase. I didn't know what I was looking for, or what I expected to find. A force inside of me pressed me to move. I began to hear voices. The closer I got to Doña Brígida's room, the louder they became. I was afraid, but I *made* myself go to the door, and I pressed my ear to it.

The voices became clearer. They belonged to Don Flavio and Doña Brígida; they were shouting and screaming at one another. Oh! You cannot know the cruel things they said to one another. They hurled dirty words, such that the Devil himself would not use. There were accusations that made me ashamed and afraid for them. On and on, brother and sister hurled insults at one another, offenses that I will never forget. My knees shook and my body shuddered. I wanted to run away, but something, I don't know what, kept my ear pasted to that door. I think I wanted to know *why* they were pouring so much poison on each other.

Then it came out. Doña Brígida accused her brother of having *Niña* Isadora murdered, just as he had done to Jerónimo. She screamed that she would not be silent, that she would go to the magistrates. This finally silenced Don Flavio. After that neither one said anything. All I could hear before I crept away was the ticking of the clock in the corner of her room.

After that night, Don Flavio roamed the hacienda as if demons pulled him by the hair. He was a soul escaped from Hell, a man possessed. He would not eat or sit still. He walked in and out of rooms; through the stables and work sheds. He mounted and dismounted his horse without reason. He gave orders and then contradicted or canceled them. He began to sell things: first equipment, then cattle and horses by the herd, after that parcels of the hacienda itself. He was a madman. His eyes were wild, and few of us had the courage to get near him.

Everyone gossiped about him. The mestizos said that *Satanás* was chastising him for whatever he had done to his daughter. The *indios* said that the gods of evil had been unleashed from the kingdom of the night for his having El Rarámuri murdered. Babble and *chisme* swirled over Hacienda Miraflores, expanding until it became a cyclone. People began to pack their *mochilas* and abandon the place that had once been a growing, fruitful garden. When the *huracán* was over, there was nothing left of the old hacienda. And that is when Don Flavio, dragging Doña Brígida and Samuel, began his sad way to this city.

You don't know how much it hurts me to recall those days. I loved *Niña* Isadora just as if she had been my own child. Could it really be, I asked myself, that a father could murder his own child?

I wept and did penance by crawling on my knees, by not eating food, or drinking water, hoping that she would return. I prayed novenas of rosaries to the Virgin of Guadalupe. I burnt *copal* and peyote to Tata Hakuli, but nothing brought her back. And I was not the only one. *Niña* Isadora was loved by many people among the mestizos as well as the Rarámuri. But something happened that gave me hope since those evil days. Listen to me, come closer, so that I can whisper this in your ear. *Niña* Isadora is alive! No, I don't know where she is, but my *heart* tells me that she lives, even after all these years.

It took many of us to run the kitchen of Casa Miraflores while people still lived there. How else could the *vaqueros*, croppers, milkers, harvesters, loggers, household servants, maids, and all the rest be fed? The place was run by teams of cooks, dishwashers, bakers and others, who were constantly providing food for the workers from sunrise to sunset. Well, among the women in the kitchen there was a *torteadora*. Ah, a *torteadora* is the woman who makes tortillas, and believe me, it's probably the most difficult job of all because it never ends. No sooner does the tortilla come off the hot *comal* before it's gobbled up.

This *torteadora* was not a Rarámuri, but a woman from the south, from where the pyramids loom in the distance, and where, they say, the gods dwell. She was a Mexica and she always spoke of the days before the bearded captains came to the shores of her city; it was once built on a lake. She was a good woman. She had big, big hands, just like a pair of griddles, and they were almost as black. Everyone said that her hands were huge because of kneading and patting masa over so many years.

Anyway, that *india* saw that I grieved for *Niña* Isadora, that I wept so much that my eyes had nearly shut, that my face was always swollen. I was so changed that people hardly recognized me. One day she took my face in her big hands and held it close to her face. I want you to hear what she said to me, because her words changed everything for me:

Among my people, we believe in Xipe Totec, the goddess of healing and life. This is her story: One day an evil spirit of destruction skinned her alive. But Xipe Totec did not die. She put on her skin and was restored to life.

After that the *torteadora* looked into my eyes, nodded, and walked away. I understood! I saw that *Niña* Isadora was like that goddess. When Don Flavio killed Jerónimo, when he imprisoned her, when he sent her away from her children and us, it was as if her skin had been peeled off of her. She was supposed to die. But I believe that *Niña* has taken her skin, put it back on and lived. Yes! Of this I am sure, and I know that one day these eyes will see her again. Tata Dios will make sure of it.

Let me serve you another *cafecito*. Sugar? Well, after those days, Don Flavio again shut himself into his room, but after a while, he came out. (This was when many people were leaving.) *¡Ay! ¡Santa Capulina!* He used to be handsome, but no more. Most of his hair had fallen out, and because he lost many *kilos,* skin hung on him like scales. He was wrapped in it from his head to his feet and he moved as if he had been one of those lizards that crawl the deserts.

Someone came looking for me, saying that the *Patrón* wanted to see me. *¡Ay! ¡Ay!* And I thought he had not noticed me! I was afraid, but I went to his room where he sat behind a desk. I can recite his words exactly as he uttered them, because they are burned into my heart.

Ursula, you see that everyone is abandoning Miraflores. Why not you?

Patrón, I . . . I don't know why, I said.

I'm leaving as well. My sister and grandson will come with me. And . . .

¿Sí?

I'm taking the mestiza with me.

Who?

The one who proves to the world that my daughter sinned with El Rarámuri. Go to the tribe and tell them that my people are coming for the girl. If anyone interferes, there will be more suffering.

Let me come to care for her.

No. You will be a burden.

Patrón, I'll work for my keep as well as the child's.

If you come, you must never tell her the truth. You will say that she is your granddaughter. Do you understand? If you disobey me, you'll never see her again.

Although I did not want to be near him, I accepted. I knew he meant to kill Alondra, or to give her away, if there was no one to protect her. I had promised *Niña* Isadora that I would care for the child no matter what happened. I kept my promise and I came to this place with Don Flavio and Doña Brígida.

And now you want me to explain what made him do all these things? Well, I don't know the answer. Some people were whispering that *el Patrón* was being investigated for the disappearance of his daughter. That might have been true, because although he was a powerful man, it was one thing to murder a nameless Indian, but another to tamper with someone like *Niña* Isadora. She was known by people in large cities. She had friends, other young women, who were anxious to know what had happened to her. I think that part of this is what forced him to sell everything he had and to abandon Casa Miraflores.

It's unreasonable, I know, but I have no other explanation. I tell you he was like a javelina, or a caged wolf. What reasons do such beasts have when they bite and claw and devour? Why did Don Flavio drag his sister along with him? He hated her and she hated him, we all knew it. I don't know what evil spirit prompted him to bring her with him—nor why she came, except to cling to him like a spine of the *maguey* cactus, piercing him.

It is easy to explain why he brought Samuel. But what about Alondra? He said he did it because she proved that her mother had sinned, but I did not believe that reason. I still don't. And why did he allow me to come? Such craziness! My head swam, and I could not understand what was happening. All I could do was listen to what my heart was telling me. If I did not follow him, he would murder the child. It would have been easy, like pouring water on a weak flame. So it was I who went up to the *barranca* to fetch Alondra. Narcisa did not resist. Her heart and spirit were broken because of the murder of her son and the bewitching of her husband.

And so we began the journey to this city. We came in a large automobile, bringing only what we wore and other necessities. I knew that Don Flavio had money packed into most of suitcases he allowed in the car, as well as in belts that he wore under his shirt. I held Alondra all the way as we crossed a desert, then over a mountain that almost reached to the sky, and finally down to this flat city where he got this house where you and I now sit.

Well, I've been talking for a long time. I'm sure you're tired and . . . *¡Virgen del Cobre!* What more could you want to know? About Jerónimo's family? Narcisa? Celestino? Ah! Very well, but I'm hungry. Talking so much has emptied out my stomach. I'll make a few *quesadillas*. No, please, you don't have to help. They're easy to make: a tortilla, a little cheese, a few drops of *chile,* then put it on the hot *comal,* turn it over a few times and it's ready. More than one pair of hands will only ruin what is so easy to make.

You would think that our people should be used to these things by now, but we are not. The *patrones* think that we're oxen, that we don't feel the humiliations, nor the pain, but we do. They think that because generations of us have endured the burden placed on our backs, we don't feel rage or the desire to take vengeance when we are wronged, but they're deluding themselves.

In our family, it was Narcisa who at first clamored for revenge after Jerónimo's murder. As soon as the funeral ritual was over, she gathered anyone who would listen, pressing, reminding, assuring that if we didn't do something, the lives of the Rarámuri would be like straw under a burro's hooves. Her sons, Jacobo and Justino, naturally, were with her. Remember, it was they who had been tied to trees so that they could not run to Miraflores and slay Don Flavio. At the same time, that strange spirit that I've already mentioned possessed my brother Celestino. He was a brave man, I assure you. No, fear wasn't the reason for the trance into which he fell, leaving him with a sadness that transformed him into a corpse.

After Jerónimo's voyage to the kingdom of the dead, Celestino crumpled over on his side, holding his knees to his chin, and he remained on the floor of his cave, unmoving and silent. No one could free him from the grip that held him. Narcisa, as well as her sons, along with other men, tried to straighten his body, but they could not. When the *nahual* tried to filter brews into Celestino's mouth and failed, Narcisa became filled with fear. Neither she nor the *huehues* had ever experienced such a thing.

By the time I left the village in search of *Niña* Isadora, the attention of the tribe was on Celestino. Everyone was convinced that he was under a spell, *embrujado,* another manifestation of the power which all *patrones* have. So when Narcisa and her sons demanded justice, they were reminded that it was the responsibility of the *hue-*

hues to determine if revenge should be taken. After they convened, the Elders decided that to seek justice would put the tribe in danger. When I returned to the *barranca* to get Alondra, I found that my brother had died. *De pura tristeza.* I believe that pure sadness took him and not witchcraft. Narcisa thought this way, too, and she decided to obey the *huehues.*

I'm tired now, but before we say *adiós,* I want to tell you about Doña Brígida. You must listen to what I have to say because you might hear more about her last days and you might be confused. You could be tempted to think that she was crazy and you might even dislike her, so I want to be the first to say that she was not *loca.* At the end of her life, maybe the same spirit of sadness that possessed Celestino also inhabited Doña Brígida, because if you ask me, I will tell you that it was pure sadness that drove her to say what she did when she was in one of those moments.

What disturbs me most of all was the change that overcame Doña Brígida just before she died. She rambled for hours about Don Flavio having two daughters, and even *you* know that this is not true. Her mouth filled with talk about good blood and bad blood. She made Alondra ashamed of her color by talking of superior and inferior people. And there was the story of the she-goat, *la cabra,* that hardly made sense to me. I don't know where such nonsense came from. It was as if the soul of Don Flavio had taken possession of her, weakened by years of sadness and solitude.

I think, too, that this city was a burden for Doña Brígida. Her bedroom was always locked. No one went in, and she came out only at certain times. At Casa Miraflores, she at least could speak with other people, hear her own language, enjoy the sierra, walk through the *llano,* or even stroll up and down the corridors of the hacienda. Here, that was no longer possible. But just before she died, she became herself again and she let Alondra know how much she loved her.

I told you about the photographs she kept in her bedroom in Casa Miraflores. What I didn't tell you was that when Don Flavio packed the automobile with suitcases filled with money, Doña

Brígida insisted on bringing several boxes of her own. They were filled not with her clothing or jewelry, but with her pictures. I think that one day someone will be able to put them together and discover the truth about her and her brother.

Doña Brígida died years ago. It was a lonely death. Only Alondra and I were with her, but she seemed content. It was on that night when she became herself again; her mind was very clear. As she lay in bed, she asked Alondra to take one of her hands and me to take the other. She smiled at us, and I saw a light in her eyes that I had never before seen. She asked us to forgive her for her ways, then she turned to Alondra and said, *Tu abuela fue mi alma.* Then she closed her eyes and drifted away. I had a difficult time later when Alondra wanted to know what Doña Brígida had meant when she said that her grandmother had been her soul. I explained that they must have been the words of a confused old woman, but I had to admit to myself that even I could not understand what she meant.

These are the most important things for you to know about *la familia.* As for the rest . . . Well, we're no different from most of our people who have been forced to leave our land. Don Flavio brought money with him. Over the years I've watched as people come to him with small envelopes in their hands. It must have been rent money, because he bought other houses soon after we arrived. How else could he have sent Samuel to a private school? That takes money. And you are wondering what became of Hacienda Miraflores. I know only what a *paisano* traveling through these parts a few years ago told me. He heard that the authorities had taken whatever was left on the place: some tools, old equipment, even the doors from their hinges.

For my part, Alondra has been my obligation. Don Flavio has allowed me and the girl to remain here in exchange for my service. Several years ago I did laundry and ironing to pay for Alondra's clothing and shoes. When my hands got so that I couldn't do that anymore, I set up a *tiendita,* a little store where I sold eggs and vegetables. Now that she's old enough, she works and pays for my things. That is life, isn't it? The circle turns, and begins again, over and over. I took care of Isadora, then her daughter. Now she takes care of me, although I must tell you that at the moment she doesn't have work. But I'm not worried; she's intelligent, and Tata Dios will not let us starve. The only thing about her that worries me is her questions—about who she is and who she came from. I have never been able to dispel those questions from her mind.

I think that Don Flavio will die soon, so I should be prepared. I'm afraid. Well, because even though I've wanted to, I have never told Alondra the truth. Fear was my reason. Fear of Don Flavio and what he would do if I ever went against his command. You have no idea what he is capable of. Even though I don't know exactly what he did with *Niña* Isadora, I can imagine. And if he punished *her,* what wouldn't he do to me? And to Alondra? Ask yourself what would you have done in my place.

When he dies I'll be free to tell her the truth, but as I said, I'm more afraid now. Oh, I fear what Alondra will think of me when I tell her everything. She has suffered so much because of this, and now she'll know that I allowed it. *¡Ay, Dios!* I cannot live without her love; she is my other daughter, another *Niña* Isadora.

It is time for me to begin preparing dinner. I've asked Doctor Canseco to join us, so I want it to be a special meal. Won't you stay? Perhaps you will visit me again here in my kitchen. We can sip *cafecito* and talk.

Brígida Betancourt

Chapter 15

Los Angeles, 1947

"My brother Flavio had two daughters: a good one, and a bad one."

Nine-year-old Alondra dusted the table as she listened to Doña Brígida. She glanced over at Samuel. She smiled when she saw that he was making eyes at her as he snickered at his great aunt's story. The old woman had her thin, beaked face turned toward the window and was unaware of the boy's mocking.

The elderly Doña Brígida held herself erect as she sat stiffly in a high-backed chair. The porcelain-white skin of her face contrasted with the black dress she wore, its high collar wrapped snugly around her stringy neck. When she turned to look at Samuel, she held her long, bony arms against her stomach, accentuating spotted hands.

"The good daughter was your mother, Samuel. She was lovely, and she was as white and pure as a lily. No one but your father ever put a finger on her so she was like the finest crystal. She was flawless and chaste. But she died, and the bad one drifted away. Just like a—"

"She-goat!" Samuel blurted out. He could not help it; laughter spilled out of his mouth. His face was red from suppressed giggling, but he hardly had time to enjoy himself before Doña Brígida lashed out, whacking him on the top of his head.

"Have respect for your great aunt! I was speaking to you so that you'll never forget that it's possible to have bad blood, even if a child is the offspring of good people."

"*Sí, Tía Grande.*"

The boy responded timidly as he wriggled under Doña Brígida's glare. He did not know which great aunt he liked best: the one who lingered in moody silence, or this one, who invented names and dates. He did know that he acted differently according to her swings in disposition. When he and his grandfather Flavio sat at the dinner table with her, she was almost mute, speaking only to ask for the salt or a glass of water. At those times, Samuel felt grown up, and he liked helping her. When Brígida was in one of her moments, he acted like a little boy despite his fourteen years, sometimes feeling even younger than Alondra.

"And you, Alondra, you have no right to smirk at the history of people far better than those who hatched *you*."

Alondra felt shaken, as she always did whenever Doña Brígida reminded her that she was an orphan. But then the girl thought of what *Abuela* Ursula told her: This was not the real Doña Brígida. She had only fallen into one of her moments.

"As I was saying, the bad one drifted away. Just like the *cabra* that is pulled by evil desires up to the craggy mountain, where she can do the vile things that her condition demands of her."

Alondra wondered what horrible things a she-goat could do. She had the feeling that Doña Brígida meant that she, Alondra, was like that perverted *cabra*. The girl looked up from the polished surface of the table to take a look at Samuel. His skin was as milky white as that of his great aunt. The only difference was that the boy's skin was smooth. Alondra glanced down at her own hands and arms, dark brown just like the hot chocolate they drank every morning at breakfast.

Samuel listened as intently as he could because he knew that if his great aunt even suspected that he was not paying attention, she would punish him. When Brígida was caught up in her imaginary world, the ritual of reciting the family history took place every afternoon, when she would repeat each episode with details and dates. The boy hated the long, tedious story. Nothing ever changed and he now knew it by memory.

The voice droned on, lulling the boy; he was getting sleepy. Suddenly, he began thinking of Alondra and how he wished he could be like her. Except—this thought jerked him out of his drowsiness—she, too, was forced by his great aunt to listen to the dreary story, as if part of the family.

Samuel was intrigued by this new realization. He looked up at his great aunt and saw that her eyes were riveted on the girl as she spoke. It was clear to Samuel that Doña Brígida was using her words to hurt Alondra.

"Why are your making faces, Samuel? You are hearing about your dead, saintly mother and I see you making the face of a bad, ungrateful boy."

"*Tía Grande,* I don't want to hear this part any more."

Samuel looked over at Alondra, hoping that she would be relieved because of what he had just blurted out, but she went on polishing the table surface. She did not look up or even show that she had heard his words. Doña Brígida's shoulders creaked forward; and she stretched to take hold of her walking stick, from against the wall.

"What did you say?"

For the first time, Samuel did not cringe at the thin, imposing figure. When he answered his voice was soft but steady. "*Tía,* I don't want to hear about the she-goat anymore."

"Samuel, I have no forgiveness for such disrespect. You will be punished, I assure you. And part of that punishment will be that you will not be allowed to play with that girl anymore."

Doña Brígida pointed at Alondra, who was by now staring back at the old woman. Doña Brígida had never been so grumpy; this was one of her worst days.

"But . . . what does Alondra have to do with—"

"Silence! You are *never again* to question your elders. If you do it one more time, Samuel, you will surely bring down a curse on yourself. One's ancestors are everything in this life and you have been blessed with a good family. You must never again refuse to hear the important things about those who came before you."

"I don't understand. Why can't I be with Alondra? All we do is—"

"It is not for you to ask for reasons! You must obey and that is all!"

The old woman had risen to her feet. She pointed the silver-handled cane in her hand at Samuel. Her voice was not loud, but it was steady, powerful. As she stood, she seemed to grow taller, longer, leaner; she almost reached the ceiling, he thought. He was stunned into silence.

"Because you have been so disrespectful to the story of your ancestors, you will have to hear it once again, from the beginning. And when I am finished, you will have to repeat it to me, word for word."

The old woman banged her cane on the hardwood floor. After a few seconds, she returned to the high-backed chair and seated herself. She placed her elbows on the armrests as she motioned to Alondra to go on dusting the table. Doña Brígida slowly passed her tongue over her withered upper lip and began again her demented version of the Betancourt family history.

Later that afternoon, Ursula went to the kitchen to prepare dinner and found Alondra standing by the pantry. Her back was to Ursula, and she saw that the girl was patting flour over her face and arms. Rushing to her, Ursula took her by the shoulders and turned her around.

"What are you doing?"

"I want to have white skin like Samuel."

Ursula took the sack of flour from Alondra's hands and pulled her to her, embracing the girl. She fought a knot of tears trapped in her throat. Not knowing what to say, Ursula tried to wipe off the flour with a wet cloth, but it was little use because Alondra was nearly covered with the powdery dust.

"You look like a cookie. You need a bath."

In the bathroom, Ursula undressed Alondra and helped her into the tub, which was filling with warm water. Slowly, she rubbed soap into the girl's skin, then poured water over her head and shoulders. She did this several times before speaking.

"Alondra, the color of your skin is beautiful. Look at how it glistens. It is brown like so many beautiful things that we love. It is the color of wood and of the beans that give us chocolate. It has the tones of herbs and plants that heal us."

That night, Ursula had already turned out the lights and was sitting up in bed trying to pray, but she was distracted thinking about what had happened that afternoon. Alondra was on a cot near her grandmother's; she, too was thinking of Doña Brígida.

Alondra and Ursula shared the service porch of the house as a bedroom. One side of the room was used as a laundry. Large wicker baskets filled with the day's ironing took up one of the corners. Next to an ironing board stood a washing machine; its ringer was used as a hook for dust rags and aprons. Behind this was a storage closet for brooms, buckets and mops. Alondra's and Ursula's cots took up the other part of the porch, which was screened in on all four sides. A door led out to the back yard. There was a full moon that night and its light filtered through the screens, flooding the room, casting silvery tones on Ursula's hair.

"*Abuela*, Doña Brígida was acting *loca* today."

"*Niña*, you know that's the way she is sometimes."

"I know, but today she said a lot about good and bad blood."

"Alondra, that's nothing new. You know Doña Brígida."

"It was different today. She said that Samuel's mother was the good *hija*, and when she talked about the bad one, the she-goat, Doña Brígida looked straight at me."

"*¡Ah! La cabra tira hacia el monte.*"

"What did you say, *Abuela?*"

"It's an old saying, Alondra. The she-goat yearns for the mountain."

Alondra sat up and leaned against the wall. She liked the times she could speak with her grandmother, especially at night when the light was turned off. The girl liked Ursula's way of speaking; it was full of words and sayings that captivated her.

"But, *Abuela,* what does that mean?"

Ursula looked over at the girl; she, too, enjoyed these moments. She liked Alondra's questions and curiosity and, most of all, she was fond of her manner of speaking: a tangle of English learned in school and Spanish spoken at home.

"It means that no matter what we look like, or what we tell others we are, we will always be pulled by what we really are. It means that what is inside of us is more powerful than what is outside."

"The *cabra?*"

"Sí."

"Is the *cabra* inside of me?"

Ursula cocked her head as she peered at Alondra through the darkness. She was beginning to feel uneasy with the direction their conversation was taking. It bothered her that Doña Brígida was lately concentrating on the example of the two daughters. She thought again of Alondra with flour smeared on her face and arms. She reclined on the pillow, thinking, trying to understand the meaning of the two daughters in the old woman's mind. It was clear that it was Isadora, but why the two sides? Why had the memory of Isadora split into two persons somewhere inside of Doña Brígida? Did she think that Isadora had become bad when she loved Jerónimo and gave birth to Alondra? That could not be, because the old woman had loved her niece. Everyone knew that. Ursula shook her head, trying to unravel the tangled threads spiraling in her mind.

"*Hija,* what is inside of me and you is special and different. We have our own spirit."

"But the *cabra* sounds wicked."

"Only if you want to think of it that way. Remember, it's better if a person doesn't pretend to be what she isn't. It's better to be yourself, *hija,* because sooner or later the truth will come out."

"And the she-goat?"

"If that's what is in me, that's what is in me!"

Ursula's words were charged with finality. They announced the end of the conversation and she returned to her prayers. Alondra slid back under the covers, but her eyes were open. She was watching Ursula, right arm lifted in mid-air tracing the sign of the cross in different directions. She closed her eyes, expecting the sound of her grandmother's whispered prayers to lull her to sleep.

"*¡Abuela!*"

"*Niña*, go to sleep! Can't you see that I'm praying?"

"What are ancestors?"

Ursula sighed deeply, letting her breath filter slowly through her teeth. She turned toward Alondra, squinting as she peered at the girl. "Ancestors are family, people who live before our time. They are the *abuelas* and *abuelos* who gave life to our mothers and fathers."

"Are there bad ancestors?"

Ursula's back snapped forward and she sat erect, ears straining as she listened to what Alondra was saying. She felt a pang of worry at what Doña Brígida might have told the girl about her Rarámuri side. The old woman's mind strayed more and more each day. Recently, her spells had brought out a different side, a meanness that had not been there in the past.

"Why do you ask?"

"Doña Brígida said that Samuel was blessed with good ancestors. Better than the ones who hatched me."

Ursula pressed her back against the pillow as she shook her head. Then she scratched her head and rubbed her eyes, thinking of what to say to the girl.

"Doña Brígida's spirit has lost its way and her words are messages that it is sending. It is searching for help because she no longer remembers the truth. You were not hatched. You were conceived in moonlight and born in the light of the rising sun. You do have good ancestors. Don't forget what I've told you about the Rarámuri. Our history is long and so is our memory. We have known the secrets of dreams and healing from the beginning of time. We know the arts of carving stone and of dancing. We speak the language of Tata Hakuli and Tata Peyote. Know also that your ancestors are the people who run with the wind. They are the distance runners."

"Tell me more, *Abuela.*"

Ursula smiled because she heard sleepiness overcoming Alondra's voice. She went on speaking, transported to the sierra and to the kitchens of Casa Miraflores where Rarámuri, Hicholes, Mexicas, Zapotecas and Chichimecas worked together, exchanging beliefs and legends.

"Your ancestors, Alondra, walked the floors of deserts and jungles, climbed the heights of the *barranca,* prayed to the gods of the north countless cycles before Samuel's ancestors came to these parts of the world."

"Tell me about my father."

"Your father was El Rarámuri, the distance runner who was swifter than the wind. His speed was so great that even the fastest deer could not match him."

"Tell me about my mother."

"Your mother was Xipe Totec, the one who did not die but was reborn instead."

"Tell me . . ."

Alondra's voice trailed and Ursula knew that she had fallen asleep. Rising, Ursula went to the child, fluffed her pillow, and tucked the blanket around her feet.

Chapter 16

The following afternoon Doña Brígida, propped rigidly into her chair, went on with her narrative. "Our roots are in Spain, from where our ancestors came to Mexico. The first patriarch of the family was Don Reynaldo Betancourt. His son was Humberto, and *his* son was Horacio. He was the father of Fortunato and he of Gonzalo, who had ten sons, of which only one survived. His name was Calisto. Your great-grandfather, Samuel."

The boy cringed. At the thought of reciting the list of names, he began to feel sick.

"The son of Don Calisto was Don Flavio, your grandfather and the father of your mother. God did not bless him with a son but with two daughters: one good, one bad. You, Samuel, are the son of the good daughter."

Doña Brígida's monotonous voice droned on as she recited names and details to the children. They wondered how she could repeat the same words in exactly the same order each time. She never skipped a name. Suddenly, the old woman stopped talking to gaze out the window. The children thought that she was finished so they began to rise from their seats when Doña Brígida's face snapped back in their direction.

"I'm not finished with my story. Get back to your places! Your grandmother, Velia Carmelita, was a beautiful woman . . . She was like a statue in a temple."

Doña Brígida's voice had dropped to a whisper. The children strained to hear what she was saying because it was something different. "Velia Carmelita's skin had the texture of olives in the autumn sun. Her smile was like dawn descending onto the plain, filling it with light. Her lips were soft and her breath was like perfume. Her breasts were high and firm."

Samuel shot a look at Alondra. He pursed his lips into a round circle and he stuck his hands under his shirt, puffing them out like a woman's breasts. Alondra stopped dusting the table and moved closer.

"My brother didn't deserve her."

Just at that moment, Ursula came into the parlor. "Doña Brígida, it's past the dinner hour. Don Flavio is in the dining room waiting for you and Samuel."

Ursula stood in the doorway, arms crossed over her chest. The expression on her face betrayed her concern when she saw that the children appeared to be oddly captivated by whatever Doña Brígida was saying. Alondra, rag in hand, headed towards the kitchen. When Doña Brígida, followed by Samuel, disappeared into the corridor, Ursula stopped Alondra, shaking her head.

"*Virgen del Cobre,* I don't know what's happening to her."

"*Abuela,* she was talking about Samuel's grandmother."

Her curiosity aroused, Ursula pursed her lips and took Alondra by the arm. She guided the girl into the kitchen.

"What did she say?"

"Funny things."

"Like what?"

"Well, she said that the lady's face was like a statue and that her skin was like olives."

"Like olives?"

"*Sí.* And that her things were hard."

"Things? What things?"

Alondra pecked at her blouse with her fingers, lifting it to simulate breasts. She mischievously looked at Ursula.

"Ah! What is happening? Doña Brígida said that Doña Velia Carmelita's breasts were *hard*?"

"*Sí.*"

"Did Samuel hear her say that?"

"*Sí.*"

The Day of the Moon

"¡Santísima Virgen del Cobre!"

Four o'clock could not come too soon for Samuel and Alondra the next day. When the children walked into the room, they saw that Doña Brígida had not yet arrived. They looked at one another.

"Maybe she's not coming."

Samuel whispered what he was thinking. His great aunt had never missed a session, but this could be the first time.

"Maybe she's too sad."

"Sad? How do you know?"

"Ursula told me that Doña Brígida hardly ate today. Just a tortilla with some *frijoles.*"

Samuel ran around the room giggling and pretending to be an old woman. He held one hand on an invisible cane and the other on his bent back. He bowed and wiggled his legs, tottering from chair to sofa. He pretended feeble groans, mocking Doña Brígida.

"Mi hermano Flavio tuvo dos hijas, una buena y la otra mala."

He mimicked his *Tía Grande* in Spanish, then repeated himself in English. "My brother Flavio had two daughters . . ." He was going through his antics with his back to the parlor entrance; Alondra was facing it. The boy was red-faced and laughing, but when he looked at Alondra, he realized that her eyes were riveted on a spot somewhere behind him. Wondering why he had not heard the thump of her walking stick, Samuel turned slowly to face Doña Brígida.

The boy lowered his head, expecting Doña Brígida's blow. But she walked to her chair, sat down, and motioned to him to take his place on the sofa in front of her. He smiled sheepishly as he settled himself into the overstuffed chair. The old woman looked at Alondra with a side glance that told her to begin her dusting.

"Velia Carmelita's screams echoed in the hollows of the empty, darkened patio. The ferns seemed to vibrate with her moans as she labored to give birth. Silhouettes dashed in and out of the kitchen of Casa Miraflores. Women carrying towels and boiling water rushed to the bedroom where she lay, her legs raised and spread open, while the child made its way out of her womb. "

Doña Brígida turned to Samuel. Her face was filled with sadness. He thought that there were tears in her eyes, and he moved forward in the chair, trying to get a closer look.

"You might think, Samuel, that I should not mention these details to you since you're still a boy, but remember that Velia Carmelita was your grandmother and that the child she was about to have was your mother. *¡A-y-y-y-y! ¡A-y-y-y-y!*" Doña Brígida formed an oval with her thin lips and abruptly let out wobbly moans. In imitation, the children opened their mouth in a silent howl.

"Her screams filled the house and seemed to grow longer and louder. They took form, like demons banging at windows and doors, demanding to be freed. Pain choked Velia Carmelita. I sat by her side, holding her hands. I wanted to take her anguish into my own body. Sweat covered her even while several women toweled her down."

Doña Brígida's lips again parted in a simulated groan. This time Alondra and Samuel puckered their faces, imagining the pain. "Isadora, your mother, was born before daybreak."

The old woman paused and turned toward Alondra; her expression was still sad, but the girl thought she saw something different in Doña Brígida's eyes. His expression was soft, and gentle, and it confused Alondra because the words *Isadora, your mother,* were aimed at her.

"Then Velia Carmelita died."

Doña Brígida suddenly stopped speaking. Samuel and Alondra looked up, startled. This was the first time she had told the story this way. They looked at each other in expectation, but nothing more came out.

"But, *Tía Grande,* how could my grandmother have died before she had her next daughter? You've always said that *Abuelo* Flavio had two daughters, one good, the other bad . . ."

Doña Brígida, startled by Samuel's words, slipped back into anger, dispelling the melancholy that had prompted her to relive the moment of Velia Carmelita's death.

"Get out of my sight!" she shouted as she raised her arm, stick in hand. Her body shook so much that the children expected to hear the rattle of bones. They were frightened. Samuel leaped out of his chair and dashed out the door; Alondra followed closely. They did not stop until they had run down the corridor, through the kitchen and service porch. They tripped down the wooden stairs. Once out in the yard they kept running until they reached the shade of the avocado tree. There they fell on the ground, gasping and laughing.

"She really stuck her foot in it this time. She forgot all about the she-goat and all that craziness."

Out of breath, Samuel struggled to speak. Alondra was breathing hard. She was frightened.

"I think, Samuel . . ."

She broke off. The boy got closer to her.

"What do you think?"

"I think that the *cabra* is me."

The boy's head whipped toward Alondra. He secretly agreed with her, but he did not want her to know.

"You're nuts! You're a girl, not a goat. Besides, you're too little to be my mother's other sister. How can you even think such a dumb thing?" He paused for a moment as he slumped against the tree trunk. "*Tía Grande* just gets mixed up. That's all. Anyway, Alondra, you don't even belong to our crazy family."

After a while, they decided to go back into the kitchen, where they found Ursula by the stove. When the children walked in, she looked at Alondra, trying to discern a change, something that would alert her to what Doña Brígida had said to make them run away.

"Ursula, do you remember my mother?" Samuel had gotten close to her, reaching into the pan she was stirring. He managed to pick a strand of the meat that was browning before she pulled his arm away from the heat. Hearing what she thought might be a signal, she turned off the burner and led the children to the table, where all three sat down.

"Yes, I remember her. I took care of her from the time she was three years old. Just like I've taken care of you and Alondra."

Ursula looked at the girl and saw the question forming in her eyes. It was the same doubt that had come up recently.

"Did she have a sister, *Abuela?*"

Samuel looked at Ursula. Although he had laughed at the she-goat story, he had believed his great aunt: There *must* have been another sister. Ursula did not want to speak about this, fearing that something she said might trigger Alondra's curiosity, or even her imagination. But she knew that if she evaded the question, it would be worse.

"No, *hija,* Doña Isadora was the only daughter of Don Flavio. There was no other sister."

"J-e-e-e-z!" Samuel let out a long, whistling sound through his teeth. Then he looked at Ursula, disbelief stamped on his face.

"Samuel, you know that Doña Brígida has her bad moments. The story of a second daughter has come out of a lonely, dark corner of her spirit; she cannot help it."

"Then what about the *cabra?*"

"There was no she-goat, *niña.*"

Ursula got to her feet and told the children to prepare for dinner. Samuel left the kitchen, heading upstairs to his room and Alondra went to the sink, where she began to wash her hands. When Ursula looked, she saw that the girl was rubbing her hands and muttering: "There was no *cabra!* There was no *cabra!*"

Chapter 17

The next day the children were nervous; they knew that the old woman had been so upset at Samuel's question that she had not come down for dinner in the evening. As they waited, the ticking of the clock on the mantelpiece seemed to be growing louder.

Alondra looked at Samuel and blurted out, "Don't you ever wish that you knew who your *mamá* was?"

Samuel wondered what her question had to do with the terrible thing that was about to happen to them. He blinked, wrinkled his brow and tensely nibbled at his upper lip.

"I do know who she was. Isadora Betancourt."

"You see! That proves you don't know who she was. If you really knew, you would say your *papá's* family name. Shouldn't she be called Isadora something-or-another? When a girl marries, she has to take her husband's name, no?"

Samuel's eyes opened wide; he was stumped. He didn't have the answer to Alondra's questions. He swallowed a gulp of saliva and opened his mouth, hoping the right words would come out. "I don't know why my name is Betancourt, but I do remember a little bit about her. I think it was a cave, on top of a mountain. I slept there, on the ground. And my *mamá* used to rub my forehead a lot and tell me stories."

"Is that all you remember?"

"Yea."

"I know who my *mamá* and *papá* are, but only because *Abuela* Ursula has told me about them. She says that he ran faster than wind, and that she never died, even after they scraped her skin right off of her." Alondra stopped talking to ponder what she had said. In a few seconds she spoke up again. "Do you know what I think?"

"I think that *Abuela* Ursula is hiding something from me. *Sí.* I'll bet you anything!"

"Why do you think that?"

"Because who can live after your skin has been pulled off? And who runs faster than the wind?"

The boy began to giggle, imagining a roadrunner, its legs a blurred circle, running away from its enemy; just in like the cartoon. Samuel's laughter was interrupted by the sound of Doña Brígida's walking stick. Alondra also heard it and she jumped to retrieve her dust rag. Samuel froze into his usual place opposite his great aunt's chair.

Doña Brígida walked into the parlor. She stood erect and it seemed to the children that her cane struck the floor with more authority. They looked at each other in nervous anticipation, as she sat down on her chair, let out a loud, deep sigh, and began her chronicle without an introduction. Doña Brígida spoke quietly. Whenever Alondra thought that she would not be noticed, she looked steadily at the old woman's face. Her eyes were red and puffy, and her voice was weak.

"I will soon die, but it doesn't matter because today we've come to the end. The end of our family history."

"*Tía Grande,* may I ask you something?" Samuel had left his place to kneel in front of Doña Brígida. "What was my father's name? Why don't I get to use it? Where did he go? What about my mother? Where is she? Did she—?"

The old woman's eyes snapped open and she stared at Samuel. He thought she was about to slap him, but instead she moved him aside and got to her feet. Wordlessly, she walked past him and Alondra. They saw that she shuffled more than ever; her feet seemed too heavy for her body. When she disappeared into the shadows of the dark corridor, the children looked at each other, baffled.

After Ursula had finished serving Don Flavio and Samuel, she picked up the dishes and returned them to the kitchen sink. She sat down at the table to have her own dinner. Alondra was finishing what was on her plate, but her eyes were on Ursula.

The older woman was silent, lost in thought as she tore small bits from a tortilla, slipped them into her mouth, and chewed absentmindedly. Alondra watched her, but soon began to fidget and squirm in her chair. She pushed her plate away, deliberately scraping the table top. She jangled a knife and fork against one another, then clinked a finger nail against the empty milk glass. Still, nothing pried Ursula away of her thoughts. Alondra finally cleared her throat and let out a loud, artificial cough.

"*Sí, hija.* I know you're there."

"*Abuela,* is there something wrong?"

"*Sí.*"

"Is it me?"

"No, *niña.* It's this family. *¡Ay! Virgen Santísima!* So much suffering."

"Is Samuel suffering?"

Ursula moved her plate away and looked at the girl. She had lately been listening in on what Doña Brígida was telling the children. Now she pushed her chair back and gestured to the girl to come to her. She sat her on her lap, took her in her arms and began rocking back and forth. Ursula yearned to tell her that she was not her grandmother, but her great aunt, like Doña Brígida. She longed to let Alondra know that Samuel was her brother, and Don Flavio her grandfather, and that this was her mother's side of the family.

"Come, *hija,*" she said at last. "Let's go to bed. We'll wash the dishes tomorrow."

Together they headed toward the service porch. They were almost at the door when they heard a long, deep moan. It had been loud enough to cut through a closed door, make its way along the hall down the staircase, and to the rear of the house:

"*¡Ayyyyy, Dios!*"

"*¡Santísima!* It's Doña Brígida!"

Ursula let go of Alondra's hand to run to the old woman. She was fast, but the girl was faster. Alondra was ahead by the time

Ursula sped through the parlor, up the staircase, and to the closed door of Doña Brígida's bedroom.

Ursula rapped at the door. Silence. When a second knock went unanswered, she slowly opened the door. Alondra and Ursula caught sight of Doña Brígida stretched out on her bed, fully clothed; she even had her shoes on. She held her arms crossed peacefully on her breast.

"Por favor, entren."

Doña Brígida had not moved nor turned her face. Her voice was calm, light; Alondra hardly recognized it. Ursula moved toward the bed, holding Alondra's hand. The girl had never before been in the room, so she was taken by its high ceiling, heavy wooden furniture, carved cabinets and wardrobe. Even in the dark, she could see that one wall was covered by aged, purple-tinted photographs. As she was led by Ursula, the girl's head swiveled, looking from side to side, up and down.

When they were by the bed, Doña Brígida raised an arm and gestured to Alondra to come to the other side. Alondra obeyed and the old woman held out her hand wordlessly. Then Doña Brígida smiled. She seemed content as she held Alondra's hand.

Alondra looked from Ursula to Doña Brígida, but there was only silence. The passing of cars in the street and the ticking of a clock on the nightstand were the only sounds. Alondra became aware of Doña Brígida's hand, of its warmth and softness, and she was surprised. She had imagined that the old lady must have been made of something hard.

"Ursula, take my hand." Doña Brígida stretched her other hand toward Ursula. Alondra stared at the women and for the first time wondered if they were the same age. She had never thought of how old her grandmother might be, and as for Doña Brígida, Alondra had thought that she had been born old.

"¿Qué pasa, Doña?"

"Me muero."

"¡Santo Dios! I'll call Doctor Canseco."

Doña Brígida held onto her hand. She pulled Alondra and Ursula closer to her. "No. Stay with me."

She smiled first at Alondra, then at Ursula. The girl was struck by the beauty of Doña Brígida's face. Why had she never smiled like that before?

"Take care of my pictures, Ursula. It's all there."

Ursula nodded. The old woman turned to look at Alondra. Their faces were so close to one another they nearly touched.

"*Niña*, one day you will return to the *llano* and ride in a carriage and see the sierras that tower over the *barranca*. One day you will sing songs, write poems, and walk through corridors of Casa Miraflores with the one you love. You will do that, just as I did." Doña Brígida smiled at Alondra, pulled her hand from Ursula and stroked the girl's cheeks and forehead. She traced her hairline with an index finger. Her eyes roamed Alondra's face, looking at her forehead, nose, mouth. "Your grandmother was my soul."

Doña Brígida closed her eyes and drifted away. Outside, the flow of cars had lessened and the ticking of the clock seemed to grow louder. Alondra looked at Ursula, who had tears on her cheeks. She had not known until then that Ursula loved Doña Brígida.

Ursula covered Doña Brígida's face and made the sign of the cross many times over. Alondra could not make out the prayers her grandmother was reciting, but she knew that they were uttered in her own language as well as in Spanish. Then Ursula took Alondra by the hand and led her out of the room.

"What are we going to do now, *Abuela?*"

"I have to tell Don Flavio that his sister has begun her journey to the other side of the sierra."

"Will he cry?"

"I don't think so."

"And then?"

"Then I must bathe and clothe Doña Brígida so that she will not feel uncomfortable when she meets the others."

"What others?"

"Those who have gone before her and are waiting for her on the other side."

"Samuel's grandmother?"

"*Sí*. I'm sure of that."

In the kitchen, Ursula and Alondra prepared chocolate and *pan dulce* for the mourners, who sat in the parlor. Alondra was layering the different pieces of bread in a pattern, being careful that the *cuernitos* did not crush the *conchas*.

"*Abuela*, what did Doña Brígida mean when she said that my grandmother had been her soul?"

"I don't know, *niña*. Maybe she was just confused."

"You're my *abuela*, but you're on my *papá's* side. Do you think that she was talking of the *abuela* on my *mamá's* side?"

Ursula stopped stirring the milk. In one hand she held a wooden mill; in the other, the chocolate patty that she would put in before the milk came to a head.

"Only Tata Dios knows. I think it was someone that Doña Brígida loved and who made her happy."

"Where is Casa Miraflores?"

"In Chihuahua."

"Doña Brígida said that I would go there to sing songs."

Ursula returned to stirring the milk and began to add the chocolate. She had to concentrate, so that the contents of the pot would not boil over.

"And the pictures, *Abuela*? She said that it was all there. What did she mean by that?"

"I remember some of them. There were pictures of her and Don Flavio taken even before they came to Chihuahua. Others were of people and friends they made at Hacienda Miraflores. Some were of special days like Don Flavio's wedding and *Niña* Isadora's baptism."

"She was Samuel's *mamá*. Was there a picture of the bad daughter?"

Ursula pointed the wooden mill toward Alondra and wagged her head impatiently. She had momentarily forgotten about the pot, so she flinched when she heard the sizzling of spilled milk on the burner. After she lowered the flame on the burner, she again looked at Alondra.

"I have told you many times that there was no bad daughter. That was something that came out of Doña Brígida's mouth during her moments of illness."

"*Abuela,* do you think that I'll—"

"*Niña,* the chocolate and *pan dulce* must be ready now, not *mañana.*" With that, Ursula carefully poured the steaming chocolate into a pitcher and headed for the parlor. Alondra followed, carrying the platter of sweet rolls.

Two days later, the sky was a gray and chilly current swirling around the tombstones of Calvary Cemetery. Alondra and Samuel, in dark clothing, stood shivering on the fringe of the acquaintances of the Betancourts. Snippets of the priest's high-pitched voice floated over to Alondra as he recited the prayers for the dead.

"*Absolve, Domine, animas omnium fidelium defunctorum, ab omni vinculo delictorum . . .*"

Alondra wondered of what sins the priest begged that Doña Brígida be cleansed. She shuddered as the cold wind cut through her short dress and coat. She looked up to the sky and saw gray clouds skittering across the wide expanse. Then she looked around, peering at the gathering of people. In the center was Don Flavio, dressed in black. She was afraid of him, having seen him only a few times in her life. The only person crying was Ursula.

"*In paradisum deducant te angeli . . .*"

"*Tía Grande* is not going to Heaven. I think that she's going to the other place. You know, Hell."

Alondra, jerked out of her thoughts, did not answer Samuel's whisper in her ear; she only wagged her head in disagreement. She looked over to the priest and saw that he was sprinkling holy water on the coffin and into the grave. At the priest's signal, four men lowered the box into the hole. Alondra stretched her neck to watch them as they filled in the dirt. She could hear the hollow thud as each shovelful of earth was piled above Doña Brígida's head. When Alondra tired of watching, she turned to Samuel.

"No. She's going to the other side of the sierra, where she'll meet the others."

Alondra Santiago

Chapter 18

Los Angeles, 1965

Alondra sat at the table, unmoving. Even the kitchen noises did not intrude on her thoughts. Both women were tired from a sleepless night spent tending to Don Flavio, but Ursula moved about the business of preparing dinner.

"*Abuela*, it's been a long time since the death of Doña Brígida, hasn't it?" At twenty-seven, Alondra felt that her childhood was a lifetime ago.

"Yes," Ursula answered without looking up, as she mashed a clove of garlic. When she put the pulpy dab into the skillet, it sizzled loudly, and the kitchen filled with its fragrance.

"And now it looks like the old man is going, too. He was really in bad shape last night."

"Doctor Canseco is with him now. *Niña*, you should help him. You know what you're doing."

"Because I went to nursing school?"

"*Sí.*"

"*¡Ay! Abuela.* I finished last in the class."

"You finished. That's important."

"Hmm. Maybe. Anyway, the *viejo* doesn't let me come close to him. *¡Chispas!*"

"I thought that school taught you not to mix your words."

"I try, *Abuela,* but sometimes they get jumbled up."

As she watched her grandmother move from stove to sink to table, Alondra reflected on questions that had been gnawing at her for years. As a child Alondra had been mystified by Doña Brígida's last words that she would someday return to Mexico. As her grammar school and high school days passed, the longing to find out more about herself and her beginnings grew until it became an obsession.

She had tried to quash the uneasiness that hounded her with nursing school. Although she had finished the program, nothing in it satisfied the drive inside of her. She decided to get a teaching credential. That ended with a leave of absence midway through the program. After that, Alondra decided to stay at home with Ursula for a while.

During those years, Samuel had been drafted, had been posted to Korea, and returned. Some time after that he married a girl from San Francisco and moved out of the city. Alondra had felt lonelier than ever without him. Even the young men she dated could not put out the yearning inside of her.

"Abuela, tell me about the *llano.*"

Ursula stopped what she was doing, went over to Alondra and looked at her. She knew from long experience what was coming next.

"*Hija,* please try to put that out of your head. Concentrate on your life. Think—"

"I *am* concentrating on it. I can't live *mi vida* and until I find out . . ."

"Find out what?"

This conversation was not following the usual pattern. Alondra's voice and words were charged with anguish. Ursula wiped her hands on her apron, pulled out a chair and sat next to Alondra.

"*Hija* . . ."

"No, *Abuela,* you're not going to put me off anymore. You know what Doña Brígida meant. But all you tell me are cute little details."

"Cute! *¿Qué es eso?*"

Alondra put her hand on Ursula's shoulder and squeezed it. Her face had darkened and her eyes were bright.

"Tell me, *¡por favor!*"

"Soon." For the first time, Ursula made concession: "When Don Flavio dies."

"But he's almost dead now! You know that. How can he make a difference?"

Ursula rose to her feet, her mouth clamped so tightly that it was a straight line. She returned to the stove, shaking her head.

"Perdóname, Abuela. I can't help it. Look at me, please. I'm twenty-seven years old and I can't find myself. Nothing I do helps. How many jobs have I had? You tell me. I drive the guys I date crazy. I drive *myself* crazy. I'm empty and I need someone to help me."

"Soon, *niña.* Very soon."

Dinner did not take place that evening. Soon after Alondra and Ursula spoke, Dr. Canseco emerged from the bedroom to let them know that Don Flavio's death was imminent. The old man was now asking for them, he added.

"What about Samuel, doctor? We have to call him."

"There's no time now. You'll have to call him after Don Flavio's gone."

Although she had grown to womanhood in his house, Alondra had seen Don Flavio, and been in his company, only sporadically. This was the man who had imposed rules, who had kept her and Ursula almost always in the kitchen. This was the person who had prohibited them from sitting at the table with him, tacitly reminding them always that they were servants. Yet now, on the verge of death, he had sent for them.

He was stretched out on the bed, lying on top of the covers because he couldn't tolerate the weight of a sheet. His face, taut with pain, was turned to the window that overlooked the street.

"Don Flavio, Ursula and Alondra are here. You asked for them."

The old man only fluttered his eyelids in response. His hands were on his chest, clutching at his nightshirt. His skin had yellowed since the previous night; it clung to his skull. Ursula was shaken by the deterioration that she saw. Don Flavio's spirit was already on its path to the kingdom of the dead. She made the sign of the cross over him, then turned in every direction of the room, tracing the cross in mid-air. The doctor watched her impassively.

Don Flavio's lips moved, but his eyes remained focused on the window: El Rarámuri had returned. At last he turned his face away from the glass to look at Alondra. He tried to speak to her—she thought she heard words slip through his lips—but he was unable to talk.

Alondra knelt by his side, pulled by a strange energy. Don Flavio's eyes rolled toward a corner of the room. Alondra saw nothing except a wooden chair, a desk, a photograph. She rose to her feet: It was a man dressed in black, wearing a bowler hat. *Edmundo Betancourt. 1896. Arandas, Jalisco.* The script was flowery, written in white ink against the dark background of the daguerreotype.

She brought it to Don Flavio and put it by his side. The old man seemed not to notice. His breathing began to grow shallow as he again glared at the window. When Don Flavio's congested chest began to hitch in ragged, shallow breaths, Doctor Canseco looked at Alondra and Ursula. It was time. In a few minutes, the breathing had stopped.

Alondra stared at the old man's face: It had become a yellow mask. When the doctor covered the corpse, both women left the room.

Alondra waited, listening to the telephone ring at the other end of the line. After the fourth ring, a thin voice piped, "Hello."

"Is Samuel there?"

There was no answer, just a pause. She heard the receiver being put down, then a brief shuffle.

"Hi, Alondra. How's—"

"Don Flavio died this morning."

Samuel was quiet, but Alondra waited.

"I guess he went fast."

"He was very sick, but he died here because he didn't want to be taken to the hospital."

"That figures." Samuel stopped for a moment. "They're gone now, Alondra, the old ones. It's hard to believe, don't you think?"

"Yes." When he didn't say anything, Alondra went on: "His body is on the way to the mortuary, but you're the one with the final say about where he's to be buried and how much money you want to spend."

"It's not going to be that way. The old man left a will. I have it. He wanted to be cremated and that's the way it'll have to be."

"Just like that, Samuel? No prayers, no ceremony, *nada?*"

"That's the way he wanted it. I'll make the arrangement from this side." Again he paused. "I'll try to come down as soon as I can. I'll let you know when I'm coming." Then he said, "Alondra, you and Ursula can stay in the house, if you want."

"I can't pay rent right now, but I'll get a job soon."

"Take your time. It doesn't matter. Do you want to live there?"

"*Sí.*"

"With all the memories?"

"*Sí,* and with *Abuela.* Samuel?"

"Yeah?"

"What's going to happen to his ashes?"

"He made me promise to throw them in the ocean."

"*¿Qué?*"

"In the ocean, Alondra. He said he didn't want the fuss . . . more than likely because he knew that no one would come to his funeral."

"Don't say that!"

"It's true."

"Okay. I hope you can come soon."

"I'll try."

Alondra walked over to the kitchen: It was early afternoon; the sun shone through the large windows, flooding the room with pale November light. She found Ursula sitting at her usual place, but when she looked up, her eyes were red and her face swollen and blotched. Ursula sprang to her feet when she recognized Alondra by her side.

"*Niña,* let me get you something to eat."

"*Gracias,* but I not hungry. Maybe a *cafecito.*"

While Ursula rattled the kettle on the stove, Alondra slumped over the table. She felt sorry for Samuel for his not having been with his grandfather during those last hours.

It struck her how she and Samuel were alike. Like her, Samuel was an orphan. Alondra reminded herself that she at least knew some things about her mother and father. Samuel never knew who his father was—not even his name. Most of Samuel's questions, too, were unanswered. Yet he did not let his heart be troubled with these thoughts. Alondra wished to be like him and accept that if some things had been kept from her, it was probably for the best.

The two women were quiet. Only the soft clinking of spoons stirring coffee broke the silence. Alondra kept her eyes on Ursula, remembering that it was she who had brought her up, she who had cared for her. Why, despite Ursula's love, had she always been hounded by the desire to know more about her mother and father?

"I'll get a job and we can both live off what I earn. This time I'll hang onto it. Samuel says we can stay here, but maybe we can find another house. What do you think?"

Alondra was grateful for the surge of affection she felt for her grandmother. She looked at her, and saw that she had grown old. Ursula's face and hands were wrinkled, and her shoulders were frail.

"I think I like it very much, *niña.*" Suddenly, she looked up at Alondra. "What about Don Flavio? When are we going to bury him?"

"We're not. Samuel says that the *viejo* left orders to be cremated. There's not going to be a service either—not even a rosary. "

"No prayers! What will guide him to the other side? How will he know where to go?"

"Don't think about it, *Abuela.* He's gone and we can't help him."

"Yes, we can! We'll recite rosaries for him. No one can stop us from praying, can they? Maybe he'll find his way to the kingdom on his own, or maybe a friendly spirit will be waiting for him."

"Maybe, *Abuela.*"

Ursula fell into silence, thinking of the old man who had lived in loneliness and had now chosen the same existence in the land of the dead. But as she looked at Alondra, she sensed a peacefulness in the young woman she had never seen. Perhaps, she told herself, there was no longer a reason to have the conversation she had so long dreaded. If Alondra did not press her, why should she tell what might only sadden her? Putting her thoughts aside, Ursula pulled a handful of keys out of her apron pocket.

"I've cleaned his room and there were just a few things. Mostly old clothes and shoes. Besides his father's picture, there was nothing, only these keys."

Alondra pushed the empty cup aside with her forearm as she took the keys: front door, back door, garage, tool shed, the old Ford. She did not recognize the one with masking tape wrapped around its top.

"Do you know what this key is for?"

Ursula took the key from Alondra, holding it at arm's length. She squinted as she turned it over in her fingers.

"I think that it's the key to Doña Brígida's room, but don't even think of going in there. No one, not even Don Flavio, has gone in since she died. It must be filled with her spirit, and if you open the door, it might escape to roam the world on its own."

"I don't believe in those things."

"Well, you should believe. A spirit can be a prisoner in a room or in a house for years. Once it has been set free, no one can tell what it will do in vengeance for having been kept captive."

Alondra slipped the key into the coin pocket of her jeans and smiled at her grandmother's superstitions. Sometimes Ursula talked of spirits that went on to inhabit their own kingdom. Now it was one trapped in a room. But she decided not to say anything. Sometimes Alondra secretly hoped that Doña Brígida *would* reappear somewhere, sometime. Alondra would have liked to converse with her now that she was a woman. She yearned to ask if she was truly meant to return to Casa Miraflores with the person she loved.

The next morning, Ursula awoke for the first time in her memory to the smell of brewing coffee. Light streamed from the kitchen, where Alondra sat quietly at the table.

"*Buenos días, hija.*"

"*Buenos días, Abuela.*"

"I think you were restless last night."

"*Sí.* I couldn't sleep. I kept thinking of the old man and other things, until I remembered the key."

"What key?"

"The one you found in Don Flavio's room."

"Oh."

"I went up to Doña Brígida's room to try it."

"*¡Santísima Virgen del Cobre!* How could you *do* such a thing?" Ursula appeared to be paralyzed, her face reflecting the dread that had taken hold of her.

"*Abuela, cuidado,* sit down, you look like you're going to have a heart attack. Sit here. Let's have a *cafecito.* I never made it into the room. The key didn't work. It must be to something else."

"*¡Gracias a Tata Dios!*"

Ursula began to sip her coffee, making loud, slurping sounds. The rain had returned, drumming against the windowpanes. Both women held their mugs in both hands, trying to capture the heat radiating from the coffee.

"I'm going to find the door that matches the key. I'll begin up there—with the attic."

Ursula pinched her lips impatiently. There were other things that had to be done instead of trying to uncover what ought to be left alone.

"I must, *Abuela.* We can't live in this house without knowing what's in it. Don Flavio had his ways. But now the place is ours, and I want to know what's in it."

Ursula sat back, thinking. If Alondra's attention were taken by the house, then she might forget her questions. For years, Ursula had been afraid of something that probably would never happen. This was a new project, and it would take up most of Alondra's time. After that she would propose that together they paint and clean the entire house.

"Yes! I think it's a good idea!"

Alondra was startled by the reversal in attitude. As she sipped more coffee, she cocked her head to one side, narrowing her eyes as she studied her grandmother.

The attic had fascinated Alondra when she was a child, but neither she nor Samuel had ever dared go into it: Don Flavio had laid down the law against it. He was even stricter about the prohibition after Doña Brígida's death. Now that she was about to enter it, she wished that Samuel were with her.

She had wrapped her head in a red bandana and had put on gardening gloves and boots; it would be dusty. When she reached the door at the head of the narrow stairway, she inserted the key in the rusty latch. With a scraping sound, the lock resisted, but with some pressure, she heard it click open. The catch disengaged easily, but the door made loud, creaking sounds as it began to slowly open; its hinges were rusted, and litter on the floor blocked its path. The attic was dark except for one shaft of light that filtered through the dirty panes of a small window facing the street. Alondra's fingers groped up and down the wall for a light switch, but there was none. She then shuffled toward the center of the room, holding one of her arms outstretched before her and the other stuck rigidly upward— in hopes of finding a string dangling from a ceiling light. As she walked, Alondra felt her boots slipping and crunching against the floor.

Suddenly, she was surrounded by the whir of flapping wings. From the darkness, a nest of birds, a cloud of pigeons, descended on her, whipping around her head and body, scraping her face and hands, pecking at her eyes. She tried not to scream, but terror gripped her throat. She fell to her knees and wrapped her arms around her head, trying to shelter herself against the claws and beaks. Groveling on her elbows and knees, she began to crawl, in circles, searching for something with which to defend herself. With one arm still protecting her head, she fumbled with her other hand until it landed on something that felt like a broomstick.

Alondra grabbed the broom with both hands and began to swing it in broad circles above her head. As the momentum of the paddling increased, she rose to her feet, where she was able to whack the birds until they backed away. The room filled with the sound of her stick cracking and thudding indiscriminately against the attic walls, followed by weak chirping. She kept up the assault until she was certain that the birds had retreated. Her eyes had become used to the gloom by then, and she saw the last of them as they fled through the same hole in the wall through which they had first invaded the place.

Sweating, panting, and exhausted, she had to hold onto an upright beam. She would fall if she did not hang onto something. When she finally made out the dangling light cord, the sudden flood of brightness made her blink and squint. As her vision adjusted, she saw that the floor was piled high with the white crust of pigeon droppings. Her eyes opened wide, pupils dilated. The entire room was smeared with bird excrement.

Alondra's stomach turned, forcing her mouth open as she gagged. She gasped foul air through her mouth and aching chest. She sloshed her way to the window and forced its rusted, creaking hinges open. Hanging her head out the window, she vomited until her stomach emptied completely. She stayed slumped over the windowsill for several minutes until the damp November chill revived her. Taking long, deep gulps of air, she peered into the mist hovering over the rooftops.

When she finally pushed herself away from the window, she yanked the bandana off her head, wrapped it around her nose and mouth, and forced herself back into the room. The attic was huge, and she knew that it would take hours, if not days, for her to scrape away the blanket of excrement covering everything. There were certain things that Alondra could make out despite the filth. Piled high in one corner were several broken chairs; one had a leg missing, others had splintered backs. In another nook, she saw the remains of several of Samuel's childhood toys.

Alondra stood under the circle of light cast by the bulb, turning slowly, taking in shapes and containers. She shuffled towards a wall. When she got close enough, her eyes made out the shape of an old-fashioned upright wardrobe, its spindly legs visible through the caked slime. She grasped the handle, but it was locked. The doors were solid hardwood, and they would not give way.

Alondra backed away from the cabinet. After a while she found a piece of metal which she forced into one of the handles. She pulled sharply, and the panels snapped apart with a dull crunch. She flung the doors open and a black figure threw itself upon her. Alondra let out a muffled scream as she fell to the floor.

When she recovered from her fright, Alondra cursed: Her rear end was smeared with pigeon shit.

She sat on the floor, legs sprawled apart, as she gawked. A row of long, black dresses hung from the wardrobe, and the first of these had fallen onto her at her violent yanking on the wardrobe door. When her terror passed, she realized that it was not the old woman, after all. She had not uncovered Doña Brígida's body. It was only the dresses she used to wear.

Alondra pulled her heels toward her and put her elbows on her knees while she giggled nervously. At last she cupped her face in her hands and let herself laugh until she felt the tension melt away. When she looked up again at the garments, she was struck by the realization that when she was a child, she had always thought that Doña Brígida had only one dress, which she wore always. The old woman had had many dresses: All identical, all cut from the same material, all in the same end-of-the-century fashion.

Alondra flopped back on her elbows, indifferent to the crud that now clung to her. She did not know what she had hoped for, but it had to be more than old dresses.

"Shit!"

As she got back on her feet, Alondra wiped her hands and arms on her pants. When she moved closer to the cabinet, she noticed that there were two drawers at the bottom. She tried opening one and was surprised to discover that it slid out easily. There were several strings of pearls, a set of earrings, and a broach watch with a chain. This was Doña Brígida's jewelry.

Alondra took the watch in her hand and laid it in one palm. She remembered the old woman fingering the ornament. She shook her head and returned the watch to its place. The other drawer was locked, so she inserted the metal bar and broke the lock with a snap: It was a packet of letters, bound by a ribbon. She took the bundle and turned it over, scrutinizing the yellowed, crinkled envelopes. Then she went over to the window; she needed more light to read the writing. On each of them was written: *Brígida*.

Alondra stuffed the letters into the bib of her overall. She would check their contents later. She returned to the cabinet and was about to close it when she made out a cardboard box behind the dresses. Alondra spread the garments apart to get a better look.

She pulled the box toward her; it was heavy, but she could manage it. It plopped onto the floor. A thick cord held down the flaps. It was filled with photographs. They were old, and many of them were daguerreotypes. She took out the first one; it was a young Brígida, fifteen or sixteen years old. Her posture, the way in which she held her head and cocked her eyebrow, along with the broach watch—it could be no one else. She looked on the reverse side and made out the date: 1901.

Alondra picked up the entire box and carried it from the attic. When she got to the service porch, she put the box and letters into the broom closet, then went to the bathroom, where she stripped.

She stood naked for a long time, holding her head back, taking large gulps of air, struggling to steady her pounding heart. Don

Flavio had stashed it away from sight after his sister's death, she knew. It must be important. Alondra wondered if he had gone through the contents of the wardrobe, as she was about to do.

"Probably not. The old *loco* more than likely had a bunch of guys take the thing up and lock it in the attic. Then he put the key on a chain and forgot about it."

Alondra mumbled to herself as she shampooed and scrubbed, trying to wash away the stench that had seeped into her skin. After dinner, she stayed in the kitchen alone.

Alondra put on a pot of coffee, then plopped the box under the light and began to unpack it. When she reached into it, her fingers found the packet of letters. The ribbon disintegrated as she pulled it. She opened the top envelope carefully and removed the letter. She made out the date, then the greeting.

3 de enero de 1913.
Querida Brígida,

It took Alondra a while before she could read the words that followed. She mumbled, irritated that she had not listened to her grandmother, who had frequently advised her to practice speaking and writing Spanish. She glanced down ahead, to the signature.

Te ama, Velia Carmelita.

Alondra leaned against the backrest of the chair to relieve the pressure on her back as she read the letter word by word. It was short, but, the message became clear: It was a love letter written to Doña Brígida by Velia Carmelita. Alondra closed her eyes, mentally arranging names and relationships: Velia Carmelita was Samuel's grandmother, Don Flavio's wife.

"*¡Chispas!*"

Alondra, staring at the yellowed paper, felt guilty and awkward for having pried into what was private. But she could not help herself. She looked out the window, at the dark and wet outside, but she was not thinking of the weather; she was calculating dates.

Doña Brígida must have been Alondra's age when she had read the letter. Alondra had never heard such words—words that expressed a love that transformed plains, sierras, and *barrancas* into paradise. At her age, no one had told her, *Because of you, the world has meaning*.

Slouching against the chair, Alondra stared out at the night, listening for street sounds, but the barrio was asleep; nothing stirred. She held the fragile letter in both hands as she pondered the mystery of love between the two women. She was perplexed; this thought had never entered her mind when thinking of Doña Brígida, but now that it was in front of her, Alondra felt glad and, in a strange way, envious.

She returned the letter to to the packet and put it aside. Now that she knew what was in the other letters, she decided not to read them. One said it all and the others should remain secret, even to her. But she decided to keep the letters; to cherish them as her own.

Chapter 19

Alondra awoke the next day grumpy and belatedly disappointed. She had hoped to find something that would help her to discover herself, but what she found instead was about Doña Brígida. She tried to soothe the irritation she felt by telling herself that the photos might help her come up with something.

Alondra stayed behind after dinner once again that night to examine Doña Brígida's photographs. She put the coffeepot to brew, pulled the box out of the cupboard, and began to go through the pile, separating the pictures according to size. The larger ones were mounted on gray cardboard frames; the smaller ones were loose, and most had frayed, ripped edges.

The first large one was Don Flavio's wedding picture. He was seated on an elegant chair with gilded legs and armrests. Next to him was a column crowned by a large bouquet of flowers, and Alondra could make out a cloth backdrop showing a snowy volcano. He was young—in his late twenties or early thirties. He was dressed in black, high boots and he held an elegant hat in his hands. His chin was forced up by a starched, broad collar, and his tie was wide and delicately knotted; a stud adorned its center.

"Hmm. You were good-looking. How come you became such a *loco?*"

The faded picture did not diminish his handsome appearance. His hair was wavy, thick, and blond, and even his mustache, shaped like two handlebars, was light-colored. Alondra could also see that his eyes were blue, almost transparent. When she concentrated on his face, she saw Samuel's face reflected there.

Standing next to Don Flavio, one hand delicately placed on her husband's shoulder, was Velia Carmelita. Her height was medium;

not much taller than her seated husband. She was dressed in the end-of-the-century fashion; Alondra calculated that she was not more than seventeen or eighteen years old. Alondra thought that she was beautiful. Her eyes, mouth, and nose reminded her of statues she had seen in books. Even the coils of hair that had slipped out of the veil made her look like a figure in an art book. She was smiling, but she had a faint, almost painful look.

"Maybe your shoes were tight and your feet were hurting you."

Fatigue was overtaking Alondra, so she began to flip through the pictures with less concentration. She stared briefly at one showing elegantly dressed *rancheros* in *charro* suits. There was another picture showing Don Flavio, Velia Carmelita, and Brígida on a picnic. They smiled self-consciously at the photographer as Indian servants catered to them.

Alondra was losing patience. That was the only picture with Doña Brígida in it. She grabbed the box, dumped its contents on the table, and began picking out pictures randomly. She took a quick look at each one, then flipped it to one side. Patios with shining tile floors and potted plants leapt out as she scanned each photo. Formal dances, weddings, baptisms, and other occasions wearied her even more.

Here was Don Flavio, stiff and arrogant, mounted on a large black gelding; he held a riding whip in his hand. Alondra's attention was taken by an Indian who stood by the horse, holding the bridle. An oversized sombrero covered his forehead almost to the eyebrows, but his features were in focus. She examined his face closely; something in her memory moved. She gazed at the picture for some minutes, turning it in different directions to catch light. Unable to recall anything, she shrugged her shoulders and went on to another picture.

Alondra slumped against the chair in exasperation, accepting that there was nothing in the box for her. Then her attention was caught by a photograph of an infant dressed in baptismal garments. She flipped the picture over: *El bautizo de Isadora Betancourt. Hacienda Miraflores, 1913.* She turned the photo to its front, wanting to see what she looked like, and if Samuel resembled her, but Alondra saw nothing but the tiny, puffed-up face of a newborn child. Then she remembered Isadora's sister, *la cabra,* and she shuffled through other photos, but there was nothing. Frustrated and angry, she threw the picture on the pile that had built up in front of her.

"There wasn't a she-goat after all. There's nothing here but a bunch of Betancourt shit."

She stretched and flexed her legs, as one of them was cramping painfully. Then she got to her feet and poured another cup of coffee. Alondra had not noticed the day beginning to break, the first rays of sun were creeping into the kitchen, diffusing the light of the overhead bulb.

"Something is missing. Someone's been messing with these pictures," she muttered to herself.

"What pictures?"

Ursula, her hair still wet from her morning bath, walked into the kitchen.

"*Buenos días, Abuela.* I didn't know that I was talking out loud."

"Have you been here all night, *niña?*"

"*Sí.*"

"Where did you find these photos?"

"In the attic. They were in Doña Brígida's wardrobe, along with other things."

"Hmm." Ursula absentmindedly poked a pudgy finger, pushing one picture to the left, the other to the right. She cocked her head, an inquisitive expression on her face. "I've never seen these before."

"No? I thought you said that you used to look at Doña Brígida's pictures all the time."

"Yes, but these were not hers. I'm sure."

Alondra's face showed satisfaction: Someone *had* substituted these pictures for Doña Brígida's. She got to her feet as she felt a surge of new energy, despite her sleepless night.

"Today I go into Doña Brígida's room."

"No, *niña!*"

"*Sí, Abuela.* There's more to see. Maybe I'll find it there."

"*¿Qué?* What are you looking for?"

"I'll show it to you when I find it. In the meantime, let's have breakfast. I'm starving."

Equipped with a crowbar, Alondra went to Doña Brígida's bedroom door. Her hands shook slightly as she inserted the clawed end of the tool between the door and its jamb. She yanked and there was a crunching sound. The door popped open. Alondra did not move.

She was afraid, she had to admit it. Especially when she felt a current of air seep through her overalls, making her shiver. A dank, sour smell drifted into her nostrils.

She remembered the room as it had been on the day Doña Brígida died. Alondra looked at the high ceiling, the drooping velvet curtains, the ancient chandelier, the four-poster bed. These images floated in the gloom, and she was not certain if she was seeing real objects or memories.

It suddenly occurred to her that the room must have electricity. Her fingers fumbled up and down the side of the door sill until she located the old-fashioned button switch. Even when the room lit up, she still felt like the child who had timidly walked into the bedroom clutching her grandmother's hand. Alondra had to shake her head to come back to the present.

She took a few steps into the room, and saw that everything was as it must have been during the life of Doña Brígida. She had almost begun to lose interest when she noticed a wardrobe; it stood upright against the wall.

It was empty. The bottom drawers, too, had been cleaned out. Don Flavio had seen to it that nothing remained behind. Alondra turned, intending to leave and tell her grandmother that the bedroom did not have an evil spirit waiting to be freed, after all. As she was leaving, however, she noticed that the wardrobe stood in front of what appeared to be a door. She went back and tried to push it aside with one shoulder, but although empty, the wardrobe was too heavy for her to budge. Then she tried backing into it, pressing her buttocks and upper back against its side as she dug her heels into the floor. Breathing hard and muttering under her breath, Alondra was finally able to push the wardrobe away from the wall. The wardrobe concealed a closet door.

She found stacks of boxes. There was not enough light for her to make out the inscriptions, so she ran to the service porch for a flashlight. Alondra was so engrossed in her task that she did not notice Ursula standing at the stove as she sped through the kitchen.

When she returned to the room, Alondra pulled out a box and took it to the window. She sat on the floor to examine what it held. She cried out: It was Doña Brígida's collection of pictures. Here was Brígida with Velia Carmelita by her side. Dressed in gauzy white dresses, the two sat outdoors on a wicker seat, their heads cocked toward one another, nearly touching. Alondra looked carefully and saw that Velia Carmelita was showing signs of pregnancy. Both figures smiled, holding hands.

There were dozens of pictures, but Alondra looked at each, studying, comparing, absorbing the young Brígida and Velia Carmelita. Her eyes took in their beauty and the happiness stamped on their faces. Here they held guitars; over there they walked arm in arm under shaded arches and colonnades. In a carriage, seated under a tree or next to a stream, each photo showed Velia Carmelita's growing pregnancy and Brígida's attachment to her.

Alondra's head began to swim as she became dizzy with fatigue. She closed her eyes while the spell passed. When she looked again, she saw a picture that captivated her: two children—a boy and a girl. Alondra recognized them as Don Flavio and Doña Brígida. Behind them stood a young Indian woman; her image sent a vague shudder through Alondra. She brought the picture closer, and she confirmed what she had thought at first glance: She, Alondra, looked like the dark-skinned woman. She put the picture into the bib of her overalls. She would ask Ursula about it.

When she returned to the closet, she flashed the light on a shelf that held several small boxes. The inscription on one read: *Sanatorio de San Juan de Dios—Zapopan*. Stacked neatly inside of it were receipts, each one marked PAID, along with its canceled check. Each check bore Don Flavio's endorsement. The date of the first bill was October, 1939. She returned to the closet, skipped the other boxes and yanked out the last one. She went to the window and forced herself to translate: *Services and assistance provided for Isadora Betancourt*. It was dated a month before Don Flavio died.

"Isadora Betancourt! *¡Chispas!* That's Samuel's *mamá.*" Alondra leaned against the wall and stared at the wardrobe. Don Flavio had taken over his sister's room after her death to store the things he kept a secret. "But how did he move that wardrobe when he was so weak?"

She frowned, trying to imagine the frail man moving the heavy piece of furniture that had taken so much of her energy to budge. She shook her head, pondering his obsession with secrecy.

"You old *loco*. If your daughter is sick, she's sick. What's the big deal? Why try to hide it?" Alondra stuck the invoice into her bib with the intention of showing it, too, to Ursula. Without bothering to put things back into place, she walked out of the room and went downstairs.

Ursula was ironing a sheet when Alondra asked her to join her. She disconnected the iron and followed Alondra into the kitchen, and together they sat down at the table.

"*¿Qué pasa?*"

"Look at this picture, *Abuela*. Have you seen it before?"

Ursula squinted as she tried to focus on the photograph, but it was not until she held it at arm's length that she recognized it. She smiled, remembering the time when she had first seen it.

"*Sí*. This is Doña Brígida and Don Flavio when they were children."

"And *la india*? Who is she?"

Ursula put the picture on the table and clasped her hands on her lap. She squinted as she pursed her lips.

"Doña Brígida told me that it was her mother."

"*¿Qué?* Her *mamá?* But this is an *india, Abuela.* I thought they were white people."

"*Sí.* I thought that too, but I believe that she was telling the truth. She said it to me many times; every time I dusted the picture. She told me that her *mamá* was an *india* from the tribes of Jalisco."

Alondra shook her head and rolled her eyes. She took the picture and looked at it again for a while, turning it toward the window for better light.

"I look like her."

Ursula tensed, and her fingers pressed against one another, leaving yellow blotches on the back of her hands. The moment she had feared had come. It was staring at her, telling her that she must tell Alondra the truth. Her mouth suddenly grew dry, and she tried to scrape saliva from the roof of her mouth with her tongue so that she could speak. She stared at the tabletop, wondering where to begin.

Both women were quiet for a long while; dripping water from the leaky faucet splashed against the sink. Ursula's face was set in concentration, and she seemed to be listening to something far away. Alondra sat looking at her, noticing how the overhead lamp cast deep furrows in her face, as if it had been carved from brown wood, or cast in hardened earth. Her hair, still thick, had grown nearly white, and her braids were like tight, gray ropes.

"I found this paper up there in the closet, too."

Ursula breathed a sigh of relief when Alondra interrupted. Anything would be easy to deal with in comparison with the photograph, because Ursula had long ago seen that Alondra did indeed look like her Indian great-grandmother.

Alondra spread the invoice on the table, smoothing the creases out of it with the palm of her hand. She paused, waiting for Ursula to read it, but then remembered that her grandmother did not know how to read or write.

"It says that Isadora Betancourt is in a hospital of some kind."

"*¿Qué?*" Ursula whipped forward to the edge of the chair. She put both hands on the paper as if wanting to *feel* what was written on it.

"*Sí, Abuela.* Right here it says her name, the place of the hospital, and down here is the date."

"A long time ago?"

"No, just a few weeks ago. Look. Don Flavio was still alive."

"What is the name of the hospital?"

"Sanatorio San Juan."

Ursula shut her eyes and slipped back in the chair, trying to find support for her body. She had never doubted that Isadora was alive, but to know that she had been in an asylum for so many years made her heart shrivel. It took Ursula a few seconds to bring together what had happened during those sad days that ended with Isadora's disappearance. She now knew that when Don Flavio had vanished with the driver, it was to condemn Isadora to live in a tomb.

"*Abuela,* are you okay? You look sick."

"I'm okay."

"Why do you think the old *loco* kept it a secret? It was his daughter, and he pretended she was dead. And what about Samuel? He thinks she's dead, but she's not. Look, it says so right here. What sickness could anybody have that would make a father hide it?"

Ursula struggled to control the ringing in her ears. She held her breath until she was able to gather the courage she needed. She prayed silently. Alondra and Samuel had been cheated of their mother, and Isadora had been deprived of them, and of a lifetime of freedom. Her heart ached to think of Isadora's years of imprisonment, and she felt ashamed for having played a part in the web of deceit spun by Don Flavio.

"*Hija.* Listen to me. This sanitarium is not a hospital. It's a place for those sick up here." Ursula put an index finger to her temple and made a circular, churning motion. She waited for Alondra to say something.

"Samuel's *mamá* is a *loca?*"

"No! Now I know that Don Flavio put her there in punishment."

"For what?"

"For loving El Rarámuri."

Alondra stared at Ursula, momentarily stunned, putting memories and stories together. She did not take her eyes from those of Ursula. When she finally spoke, her voice was barely a whisper.

"El Rarámuri! You've told me he was my father."

"*Sí.*"

"Isadora loved him?"

"*Sí.*"

"What happened to him?"

"Don Flavio had him killed."

"And he imprisoned Isadora in the *sanatorio?*"

"*Sí.*"

Alondra stood, walked over to the sink and stared out the window. Night was overtaking the streets and rooftops; more rain had begun to fall. She turned to face Ursula, struggling to silence the roar that grew inside her head. She stared at her grandmother for minutes that seemed endless while she relived her childhood of loneliness and doubts.

"She was my *mamá?*"

"*Sí.*"

"And Samuel is my brother?"

"*Sí.*"

"Don Flavio was my *Abuelo?*"

"*Sí.*"

"Doña Brígida was my *Tía Grande?*"

"*Sí.*"

"And you—who are you?"

"*Niña,* here in my heart, I'm your *abuela,* but in truth, I am the same to you as was Doña Brígida your *Tía Grande.*"

Ursula had long imagined Alondra's rage for having the truth concealed from her. Inwardly she had grieved for this day, because Alondra's love meant everything to her. She did not understand when Alondra came, knelt next to her and put her head on her lap. Ursula responded by embracing her; she felt that the young woman's body was serene.

"*Niña*, do you forgive me for not telling you the truth?"

"You did tell me the truth. El Rarámuri was my *papá* and, as you said, my *mamá* was she who did not die, even though her skin had been torn from her. What you left out was what the old *loco* did to his own daughter, and that was because even you didn't know the truth."

Ursula was astounded. She had not expected this, but she was happy beyond words. She took her by the shoulders and looked into her eyes.

"What are we going to do, *hija*?"

"First, we're going to tell Samuel that he's my brother. Then we'll go to Mexico to get our *mamá*."

While Alondra waited for Samuel's arrival, she pondered Don Flavio's motives. No matter how many times or the ways she tried, she found his rancor incomprehensible. Alondra asked herself why her grandfather had murdered her father: Was it because he was an Indian? Don Flavio's own mother had been a native of the tribes of Jalisco. Did he so detest that part of himself which was inhabited by his mother's spirit? And Isadora? What about her?

The loneliness that Alondra had felt as a child returned, more intense, deeper. Restlessness possessed her. She spent nights packing and unpacking the suitcase she intended to take in search of her mother. She stared into mirrors, trying to see Isadora's features, traces of Brígida and Velia Carmelita. But what she saw was the brown face of Don Flavio's mother.

Days passed before Samuel arrived in Los Angeles. Alondra and Ursula met him at their front door, hugged and kissed him, then headed straight to the kitchen, where Alondra served coffee. Alondra hardly took her eyes off Samuel's face as Ursula told him their mother's story: her wedding and Samuel's birth; her abandonment by his father, Eloy; her love for Jeronimo, El Rarámuri;

Alondra's birth and her father's murder; the disappearance of their mother; their self-exile to Los Angeles.

Samuel listened in utter silence, holding his face in cupped hands, elbows balanced on the table. His eyes were nearly shut; now and then a lid fluttered. His lips were compressed into a tight line, giving him a mask-like appearance. Alondra saw that he clenched and unclenched his jaw as he swallowed; the muscles in his neck were taut. As Ursula spoke, he sometimes passed a hand over the certificate that verified Isadora's whereabouts.

When Ursula finished, he looked at her for a long time, his face expressionless. His memory dipped back to the vague shadows of a cave, and a brown man with long hair who showed him plants, birds, and insects. Samuel called up images of arched and colonnaded corridors, of a stable and of a golden-haired woman who stroked his forehead. Loud noises and shouts of servants running around, disoriented, calling for a doctor, for hot water, for bandages, echoed first dimly, then with more focus in Samuel's recollection.

He moved his head from one side to the other, listening to a voice only he could hear.

"You don't believe me, Samuel?"

He held his hands clasped tightly, and he hunched over, nearly hiding his face. He shook his head, pulled on an earlobe, licked his lips, but even after minutes had passed, he appeared unable to speak.

"You don't believe me?"

"Ursula, why didn't you at least tell Alondra? She's been a grown-up for a long time. Why now?"

"I was afraid."

"Afraid? Of what?"

"Don Flavio."

"*Abuelo* had been so weak for a long time. What could he have done to you?"

Ursula was unable to deny the truth of what Samuel hurled at her. Still, an inexplicable dread had gripped her, convincing her that

Don Flavio, even as he faded more with each day, still somehow had possessed the power to destroy Alondra. Ursula did not answer.

Samuel shook his head again, then sighed with exasperation. Nearly forgotten impressions of his mother, the feeling of her hands on his face, tormented him. He wanted to believe that his mother still lived, but he could not.

"She's not alive."

"¿Por qué no?"

"Too many years have passed, Alondra. Who could stand so much misery?"

"Prisoners last longer in penitentiaries."

"Maybe, but I can't believe that she's still alive."

Ursula at last spoke up. "What about this paper? Don't you think it proves that she's alive?"

"No. I think that it's a fake certificate. The old man was being taken in by someone down there, someone who made a lot of money off him over the years. Even if she is alive, have you thought that she might be better left alone? Leave things as they are, Alondra. Marry, have kids, make your own family."

Alondra stared at Samuel, and her eyes clouded. Her body tensed as she pressed her fists on the table.

"I can't do anything until I'm sure of what happened to her. I'm going to search for her."

"What will you do if you do find her?"

"I . . . I'll bring her back here to live with us!"

"I'm going with Alondra," Ursula broke in. The determination in her face and body made her seem less old, less frail as she pressed her hand on the table.

"¡Ay, Vieja! You're too old for these—"

"Who's too old? Samuel, *¿por qué?* What makes you think she's not alive?"

"I don't know *what* to think anymore! How do you think I feel after hearing what I've just been told? My father is a deadbeat; my grandfather is a murderer; my mother is in a loony bin—and you ask me what I *think!*"

"Why don't you add the part about me?"

Samuel's flushed face whipped around to look at Alondra. He opened his mouth several times, but words would not come out. Finally, he was able to say, "Alondra, I've always thought of you as my sister. I've always loved you that way. What Ursula has just said doesn't add or take from my feelings for you. I don't have to be told that you're my sister. I've always known it in here." He stopped speaking abruptly, but he went on patting his chest with one hand, deeply moved.

"Still, I wouldn't go if I were you," he continued doggedly. "It's too risky. Mexico is not easy on strangers."

"Ursula and I can make it. Right, *Abuela?*"

"*Sí.*"

Samuel got to his feet and began walking around the kitchen as Alondra went on speaking.

"I need money. Please lend it to me. I'll pay it back as soon as we return."

"It's not the money."

"Then, what's the reason?"

"I already said: It's dangerous, Alondra."

"Come with us."

"I can't leave my family."

"Then lend me the money, and I'll find our *mamá.*"

Samuel halted mid-step and stared at Alondra as if he had just seen her. He nibbled on his upper lip nervously.

"Our *mamá.*" He returned to the chair and sat on its edge, bouncing his legs up and down on his toes.

"Okay. Let me find out how much a plane ticket costs to the closest airport to Zapopan. I think it's Guadalajara."

"A plane?" Ursula's small eyes rounded, and her lips beaked. "*¡Nunca!* I'm afraid of those machines made by the devil!"

Alondra shrugged her shoulders, reached over the table and patted Ursula's hands. "We can take the train. I already checked it out. It leaves out of Mexicali. From there, it'll take us to Guadalajara. When we make it to that city, we can take a bus to Zapopan."

"How do you know all of this?" Samuel interrupted.

"I've made phone calls. That's all I've been doing while we waited for you."

"Okay! Okay! I'll drive you to the station. We can get the tickets when we get there."

"Let's go tomorrow."

"That soon?"

"Our *mamá* has waited too many years. I don't want her to wait longer."

The drive from Los Angeles to Mexicali began early the next day. It was a gray November morning and the long ride through the desert was monotonous. When they crossed the border at Calexico, Samuel headed for the train station, where he bought tickets for a Pullman coach. When it was time, Samuel walked Alondra and Ursula to the platform, where he helped them get on the coach and place their bags on racks above the seats. The two women were excited; neither had traveled on a train before. When the signal was given for visitors to leave the coach, he hugged and kissed them good-bye. Back on the platform, he stood beneath their window, smiling as the train surged forward. Ursula and Alondra returned his smile, waving at him until he disappeared from view.

Chapter 20

The trip through the northern Mexican states took the two women across vast expanses of desert. Alondra spent hours gazing at the passing landscape, captivated by the changing light of the sun on the sand and cactus. She thought of her mother, and of Brígida's love letters, which she had packed along with her other things. But most of all she and Ursula talked. The older woman told of her memories of Isadora, Brígida, Celestino, Narcisa, and Jerónimo. Alondra was hungry to hear about the Rarámuri, their life in the caves, their language. Ursula told Alondra about her days as a baby and child.

Towns and cities drifted by as the train slid on its iron rails. Benjamín Hill. Guaymas. Hermosillo. Alondra also enjoyed the nights, when she fell into a trance induced by the soft clacking of the wheels and the swaying of the coach. During those nights she relived her childhood, when she played with Samuel and listened to Doña Brígida's tales of the family.

They arrived in Guadalajara at midnight. They were fatigued, yet Ursula was alert and evidently energized by being back in Mexico. From that point onward, Ursula became their voice to the surrounding strangers.

As soon as there was daylight, the two women made their way to the central bus station, where Ursula bought tickets to Zapopan. The station was already crowded, but they found a corner away from the stream of travelers, the screaming children, the squeaking carts, and the people shouting out good-byes. Some travelers carried not only bundles and suitcases, but small cages stuffed with chickens and ducks. Ursula grew happier with each hour.

Alondra was jerked out of her fatigued thoughts by the blast from the loudspeakers:

"¡Autobus número 31, destino a Zapopan! ¡Vámonos!"

"¿Señorita? Señorita, ¿está vacío?"

Alondra looked away from her window and saw a woman pointing to the seat behind her. Alondra nodded her head, and the woman took the place after pushing a cardboard box under the seat. Alondra craned her neck to look back at the woman, who smiled and began to chat with her and Ursula. Where were they from? What were they doing so far from home? Yes, she was a native of Zapopan and could give them necessary information.

Alondra stretched and looked back as the bus pulled onto the highway. Looking at the twin spires that dominated the skyline but were receding quickly, she plucked up enough courage to ask the woman behind her what they were.

"Señora, esas torres, ¿de qué son?"

"Es la catedral de Guadalajara, Señorita."

Alondra knew that she or Ursula would have to ask the woman how to get around town once they arrived, but first she wanted to relax for a few minutes and look at the countryside. The trip, she knew, would take almost an hour. There would be time, she told herself, to get the information she needed.

"This is my grandmother, Ursula, and we're here looking for a hospital," she said at last. "Its name is Sanatorio de San Juan. I wonder if you could tell me how to find it."

"Zapopan isn't that big, Señorita. What is best for you to do is to go straight to the basilica; all our streets begin and end there. That hospital is a very large one, and you will see it immediately once you're in front of the church. It's located on the highway that goes out to Tesistán. Don't worry. Just ask anyone, and they will point you in the right direction. Do you and your grandmother have a place to stay?"

Alondra had not taken the time to find out about hotels or boarding houses, confident that she would find something. It was

1965, after all (as she had pointed out to Ursula, who feared the worst); even Zapopan was sure to have a hotel. The woman passenger had a worried look as she waited for Alondra's answer.

"No, Señora, we don't."

The woman rubbed her chin, thinking. "I would invite you to my home but I don't even have a sofa, much less a bed for the two of you. But I've got an idea. The nuns at the convent of El Refugio rent out rooms to young women like you."

Ursula spun around, a look of irritation on her face. The woman turned her attention from Alondra to her. "Señora, a thousand apologies. When I said *young women,* you were, of course, also included. We were all young at one time or another, weren't we?"

Ursula did not respond, but looked at Alondra with annoyance. Alondra guessed at what was behind Ursula's anger.

"*Abuela,* I have to speak for myself sooner or later," she whispered. "You should be glad that I can speak pretty good *español.*"

"You can't. You sound like a *pocha.*"

As the bus pulled into the terminal station, the passengers got to their feet, taking their possessions, pressing to get out of the vehicle. Once on the pavement, the woman pointed in the direction of the basilica.

"Just follow this street until you reach those towers. Do you see, over there?" A chubby finger pointed out the cathedral spires. As the woman began to walk away, she stopped abruptly and turned to Alondra.

"Señorita, it occurs to me that the hospital you're looking for is for the insane. Are you sure that you have the correct name? We have another hospital, you know, for other afflictions."

"Yes, Señora, I'm sure. *Muchas gracias.*"

As the two women made their way on the cobblestone street, Alondra felt that she was leaving her time and entering a world of the past.

When Ursula yanked vigorously on the rope at the convent's entrance, a deep bell rang, startling Ursula from her revery. The two waited for a few minutes, looking through the grates at a patio filled with potted geraniums and carnations. It was silent. Only the chirping of caged birds and the gurgle of a fountain reached them. Alondra pulled on the cord again, and this time a nun ran to the gate. She was young, and it appeared that she had been washing dishes; her arms and hands were smeared with soapsuds.

"Buenas tardes."

"Buenas tardes, Señorita." The sister's stare seemed to reflect surprise at the presence of the two women.

"I understand that your convent sometimes rents rooms to—"

"Please come in."

The nun turned several times to look at Alondra and Ursula as they made their way through a courtyard, across an arched cloister, and into a small, dark office. When she opened the door, she smiled for the first time, indicating with her hand that they should sit. Alondra obeyed and took an oversized wooden chair, its seat and back covered in hard, worn leather. Ursula rested in a similar seat. They were alone. Not even the birds or the fountain could be heard through the thick adobe walls. All they could see of the garden were the clustered fronds of a palm tree that leaned against the latticed window. Most of the room's walls were taken up by shelves loaded with books. They seemed to be old manuscripts; most of them were bound in faded leather, and from where she was sitting, she could make out that some of the titles had worn away.

"Buenas tardes, Señorita."

Neither Alondra nor Ursula had heard the sister enter the room, and they were startled by her sudden presence. Like schoolgirls, they responded with one voice:

"Buenas tardes, Madre."

Alondra felt a sharp jab of apprehension for the first time since leaving Los Angeles. During that instant, she wondered if Samuel had been right—that all of this might be a mistake.

The Day of the Moon

The woman was dressed in a coarse brown habit that hung to the floor, and her head was covered by a wimple and black veil, highlighting the transparent skin of her face. The sister appeared to be in her mid-forties. Her eyes were bright and deeply set, her nose was beaked, and her thin lips curved slightly downward. *She looks like a bird,* thought Alondra.

"I understand you need a room?"

"Yes, *Madre.*"

"Where are you from? You're not from these parts, I see."

"No, I'm not from this area. But my grandmother, Ursula, is from Chihuahua. I'm from Los Angeles, and I'm visiting Zapopan, hoping to find someone."

The nun's eyebrows shot upward. She held that expression steadily as she looked at Alondra.

"I'm here looking for a person who is interned in Sanatorio de San Juan de Dios."

"A relative?"

"Yes. My mother."

The nun motioned for Alondra and Ursula to return to their seats, then she took another chair. Her face softened as she reflected. She looked out the window for several minutes, making them uneasy. At last she turned back to look at Alondra.

"I'm sorry, Señorita, I've been rude. My name is Sister Consuelo, and I'm presently the superior of this community. Your grandmother's name is Doña Ursula. May I ask your name?"

"Alondra Santiago."

"Well, Alondra, let's talk for a few moments. You and your grandmother are welcome here, and you can depend on a room to live in while you go about your project. Although our guests do not live inside the convent itself, we have a few rooms on the other side of the courtyard which most visitors find comfortable. We have a dining room for you, small but adequate, in which you can take your meals. You will have to share a bathroom, and you will get fresh towels and soap every day."

Alondra smiled, turning to look at Ursula whose expression showed that she, too, was pleased. She mouthed silently: *Doña* Ursula.

"There are a few rules that must be kept. First, we ask you to attend morning mass with the community. The celebration begins at seven-thirty; after that, your breakfast will be ready. The sisters chant Matins at seven. You're welcome to join us at that time, though you don't have an obligation to do so.

"The most important rule of our convent is this one: Our gates are opened at eight in the morning, and locked at eight at night. During those hours, our guests can come and go as they wish. However, anyone not indoors by the time the door is closed will have to sleep elsewhere."

Sister Consuelo looked at Alondra steadily; she was now smiling.

"Yes, *Madre*. How much should we give as a deposit? I'm not sure how many days we're going to be here."

The nun rose to her feet and stood gazing down at Alondra. "I don't deal with that part of our household. Sister Sarita—she let you in—is in charge of our guests. She'll tell you how much the room will cost you and when you should pay." Sister Consuelo turned to Ursula and gave her an equally bright smile.

"How long has your mother been a patient?"

Alondra's eyes widened, and she turned to Ursula for help. It struck her that she couldn't answer the question.

"Since 1939," Ursula said.

The nun's eyebrows arched, and she pursed her lips. "You mustn't be disappointed if you cannot find information regarding your mother. The place is notorious for its secrecy."

"Secrecy?"

Sister Consuelo sighed. "It's an asylum for the rich, and most of the patients are interned in silence—even concealment. Some of the families involved are ashamed that such a thing as insanity has struck them. I must confess to you that I've never been able to understand it. However, people are strange, and they feel that madness is the same as disgrace, or even scandal."

Alondra moved away from Sister Consuelo and went over to the window. From that point, she could see the fountain and the caged birds. The doubts Alondra had experienced minutes before melted away. She turned back to look at the nun.

"Where should we begin?"

"Do you know anyone of influence in Zapopan?"

"We know only you."

The nun smiled wryly, and her small eyes brightened. She plunged her hands under the long scapular draped over the front of her habit and furrowed her forehead.

"Doctor Silvestre Lozano, the director, is a patron of this convent and has often assisted us when we've needed help. He's a kind man. He's been head of the asylum only briefly—not more than two years. Give me time to approach him regarding your mother. I believe that would save you time and, hopefully, disappointment."

"*Gracias, Madre.* While we're waiting, I think it would be a good idea to see the place. Where is the hospital?"

"Very close. *Everything* is close in Zapopan. If you take a wrong turn, all you have to do is to return to the basilica and start all over again." Sister Consuelo was smiling, but Alondra thought she detected a sudden glimmer of pity in her eyes.

"Those stricken with madness are sometimes better off left alone, Alondra. It might be more prudent to leave things as they are."

"What if someone has been put away for another reason, not for insanity?"

"Then all the more reason not to intrude. If a person has been put in that asylum unjustly, it means that there are powerful people behind it. Anyone, especially a foreigner, unknowing of the ways of this place, might well keep a distance."

"*Madre,* my mother was put in that place as a punishment by her father; she was not insane. He's dead now, so unfortunately he's escaped what he deserves. But if she's still alive, nothing will keep me from taking her away with me."

"It's late," Sister consuelo said gently, "and I'm sure you're tired after your journey. Sister Sarita will show you to your room. I'll see you tomorrow morning at mass. By the way, what is your mother's name?"

"Isadora Betancourt."

Chapter 21

Alondra and Ursula's room was small but comfortable; it had a large window through which early sunlight flooded. Alondra rose early after a fitful sleep. After she and Ursula dressed, they stepped out to the patio and into an old garden, filled with potted flowers and ferns. In the center was a weather-beaten stone fountain, where water spurted from the open mouth of a sculpted carp. Ursula drifted to one side of the garden while Alondra looked around, seeing that someone had already uncovered the bird cages. She leaned against a pillar and listened to the singing of canaries and *zenzontles*.

She looked at her watch and realized that it was still too early for mass. For a moment she considered going back to the room, but the morning was so beautiful that she decided instead to stroll through the porticos and courtyards of the convent grounds. Sister Sarita had pointed out the chapel the evening before, saying that she would be welcome there at any time. Alondra turned away from the garden alone and walked over to take her seat before the nuns began to chant their prayers. When she went into the small church, she found several nuns already praying. Fearing her footsteps would disturb them, she was about to turn away from the doorway when she bumped into Sister Consuelo, who nudged her toward the benches, smiled, and silently led her to a side pew. She handed Alondra a thin, black book, then went to her place at the rear of the chapel.

The paintings on the walls were all large, dark representations of saints and madonnas, most of them mounted in ornate, gilded frames. A statue of the Virgin Mary, garbed in a light blue gown, stood near the altar. Alondra noticed with surprise that the altar was strangely bare, in contrast to the intricate paintings surrounding it.

All that she could make out on it were the tabernacle and two bronze candlesticks.

Alondra leaned back, absorbing the peacefulness of the chapel. She listened to the soft treading of the nuns as they arrived and seated themselves at their place; a clock striking seven, its chimes filling the high vaults of the place with their silvery tinkle; the echo reverberating off the statues and stained-glass windows. She turned in the pew and saw that Ursula had taken a place a few benches behind her. Suddenly, the silence of the chapel was ended by a startling, high pitched note.

¡Ave María!

The phrase had been chanted out by a single voice, and even though it went unanswered for the moment, Alondra saw that all the nuns rose to their feet and began to chant the prayers.

Deus, in adjutorium meum intende.

Alondra did not understand the words, but after a moment she remembered the book that Sister Consuelo handed her, and she opened it to find that it showed the Spanish text alongside the Latin. As she became more engrossed in the meaning of the chanting, she felt her spirit moved by the cadenced verses and rhythmic responses. The ritualistic standing, bowing, and sitting of the nuns gripped her imagination, slowly mesmerizing her with every verse, and she followed their movements, captivated by the spiraling voices:

I was exalted like a cedar in Lebanon, and as a cypress tree on Mount Sion. Like a palm tree in Cades, and as a rose plant in Jericho was I exalted. I gave forth a sweet fragrance like cinnamon and aromatic balm. I yielded a sweet smell like choicest myrrh. I am black, but comely, O daughters of Jerusalem.

Alondra felt her breath catch in her throat because she had never heard such words before. Her mind raced. She was copal. She was mahogany. She was cacao. She was peyote.

Nigra sum, sed formosa, filiae Jerusalem:
I am black, but comely, O daughters of Jerusalem.

The verse was again intoned by the lead chanter. The words swelled over Alondra, and she closed her eyes. These were just prayers, she told herself, nothing that should move her so profoundly.

Surge, amica mea, et veni. Iam hiems transit, imber abiit et recessit. Flores apparuerunt in terra nostra. Tempus putationes advenit.

Rise up, my beloved, and come away; for the winter is past, the rain is over and gone; flowers appear on our land; the time of renewal is come.

Alondra listened to the canticle, clinging to it. She was listening to her mother's words, inviting her to come to her. The winter of despair and emptiness was over. Lost in the thoughts and sensations she had just experienced, Alondra remained in her seat long after mass ended.

Afterward, she had breakfast with Ursula. She sipped hot chocolate and munched on sweet rolls brought to her by a nun who smiled as she silently handed over the dishes. Later, they left the convent and began to make their way to the basilica, passing the open market with its vegetable and meat stands, fruit vendors, shoe peddlers, stray dogs, and bawling children. When they reached the church, Alondra and Ursula stepped out onto the cobblestone street and began to make their way down the incline toward the brick buildings surrounded by austere walls. All the while, Alondra pondered on her experience in the chapel. Words swirled in her mind as she walked by Ursula's side, and she repeated the chant because it gave her comfort. *I am black, but comely, O daughters of Jerusalem.*

The next day, Alondra and Ursula sat in the library waiting for Sister Consuelo. They expected that she had news from Doctor

Lozano. Now and then the splashing in the fountain and the chirping of birds penetrated the walls, soothing their anxiety.

"*Buenos días, Doña Ursula. Buenos días, Alondra.*"

"*Buenos días, Madre.*"

The nun took the same chair she had sat in during their first meeting, taking time to arrange her habit around her arms and wrists. After she did this, she looked first at Ursula, then at Alondra.

"I have news for you. Doctor Lozano has agreed to meet with you."

"When, *Madre?*" Alondra was sitting on the edge of her chair, trying to get closer to the nun. She was tense and what Sister Consuelo had just said had a strange effect on her. It filled her with fear but at the same time with excitement and joy. The memory of the transport she had experienced during the chanted prayers returned to her.

"Tomorrow."

"She's alive!" Alondra nearly shouted that her mother was alive, just as she had thought from the beginning. Ursula put her hands to her face. Her body rocked back and forth on the chair. When she pulled her hands away, she was mouthing prayers to Tata Hakuli and the Virgin Mary.

Sister Consuelo, jarred, did not know what to say. After a few seconds she picked up where she had broken off, her voice betraying uncertainty.

"He didn't say that, Alondra. As I explained yesterday, Doctor Lozano is relatively new to the position, and the number of patients in the sanitarium is considerable. He said only that he would meet with you and your grandmother."

"We're very grateful for your assistance. I'm sure that without you this would not be happening."

"Thank you, Alondra but I'm certain that my intervention was not absolutely necessary. Things happen because they must."

Alondra, still nervous and agitated, went on to relate to the nun as much as she knew of her mother. Ursula piped in many times, filling in gaps left by Alondra's account.

"I don't know what to say except that, unfortunately, this story is like some others. Not many, but it is not the only time that a father has done such a thing. I'm sorry, Alondra."

Alondra explained that she and Ursula had tried to go into the asylum the day before, but had gotten only as far as the lobby before being stopped and told to leave the premises.

"They did?"

"*¡Sí, Madre!* They were quite rude."

Sister Consuelo turned to look at Ursula, startled by the sentiment in her words. She listened attentively as Ursula went on speaking.

"But that did not stop us. I said to Alondra, '*Niña,* we haven't come this far to be thrown out as if we were beggars!' So, we left the building and made our way to its back. We did this by walking outside of those immense walls that circle to the rear. And what do you think we found, *Madre?*"

"What?" Sister Consuelo had crossed her legs and removed her hands from under the scapular, clasping them on her knees as she leaned forward.

"There is a gate back there, and one can look inside through the iron bars. Alondra and I crept up, careful not to be seen, to where we could look at what was happening inside. There, in the light of the sun, we saw a large area with stairs leading up to an indoor patio, and because the entrance doors were open, we caught glimpses of people in white gowns. Isn't this what we saw, *niña?*"

"Yes. We think that those people were patients. Last night we hardly slept, thinking that one of them could have been my mother."

Sister Consuelo was fascinated. She had lived all of her life in Zapopan and had never seen that part of the asylum. Visitors were always shown to the more modern street entrance. However, she remembered seeing photographs of the original entrance with its iron gate and stairway leading to the central patio.

"Well! Maybe you're right, Alondra. Tomorrow will tell you much more, I assure you."

"What time should we meet with Doctor Lozano?"

"He's expecting you in his office at two in the afternoon. One of the sisters will show you the way."

The nun got to her feet and headed for the door. Before leaving, she turned to Alondra.

"I pray that you find what you desire, and that your mother is in good health. Be strong and prepare yourself for what you don't expect. Remember that we're in God's hands, and that certain events in our lives, good or evil, happen because they must happen. If my sisters and I can help you, please come to us."

"Gracias, Madre."

That day, the night, and the following morning were endless for Alondra and Ursula. They arrived at the front entrance of the asylum at the appointed hour and identified themselves, saying that they were expected. The receiving attendant checked the appointment roster, nodded, and, without uttering a word, showed them into Dr. Lozano's small office.

The room was filled with filing cabinets and piles of papers. The walls held frames with certificates, awards and diplomas. An electric clock hung crookedly on one of the walls, its cord dangling limply. Alondra stared at it, noting that it was a few minutes past two o'clock. She felt her hands growing clammy, and there was perspiration gathering on the small of her back.

"Abuela, I'm afraid."

Ursula, too, was scared. Twenty-seven years had passed since the day when she had sworn to Isadora that she would never separate herself from Alondra. She thought of the years that had intervened, years of doubt and fears and loss for Isadora, years during which the baby had grown to become a woman.

"Hija, I'm scared just like you. But you'll see, everything will be right after we meet with Doctor Lozano."

"What do you think will happen?"

"I don't know. Let our spirits guide us."

They were interrupted by the sound of the opening door, and a medium-sized man entered. He had a long, dark-complexioned face, graying hair, and myopic eyes. His rumpled linen suit was frayed, and his tie slightly askew.

"Señorita Santiago?"

"*Sí, Doctor.* This is my grandmother, Ursula Santiago."

"I'm happy to meet the both of you."

The man's voice and expression were gentle. When he sat at the desk, he opened the first file; Alondra saw that it was stacked on top of several others, each one stuffed to capacity. Instead of speaking, the doctor shuffled pages, nervously turning and stacking them one on top of the other. After a while, Alondra realized that he was hesitating. When he finally spoke, his voice was soft, and he did not look up.

"I regret to tell you that the patient is no longer here."

"Not here? Then where is—"

"What I mean is that the patient died several years ago."

Alondra and Ursula stared at the doctor. There was silence except for the sound of muffled conversations beyond the closed door. Ursula rose and embraced Alondra, hoping that her arms would soak up the sorrow. After a few minutes, Alondra spoke.

"When?"

"The record shows that she died seven years ago."

"Why wasn't her father informed?"

"I don't know, Señorita."

"Why was the money not returned?"

"Because someone here is a thief."

"Is there nothing left of her? A notebook? Letters? Anything?"

"I'm afraid not."

Alondra got to her feet and put an arm around Ursula's shoulders, opened the door, and pressed her in the direction of the hallway. She felt as if there were two Alondras. One was the child who had wondered about her identity, the other one was the woman who had found her beginnings, despite having come too late to find her mother.

"Señorita, if there is anything I can do for you, I will do it."

"No. Nothing. Except . . ." Alondra faced the doctor while she framed her words.

"Except?"

"Allow my grandmother and me to leave through the same doors my mother entered."

Together, Alondra and Ursula walked down a path toward a man in uniform. He put his hand to his cap in greeting and turned to open the gate, but it took several twists before the lock snapped open. He pushed the iron grill until it moved, creaking on its rusty hinges and letting the two women pass through the gate which had opened to Isadora Betancourt's imprisonment twenty-seven years before.

They returned to the convent to stay for some days. Alondra telephoned Samuel and gave him the details of what had happened. Although he tried to sound calm, she knew that it was a cover for disappointment. She, too, wrestled with anger and sadness. The question of what to do next, or where to go, nagged at her. Ursula tried to help Alondra's distress, but she herself was grieving—for the second time—the loss of Isadora Betancourt. After a while they decided that before returning to Los Angeles, they would head for Chihuahua and try to meet with the Rarámuri people. Alondra felt that although her mother was dead, she might still find her spirit in the sierras of Chihuahua.

Chapter 22

The swaying and the lulling clatter of the train did not make Alondra drowsy because the view was so imposing. Her eyes were riveted on the heights that appeared beyond each curve as the train headed deeper into El Cañón del Cobre.

Both women were fascinated by the speed and the path of the train; they had never experienced anything like it. They craned their necks to catch the underside of the canyon floor and to see the elevations of the *barranca*. It was the end of a trip which had begun with the bus from Zapopan to Guadalajara, from there on train, until reaching the Pacific coast and the town of Los Mochis.

Alondra, whose mind was filled with thoughts about her mother, was gripped by a desire to speak to her.

"Mamá, what did you think of during those years?"

"Of you, Alondra."

Alondra shut her eyes as her mother's words seeped into her, filling the emptiness buried inside of her. She opened her eyes and looked into Isadora's blue gaze.

"When you were born, I saw that you were the color of a chestnut, and it filled me with happiness."

Alondra glanced over to look at Ursula and saw that she was pretending to be asleep. The echo of her mother's voice returned.

"Samuel also filled my mind, as did Brígida, Ursula, Narcisa, Celestino, but especially your father Jerónimo."

"Jerónimo."

Alondra mouthed her father's name, feeling it strange on her lips. She tried to picture him in her imagination, fashioning his image beginning with his feet up to his head.

"What was he like?"

"You look like him."

Alondra was startled: She was certain that she looked like the grandmother she had seen in the photograph showing Don Flavio and Doña Brígida as children.

"What's the matter?"

"I've seen an old picture, one that Doña Brígida kept. Ursula told me that it was Don Flavio's and Doña Brígida's mother, your grandmother."

"I remember the photograph."

"I think I look like her."

"Yes. You look like my grandmother, but you look like your father, too."

Alondra felt energy rushing through her knees up to her body, where it lodged in her chest. She thought that she smelled the fragrance of clay and cactus flowers.

"Were you angry or bitter?"

"Yes. I spent years thinking of the man who gave me life, but extinguished the person I loved and then imprisoned me. I detested my father. Did you know that I tried to kill him? Yes, you do know. I regret only that he did not die. I punished myself because I had failed to take his life as he had done to Jerónimo . . . and to me and to you. Loathing my father grew larger than my life itself. It became a monster inside of me, dominating and controlling me for years. But the day came when I knew that I had to fight the ugliness that had taken possession of me if I were to live to see you and Samuel again. I had to make a choice, Alondra, because you and hatred could not inhabit me at the same time. I chose you."

Isadora's voice stopped abruptly. The clatter of the train's wheels filled the car with a hum, snapping Alondra back into reality. Soon after, one of the conductors bellowed out an announcement of the train's arrival at Ciudad Creel, and the train began slowing down. Alondra jumped up and took hold of Ursula's suitcase, then her own.

Once out of the station, they found a hotel in which to spend the night. Alondra telegraphed Samuel, telling him that she and

Ursula were heading for Copper Canyon; she would let him know when they planned to return to Los Angeles.

Early the next morning, they hired a taxi to take them to Divisadero, and from there they found a place that provided tourists with mules to trek the paths across the *llano* to the skirt of the sierra. After that, only experienced hikers continued on foot. Because there were still several hours of daylight left when they reached the base of the *barranca,* they decided to go on until they reached the church of Nuestra Señora de los Dolores at the village of the Samachique, which marks the beginning of the road to Batopilas. From there, the two women struck upward, to the caves of the Rarámuri.

Alondra followed Ursula as she trekked up the rocky paths, imitating her steps, which seemed to mold with the stones. When they arrived at the village, Ursula told people that Alondra was the daughter of El Rarámuri. Some remembered. Ursula took Alondra to her grandmother Narcisa, where she received the old woman's blessing. Then they went to the caves of Alondra's uncles, aunts, and cousins.

She and Ursula stayed with the family with the intention of remaining there for a short time only. But as the days merged and weeks passed, Alondra began to experience a peace that she had never before felt. The tribe needed a teacher and someone to tend to their health. When she realized this, she decided to stay on for a longer time.

At the end of each day, Alondra walked. It was then that she conversed inwardly with her mother. They spoke of what they had done during the years of their separation. Alondra spoke of her school years in Los Angeles, and about Brígida, Ursula, and Samuel. Isadora told Alondra about her father and of her solitude in the asylum. She showed Alondra the *llano* where she used to ride with Don Flavio as a child, and where she ran foot races with Jerónimo and his brothers.

Alondra frequently hiked down the sierra to the ruins of Casa Miraflores. Most of the walls had caved in, but she could make out the walls of the bedrooms. The corridors were still there, as well as the archways and columns, reminding Alondra of the photographs of Doña Brígida and Velia Carmelita.

Ursula showed Alondra the niche in the rocks where Isadora was sitting when the Rarámuri carried her father's body up to the caves. This became a favorite place for her. She felt that her mother was still there, watching and waiting for El Rarámuri.

Dear Samuel,

Months have passed since Ursula and I came to the caves, and although I've written to you saying that we're coming home soon, things keep happening to make me decide to stay a little longer. I can't help it, Samuel, *me gusta aquí*. Although it was rough in the beginning (sleeping in a cave isn't easy), I'm getting used to life in the mountains. And since I see that I can help the people of the tribe, I feel good about staying. Who would have told us that nursing school would come in handy, after all? *¡Qué cosas!*

There's another reason for staying here. I still feel depressed and disgusted because of what happened to our mother. Do you think I'll ever get over it? Sometimes I am so full of anger that I reach out into the emptiness hoping to find *el Viejo*. I want to drag him back and make him suffer, as he made her suffer. But then her voice comes to me and I calm down. I remember the look he gave me when he was dying and I tell myself that maybe, just maybe, he was saying that he was sorry.

I know, you're thinking I'm a *loca*. But I can't get over feeling that, had we known about her a few years earlier, things might have turned out better for all of us. This place helps me deal with this terrible thought. I know, it's crazy, but being here—I think—will return something of her to me, something that will fill the emptiness and take away the bitterness.

Ursula is well but she's getting pretty old. I know that when I return to Los Angeles she'll want to come with me, so I have to think about that, too. At any rate, Samuel, I plan to stay here until after Lent. I'm told that the tribe puts on a big pageant down in the village and that people from all around these parts participate in it. Even university professors come to see it. I'd like to be part of those ceremonies and then return to Los Angeles. Well, maybe.

In the meantime, take care of yourself. Why don't you come to visit? Just write (as usual to Ciudad Creel) to let me know when you're coming and I'll be waiting for you at the airport in Los Mochis.

Tu hermana que te quiere,

Alondra